Books by Kirk Ward Robinson

Nonfiction

Founding Character
Documents that Define the United States of
America and its People

Founding Courage
Courage and Character in the United States of
America

Hiking Through History
Hannibal, Highlanders & Joan of Arc

Notes from the Field
A Diary of Journeys Near and Far

Fiction

August Roads
Novellas

Life in Continuum
Stories

The Appalachian
A Novel

Life in Continuum
Stories

A Highland Edition

Originally published May 2012
Highland Edition published January 2018

Previous versions of *Life in Continuum* and *Crossover* have appeared in various contexts.
Printed in the United States of America

Library of Congress Control Number: 2012905507

HighlandHome Publishing
Nashville, Tennessee
37215

ISBN 10: 0999604228
ISBN 13: 9780999604229

A Kindle Edition is available

Visit www.highlandhome.org

Life in Continuum
Stories

Kirk Ward Robinson

For Jarred Blane Robinson

*I know not where he lies
still I know of him, Achilles*

CONTENTS

PREFACE

Life in Continuum is a speculative exploration of time travel. Time travel itself is *not* speculative, however, since we are all doing it right now—we are traveling into the future from one moment to the next. The trouble is that we age in concert with this march through time and therefore do not perceive it as anything out of the ordinary. What we want to do is skip whole segments of time, to arrive at an alternate temporal place while our current ages remain the same. Well, this happens, too. It has been theorized and observed that clocks in motion tick slower than clocks at rest, and so anyone who has ever flown in an airplane has traveled into the future at a faster rate than the normal passage of time. This can be measured the moment the airplane lands and comes to rest at the gate. We will, however, need an incredibly accurate atomic clock to prove it.

It can also be argued that we are out of phase with the present, that we live permanently in the future. What we see with our eyes—a football touchdown, a waiter pouring wine, a shooting star—all happened in the past. How far in the past depends upon how long it took light, at about 186,000 miles per second, to bring the event to our retinas. Due to the incredible speed of light, events appear to be instantaneous over short distances; but were the sun to suddenly wink out it would be eight minutes or so before we knew we were goners. And then looking into the night sky we see stars that are hundreds, even thousands of light years away. Locate the North Star and you will see it as it was about 434 years ago, when Queen Elizabeth I ruled Great Britain. Sound is a good analogy to help visualize this concept. Sound waves are similar to light in wave form only much slower, more perceptible to human observation. When we hear the thunder, the lightening has already happened. When we hear a rifle crack in the distance, the bullet has already found its target. These sounds, therefore, come from the past—and we are in their future.

But it is travel into the past that has proved to be more quixotic, since doing so could presumably alter the very firmament of our memory, creating irresolvable paradoxes. We can hear sounds from the past, we can look at the night sky and see images from the past, *but we can't send information into the past.* And yet—were we able to find a way to tunnel through space-time, to reach that light source, that star, and do it by bypassing the speed of light, then we would be traveling into the past. There are myriad theories out there that deal with this very thing, most of them extraordinarily difficult to grasp. It may finally be as the physicist Stephen Hawking suggested, borrowing from the Fermi Paradox regarding our failure to find evidence of extraterrestrial civilizations, that were time travel possible then we should be overrun with tourists from the future.

Still, though, we suspend disbelief easily when reading time travel stories—they are just too much fun. Literary time travel into the past is a fairly recent invention, dating to the early 19th century when it showed up in a few European short stories. These evolved into full-length novels in the later 19th century, Mark Twain's *A Connecticut*

Yankee in King Arthur's Court and H.G. Wells' *The Time Machine*, among others. Time travel was (and remains) a fascinating device with which to explore human character while adding an entertaining dash of fantasy.

My introduction to the time travel genre came when I saw *The Time Machine* at a Saturday matinee as a child. This would be the original 1960 film starring Rod Taylor, not the 2002 remake. I was entranced by the concept of time travel. My mind whirled with it. I bought the book the following Monday (stores weren't open on Sunday in those days), and tore through that thing so quickly I was left wanting more. Twain followed next, Asimov and Clarke, and some obscure but delightful books by the French author Rene Barjaval. And then came *Star Trek*, the excellent scripts of D.C. Fontana and Harlan Ellison. I was ecstatic. In the 1970s, Jack Finney wrote the splendid book *Time and Again*; David Gerrold wrote a fascinating thought experiment about looping back on one's self in time titled *The Man Who Folded Himself*, and Richard Matheson published his poignant *Bid Time Return*, which was made into the movie *Somewhere in Time*. I enjoyed both, although if I could speak with Mr. Matheson I would ask him where the watch came from. The 1980s saw an explosion of time travel stories by Poul Anderson, James P. Hogan, Joe Haldeman, Gregory Benford—too many to list them all. Plots became more complex in the 1990s with the novels of Stephen Baxter and Michael Crichton, just two of many; and then in the 21st century the genre crossed back into literature with Audrey Niffenegger's brilliant *The Time Traveler's Wife*.

With this much enthusiasm I was bound to eventually write my own time travel stories. I wrote two of them, the dystopian *Life in Continuum* and the metaphysical *Crossover*, in the early 1980s. It was a shock to pull them out of my files after all of these years to discover that they were so dated as to be practically unreadable today. Their backdrops were contemporaneous with the Soviet Union and atomic bombs, 1970s hairstyles, LSD, and polyester clothing. In order to include them in this book I essentially had to rewrite them. They are, for all intents, new. *In Whose Time* came to me in 1991 over coffee with a friend named Kurt Haslbauer at the West Hollywood IHOP at 2:00 a.m., when struggling writers and actors fill the booths because IHOP is the cheapest place to pass the night in Los Angeles. I distilled this story in my mind for two decades, and wrote it only recently. In this effort I must thank Kurt, who asked the crucial question, a question that took me a long time to answer: What does their history show?

Kirk Ward Robinson
Smith County, Tennessee
March 2012

IN WHOSE TIME

Sha'raelon looked up the ramp toward her future, which existed 575 years in her past at year one, the Focal Point. Studying her reflection in the gleam of the ship, she subtly clenched her teeth to steel herself against the glimmer of doubt she could discern in the emerald green eyes that looked back on her.

"Why must I go? Why must it be *me*?"

This was a rare display of self pity from Sha'raelon. Pa'ket, her aide, put a steadying hand on her shoulder and said, "Because our history *records* that it was you."

Sha'raelon allowed a tight smile. "But no mention of my devoted and deeply perceptive aide?"

Pa'ket's left hand rested on the Sha ceremonial baton, which hung over his shoulder by a leather thong. He absently traced the etchings in the ancient wood, smoothed by the fingers of the generations that had carried it before him.

"Not all of us are destined to have our places in history known, and yet we shape history just the same," Pa'ket answered warmly, in a voice Sha'raelon imagined her father would have used had she ever known him.

"It is time, Mistress Sha," Pa'ket urged gently. He took her by the elbow, placed a palm lightly in the small of her back and guided her aboard ship, where their past awaited her future.

She approached the dais with the statuesque poise for which she had been chosen, or would be chosen. She was tall, a full head taller than Pa'ket, and dressed in a shimmering gold gown similar to the ancient Greek *chiton*, which draped over her left shoulder and flowed like a sun-lit stream down to her white strapped sandals. Her hair fell to her waist in long golden curls, gathered above her left shoulder by an emerald comb that matched her eyes, baring her elegant neck, smooth as porcelain but tinted by the sun. Her lips were full, pink. She wore no cosmetics, no jewelry. Her bare arms were firm, hinting at quiet strength. Certain graceful movements would part her gown below the waist to offer glimpses of an equally toned right leg. The women from the West regarded her with competitive suspicion. The women from the East regarded her with nervous envy. The men, from West and East, consumed her with their eyes. This was as planned. Women were formidable but men still held the power in this time.

Sha'raelon scanned the General Assembly with the political astuteness and feminine mystery of Nefertiti, using only her peripheral vision. She could make him out, obliquely to her left, huddled among men dressed in the dark business suits that the contemporaries wore, his face in profile although she could feel his eyes upon her just the same. He was handsome, actually, with a wide jaw that formed hollows in his cheeks, lending his face a muscled, masculine appearance. His chin was strong, with a shallow cleft. He had thin lips and an easy smile. His hair was black, looked soft, cropped at collar and ears, anachronistically parted on the left; and his eyes were...blue, like steel, like the sheen of his hair, but his eyes were not hard. He used them when he smiled, and he must smile a lot, she thought, because the fine lines in the corners lifted with his lips. Still, he was dangerous—he was her enemy.

"Ladies and gentlemen of the United Nations," she began, turning her attention toward a speech she had been practicing for fully twenty years, since her thirteenth birthday, when she had been handed from one set of minders to another set more adept at managing the process of puberty. She needed no notes; there were no papers on the podium. She stood regally, confidently, her hands at her sides, palms gesturing slightly outward. She continued:

"I know that for you these events are extraordinary, but for me, for us, for *my* time they are history. They are who we *are*, and history proves that we are *you*."

Sha'raelon paused to search for the recognition that line was designed to elicit, saw it flickering in a few faces. She was speaking in English Standard, in a warm contralto that was designed to appeal to the women as a balance against her visual appeal to the men. Many in the assembly wore translator headphones though, so there was a delay in their reactions. Most of them sat stone faced, waiting, inherently suspicious. One line crafted in English Standard would not influence them. Sha'raelon had foreseen this. The speech, she had argued, should have been delivered in Swahili or Arabic, but the historians had disagreed. They had countered that there were still many racial and cultural negatives extant in the mid twenty-first century, as well as serpentine political machinations. English Standard would not evoke concerns of a hidden agenda, but any other language, even French, *would.* And besides, the speech had been delivered in English Standard. This was a known fact.

Sha'raelon sighed, although her face remained relaxed, open.

"We are *you,*" she went on. "Your future, your shining city on the hill, where your work today, your struggles, your dreams are fulfilled. All that you aspire toward has been realized. I live in a world of equality and peace..." she paused again mentally. This had also been an issue, the present tense. *I live,* not *lived,* even though she could never go back, would never *live* there again. But the past tense sounded like a defeat, a loss, as if she had been cast out. "...where human beings live full, healthy lives; where there is no war, no poverty; where the scourge of disease is mostly unknown; where our Earth has been healed and where our species now resides upon every major body orbiting the sun. This is *my* world, the world *you* created, and I thank you."

That line *did* work. The applause was rapturous. Sha'raelon beamed. Color rose in her cheeks. She put on her most joyous smile, made eye contact from one end of the hall to the other, and then her eyes fell on *him.* He held her there for a moment. There was no consternation in his face. The fine lines at his eyes had lifted and he was smiling, but with...amusement. She quickly looked away, took a breath and concluded: "My present but *your* future, *your* world. You need only choose it and it will be. Thank you."

Sha'raelon bowed as applause roared over her again. Most in the assembly had come to their feet, even *he*, who clapped as enthusiastically as the others. Sha'raelon resisted letting her brows dip; she couldn't afford to look perplexed. Not now. What was he up to? What was his angle? She would soon find out. She backed away from the podium, still smiling exuberantly as he made his way forward to deliver his own speech.

He reached her as she stepped down from the dais. She kept her eyes focused on the doorway further along the curving hall, attempted to get past without contact, but even with her eyes locked ahead she could still make out the raffish smile on his face, could smell his scent, which was clean, warm and natural.

"We're not enemies, you know," he said in a smooth low voice, leaning in close as she passed by.

It took all of her will not to flinch, but she was past him now, her poise intact, Pa'ket just beyond the door. He took the first step up to the dais but then turned back to her. "My name's Jarren," he announced in a voice still low enough to be discreet, "Jarren Canto. May I call you Rae?"

Sha'raelon froze in mid step, turned toward him with icy hardness. "I know your name," she spat, struggling to control her anger, to keep her voice low. "Your use of my given name is insulting. You know this." She turned away from him smoothly, smiling beatifically as the assembly followed her movements, and carried on through the door.

Jarren grinned after her until she was beyond view and then he took his place at the podium.

"Ladies and gentlemen," he began. He had both hands on the podium, elbows locked, a casual hitch to his hips. His tie was loose, freeing a high white collar to open just below his chin. A lock of hair feathered across his brow. He wore a dark gray suit that had a platinum sheen. His wrists were bare, his skin a Mediterranean olive. He normally wore a diamond in his left ear but he had removed it for this occasion. It rested in his coat pocket, close to his heart.

"Madame Sha has described to you a future that...well, I wouldn't mind visiting it myself. *Visit*, I say, because for me her future is too small. Humanity struggles, humanity has always struggled, and it is what we have built from the ashes of our struggles that has made us the dominate force in the galaxy."

There was a sudden intake of breath throughout the assembly, and then the hall became deafly quiet, attentions rapt. Jarren smiled inwardly at their reaction.

"I must describe to you a future," he went on after a pause, "that may not be as pretty as the one you just heard, but a future that is *expansive*. I come from what is by your calendar the year AD 2656, which makes me simultaneously older and younger than my counterpart."

Jarren grinned at that, and winked. There was scattered laughter in the assembly. He continued. "I am a merchant captain. I have piloted ships to the very constellations you see in your night sky, and I tell you—they're wonderful. In my time we are loose in a frontier of eternity, where every human being can take to the stars or, if they choose, stay home on Earth or else the worlds of their births. In my time we have likewise controlled disease. We live long lives. There is no poverty or war on

Earth, although things can and do still get tense on some of the frontier worlds. But this is as it should be. It is our nature to struggle, to hold on to our own beliefs and ways of life. It is our *right* to struggle; it is what makes us reach higher. It is, truly, your future. Thank you."

The assembly remained silent, fixated it seemed. Jarren's brows lifted in surprise, but then like an eruption the assembly came to its feet and roared with applause. Jarren took a low bow at the waist, ran his eyes across the assembly searching her out. He spotted her at last, sitting rigid while the others thronged around her. Her face was a tightly controlled mask that revealed nothing, but her aide Pa'ket, a portly, white-haired man dressed in dark monk's robes, was frowning as he took her hand and led her away.

President of the United States Janine Carlyle had never attended such a bizarre briefing. The topic beggared belief; she still couldn't get her mind around it. Derrick Albertson, American ambassador to the United Nations, sat to her right.

"It's really a United Nations matter, and such a trivial one," he said.

"*Trivial*," exclaimed the president.

"Madam President—two futures, which look equally appealing to me, but based upon something as innocuous as the launch date of a United Nations *communications satellite*? I submit that this has no bearing on national policy at all. It's a United Nations matter, let the UN decide. We gain nothing by getting involved."

Joaquin Merida, President Carlyle's national security advisor, steepled his fingers and leaned forward. The former Marine major was in his late fifties, as fit and trim as he had been while fighting in Afghanistan thirty years earlier. He still wore his red hair in a flat-top cut. His friends called him Joe because he had pale Irish skin that defied his Mexican heritage, which came down to him from a great-great-grandfather who had also been the last fully hispanic member of his lineage. His squared military bearing and quiet authority drew everyone's attention.

"In neither of their speeches did I hear any mention of the United States," he said. "What governing system do they use? What happens to *us*? I think we definitely need to be involved."

Secretary of Defense Christopher Channing was nodding in agreement.

"UNCOMMSAT is going up on one of our rockets, so we *are* involved. *We* decide when the thing goes up, so the decision is *ours*."

President Carlyle pressed palms to her temples to still an oncoming headache. She was fifty-one years old, but after only twenty months in office she felt at least ten years older. Streaks of gray were already beginning to show in her short chestnut hair.

"Gentlemen," she said through gritted teeth, hazel eyes squeezed tightly, "how is this possible? This must be some kind of a fraud. It *must* be."

"Madam President," chimed in Dr. Simon Hammerskjold, her science advisor. "Both of them freely submitted DNA upon arrival; as a matter of fact, they insisted upon it. We know exactly what their lineages are—"

"Are they at least American, then?" President Carlyle interjected. She dropped her hands to the table and lifted a pair of photographs. "Neither of them has an accent. Could be Californians." She grinned, as did others around the table.

"—they could be as American as any other race on the planet. Her genetic markers are similar to yours, Madam President. His is a bit more complex but, most importantly, each of them have accumulated mutations beyond contemporary sequences. They have been evolving just a little bit longer than us."

"They're good looking people," the president mused, studying the photographs. "She looks and dresses like a Greek goddess, and he looks like that movie star from a hundred years ago. What was his name?" She snapped her fingers in thought. "Gable. That's it, Clark Gable."

"Jarren Canto could simply be playing a part, trying to look nostalgic rather than exotic so as not to alarm us," Simon commented. "But *her*...she is morphologically perfect. The width of her face to the height of her head, chin to lips, lips to eyes, neck to shoulders, arms to legs... even the shape of her fingernails and her *teeth*—in every regard these ratios are exactly one to one point six one eight. We call this the Golden Mean, or sometimes the Divine Proportion."

"Divine, huh?" mulled the president. "So this means she's a fashion model where she comes from." More laughs around the table.

Simon smiled away his annoyance. "It *means*," he said, careful not to sound petulant, "that they either have significant control of genetic design or else she was chosen very carefully for this mission."

"Or both," Joaquin Merida added. "But I am most concerned about their ships."

"Where *are* their ships?" asked the president.

"Hers is at JFK," Secretary Channing offered. "His is in low Earth orbit. Considering that they're supposedly from different places—would you say *time streams?*—the two ships are almost identical."

"Well they would be," said Simon. "Form follows function."

"And that's my concern," this from Joaquin. "Their ships are not large—the hulls are shorter than a commercial airliner, and that ring that goes around them wouldn't reach the tips of an airliner's wings—so they have found a way to generate enormous power in a small package."

Simon was nodding. "The power necessary to breach space-time must be incredible, notwithstanding the orbital maneuvers we've seen. And they're not chemical. No rocket nozzles. We can't even hypothesize how they work. We've tried to scan her ship but it's opaque to every method we've applied."

"So if that much power was made available to the world, who would control it?" Joaquin asked. "If not us then we would be at the mercy of the nation that did."

"Who's to say they're going to give it to us?" asked Ambassador Albertson.

"Who's to say someone won't take it?" Secretary Channing countered.

"Okay. Let's summarize, gentlemen." President Carlyle let the two photographs slip from her fingers. She pressed her palms flat on the table. "This is a UN matter but we can easily overrule it since they need our rocket. The greatest danger to the United States seems to be their power source, which we must somehow get control of. And," she added with a wink, "future folk are really good looking people."

That got laughs all around.

"Now, who is it that we get if the launch of UNCOMMSAT goes off on schedule?" the president asked.

"That would be Jarren Canto," answered Ambassador Albertson. "Sha'raelon has asked that the launch be delayed."

"So if we do nothing we get the movie star, and if we alter the launch we get the fashion model. Hmmm. Either future looks pretty good from here. Do any of you have a preference?" Heads shook. No one spoke up. "Then does anyone have any idea why the launch of this satellite is so significant?"

The room went silent. Simon cleared his throat and offered, "We really have no idea. Both Canto and Sha'raelon claim not to know either."

"Convenient. Okay, then, let's conclude this." President Carlyle stood, as did everyone else in the room. "Please send your recommendations by the end of the day. Thank you."

She turned to Simon. "Walk with me please."

Once clear of the others she leaned in and asked quietly, "How can there be two of them? I mean, if we had to choose one over the other then there should only be one of them here, right? They have history books too, one assumes. How can their history books say we did two different things?"

"These are theoretical matters, Madam President," Simon replied, his voice equally low, "and not my area of expertise at all. There has been very little work in this field since the days of Hawking and Penrose. Most of our funding goes to climate science and renewable energy. There's no budget for theoretical physics, and no one in the private sector's doing it any more, either. No profit in it. It's the same with the Europeans. The only functional collider today is in China, but it's been a few years since they've run the thing. There is a man, though—God, he's old, he must be close to a hundred now—named Martin Roth. He was a physics professor, came up with an equation in the 1980s. I met him at a symposium in the early thirties. He still seemed sharp then. His equation had something to do with time. It never went anywhere, but he's the only one I can think of who might be able to give us some insight, that is if he's still in control of his faculties."

"Look into it."

"Yes, Madam President."

Sha'raelon swept into the room and held out her hand to Chen Minzhe-Yu, secretary-general of the United Nations. She wore a plain white gown today, sandals strapped with gold, and her hair was gathered in looping folds at the back of her neck.

"It is a pleasure to see you again, Mr. Secretary," she announced graciously, her bright smile in perfect proportion to her face.

"The pleasure is mine, Mistress Sha."

The warmth of her hand sent a tingle down his spine and into his groin. Secretary-General Chen had a wide Han face, and epicanthic folds that creased his eyes into unreadable slits. He had cherubic cheeks, though, and a sincere smile. He was also old enough to be Sha'raelon's grandfather, so his initial reaction troubled him somewhat.

"I appreciate the respect you afford me by using my appropriate name," Sha'raelon said with diplomatic decorum.

"Oh, so *that's* what it is."

Sha'raelon turned toward the unexpected voice. Jarren Canto sat in an upholstered chair, legs crossed, one elbow propped on the seat back. He was dressed in black slacks and a black button-up shirt, open at the neck. No tie. He wore his earring today, the rather large diamond.

"Mr. Secretary," Sha'raelon said measurably, her wide smile falling into a professional countenance. "I was not aware that Mr. Canto would be here."

"It's Jarren, please," Canto said, coming to his feet.

"I apologize, Mistress Sha," said the secretary-general. His face had fallen, as if he had disappointed her somehow, while his speech had quickened, affecting the cadence of his native Mandarin. "I have not been made aware of any animosity between you and Mr. Canto."

"Please, call me Jarren."

Sha'raelon ignored Canto. "There is no animosity, Mr. Secretary. The two of us are, however, in competition. Yes?"

"That is the sad reality of our situation," Chen replied. "These are joint matters I wish to discuss, but—Mistress Sha? Mr. Canto? Would you prefer me to schedule separate interviews?"

"It's Jarren. Really. Just Jarren."

"No, of course not, Mr. Secretary. Your time is valuable, I know. I am willing to proceed jointly with Mr. Canto."

Jarren opened his mouth to comment, but rolled his eyes and shook it off instead.

"Excellent," Secretary Chen beamed. "Shall we sit?"

He gestured them into chairs at either end of a sofa. Chen took the sofa himself, sitting evenly between his guests. Sha'raelon sat as if on a throne, erect, feet together, hands in her lap. Jarren resumed his comfortable posture, legs crossed, arm thrown over the seat back.

"We have several matters to discuss," Chen continued. "You have been designated as ambassadors and therefore enjoy full diplomatic immunity, although we are unaware of the formal names of your nations."

Jarren nodded toward Sha'raelon, so she spoke first.

"We are not a nation per se, Mr. Secretary, but are rather an aggregation of all human cultures. Our racial identities are no different than yours today, and many regions of Earth are still known by their ancient nation-state designations."

"Ancient..." the secretary-general mulled. "It makes me feel anachronistic."

"I apologize. Mr. Secretary. It was not my intention to cause offense."

"Oh, no offense taken, Mistress Sha. I am only an old man who has spent his life trying to guide humanity toward peace. Come the two of you, though, and I now know that regardless the course we choose, there will be peace and equality."

"Not necessarily—" Jarren was cut off in mid breath by a sharp look from Sha'raelon.

"I beg your pardon?" Chen asked, confused.

"I think Mr. Canto *meant* to say that the science of time travel is still not fully understood—by *either* of our cultures."

Sha'raelon's eyes were razors. Canto just mouthed his first name silently as he looked away.

"Well," Chen chuckled, "I do not possess the faculties to grasp these concepts. It is enough that you are here and that your provenance is beyond dispute by the scientific community."

He paused, and then resumed with a reverence in his voice.

"Still, the circumstances of your arrival are so extraordinary that many nations, and billions of people, still refuse to accept who you are and what this means for humanity. Nevertheless..." He was caught by a stray thought. "There is a war in Somalia," he said. "Do you know this region?"

Both ambassadors shook their heads.

"Somalia is a fraction of the Earth that has never been able to reconcile itself to modernity. They have fought for decades, during the entirety of my life. Hundreds of thousands have died. I have been there many times, on relief missions when I was young, on peace missions more recently, always without success. But today they laid down their weapons. Because of *you* they laid down their weapons. You see, they *believe*. Through their hate and despair they see you as a sign from God; that we will all survive; that fighting is futile; that there *is* a future. Yes, there are billions who cannot accept the fact of your presence, but despite this we are already seeing positive signs. There are still many wars being fought, but Somalia is at peace for the first time in a lifetime. And violent crime is falling around the world. People have *hope*. It won't take long; a generation, two at the most." He exhaled with a life of pent up dreams. "Finally."

Chen's eyes misted. Jarren looked away while the man gathered himself. Sha'raelon felt her chest welling but pushed back against the emotion. *His* future seemed full of promise, but what about *her* future?

"Forgive me," Chen said after a moment. "As I told you, I am an old man. Back to business, as the Americans say. We do not have protocol for matters such as these. The Security Council wishes to meet in ad hoc session to interview each of you, but as I said, we do not know what to *call* you."

"If I might offer, Mr. Secretary," Jarren interjected quickly. "Neither of our cultures possesses the national identities with which you are familiar today. In my case we are simply 'Human Space,' while in *Mistress* Sha's case," he paused to wink at Sha'raelon, "I suppose...What would it be, Mistress Sha? Human *Solar System*?"

"Mr. Canto," Sha'raelon practically spat, although her face remained as impassive as glass. "Such sarcasm is unproductive."

"My apologies, Mistress Sha," Canto demurred with that damnable smirk on his lips. "Might I suggest then that we simply refer to our cultures as Timeline Canto and Timeline Sha?"

"That is acceptable to me," Sha'raelon agreed tightly.

"Very well then," said Chen. "On to other business. Mistress Sha, I renew my invitation for you to occupy a suite here at the United Nations."

"They're really quite luxurious," added Jarren.

"Thank you Mr. Secretary, but I do prefer to remain aboard my ship."

"Very well. I respect your wishes, although I do not envy your commute through this New York City traffic. You may, of course, continue your use of the United Nations limousine and chauffer."

Secretary Chen's mind wandered for a moment.

"That concludes our business, he said after that pause. "May I, however, ask some questions for my own edification?"

"Certainly," said Jarren.

"Within reason," said Sha'raelon.

"I am curious of history, that is to say, *your* history. Although I understand that your timelines will diverge in twelve days..."

"We call it the Focal Point," Sha'raelon interrupted. "Our calendar is based upon it."

"Yes, I understand. And your calendar as well, Mr. Canto?"

Jarren was shaking his head, looking amused as always. "No, we use Standard Galactic Rotation based upon Sol's position in Orion—to be able to consistently synchronize our clocks and calendars after FTL flights. The Focal Point is not something we dwell on in my time."

"Of course," said Chen, nodding. "Your time travel."

"Not at all," said Jarren. "From relativistic effects. Time travel is an entirely different matter."

Chen rubbed his temples.

"I should have known better than to open that topic," he said wearily. "What I meant to inquire about, though, is your history. You could describe to me how these brave new futures will unfold, especially for the next several generations of mankind."

Ah... Sha'raelon almost formed the sound out loud. It had been expected, and she had been trained for it, but no one had yet asked so she had lowered her guard. Secretary-General Chen wanted to know the future—the *immediate* future.

"Mr. Secretary," she said. "I am thoroughly educated in ancient history, but of history subsequent to the Focal Point I was carefully schooled in only the larger movements, this to prevent me from inadvertently revealing details that could evolve into self-fulfilling prophecies."

"I see," said Chen, disappointment clearly registering in the fall of his face. "And you, Mr. Canto?"

"As for me," Jarren said, "I was born and raised in deep space. I have never even *been* to Earth until now. Oh, I know some of the general things, but the particulars of Earth history are not as much of a concern out in the deep."

"So is it safe for me to assume," Chen asked hesitantly, "that neither of you knows when I will die?"

"That is a safe assumption," Sha'raelon answered, visibly discomfited by the question.

"Forgive me again, Mistress Sha. I asked in humor, not thinking that you have probably been bombarded with this question, which is a detail I truly care not to know."

"That question is best left unanswered for *all* of us," offered Jarren.

The two ambassadors rose as Chen came to his feet.

"Thank you for your time," he said, shaking their hands. He lingered with Sha'raelon, pressing her hand warmly between both of his, but not inappropriately and only for a moment. He had measured them both and had chosen his preferred future. The final decision, however, was not his to make.

Jarren followed Sha'raelon out of Secretary-General Chen's office and into a hallway. Her pace was purposeful and quick so he had to scramble to catch up.

"Mistress Sha," he called out. "Sha'raelon—oh may we please dispense with these tedious formalities?"

Sha'raelon paused, her back to the merchant captain. She could feel his presence close behind her, the gravity of him. He was taller than she, and she was taller than most.

"You may do as you wish," she said casually. "But I shall maintain decorum."

"Well, it's a start—Oh, hello Packet."

Pa'ket would not allow himself to be drawn into this insufferable man's game. He ignored the improper pronunciation of his name, reached out to guide Sha'raelon away, but she did not offer her hand. Instead she turned slowly on her heels, faced Jarren almost eye to eye.

"His name is Pa'*ket,*" she scolded. "What is this predilection of yours to insult people's names?"

"No predilection," he replied coyly, but then more serious, "just a healthy suspicion of a culture that has diverged too far from mine in only five hundred years."

"Our cultures are not the question between us," she responded with an edge. "We are simply the result of them. What is in question is your boorish behavior. How is it that *you* were chosen to represent your people?"

"Humph," he chuckled. "They came out and got me. I didn't have a choice."

Sha'raelon swayed in the face of his admission. Her own life had been devoted to this mission. Anything less seemed...demeaning to her dedication.

"Enough of this," she stated with disdain. She turned on her heels, quicker this time, offered her hand to Pa'ket even as she began making her way toward the elevators ahead.

"We need to compare notes," Jarren called after her hastily.

"And which notes would those be?" she asked as she walked on. Pa'ket had summoned the elevator. For them the conversation was over.

"What happens to you after?" Jarren asked, a tone of seriousness in his voice that Sha'raelon had not yet heard from him.

He could see her shoulders stiffen. The elevator doors opened. There were people inside. At a discreet flick of her hand Pa'ket released the door. Sha'raelon turned her back to the door and faced her antagonist again.

"What happens to you?" she asked him in a softer, Jarren thought almost vulnerable voice.

"I don't know," he replied earnestly. "They couldn't tell me."

"They would not tell you?"

"No, they *couldn't* tell me. They don't know."

Thoughts spun in Sha'raelon's mind. Jarren swore he could see her eyes go darker.

"Mr. Canto," she said after a moment.

"I beg you to call me Jarren," he got in before she continued.

Sha'raelon smiled tightly and took a quick breath.

"We should not be discussing these matters. We cannot risk inadvertently making a change."

"What can we change? You must know as well as I how futile that would be. Just by *knowing* how to come back has potentially spawned alternate realities, which will go on regardless of us. That's why it's hard for me to take all of this too seriously. There could be a multiverse out there of which we are just one insignificant thread. It is the only thing that can explain it—*us.*"

"True, that is one possibility. But it is also possible that there is no multiverse, that you, I, Pa'ket and your crew are all caught in a loop that will not be resolved until we cross the Focal Point; and that if I do not execute my duties successfully then my entire reality will be negated from one quantum moment to the next."

Jarren sighed. The elevator doors opened again, this time on an empty car. Sha'raelon tipped her head toward the elevator and Pa'ket steered her inside.

Quickly. "Have coffee with me," said Jarren. "You *do* drink coffee in your timeline, yes?" And before she could say no he went on, "I discovered a most wonderful blend at a café near here. Passes through a feline called a civet. I don't know what that means but it tastes marvelous."

"Mistress," said Pa'ket impatiently.

Sha'raelon leaned over to whisper in Pa'ket's ear. "Perhaps I should accept," she said.

Pa'ket's face went as taut as a sail before the wind.

"He is too cavalier," she continued. "I do not believe they would stake their very existence on a man who appears so...so *flippant.* This could be an opportunity to determine his strategy."

"I do not think he has any strategy at all," whispered Pa'ket. "Just a pernicious libido."

Sha'raelon flushed at that. "Come, Pa'ket," she chided him. "I am not so easily aroused, and with you to protect me I shall not become so."

Sha'raelon stood to her full height, shoulders back, hand resting on Pa'ket's elbow. "I will consider your invitation, Mr. Canto," she said with a mysterious smile.

The elevator doors closed then and Jarren found himself alone in the hallway.

"*This* is our reality," he mumbled after them. "Right here where we breathe."

Dr. Martin Roth lived in a retirement home in Jerusalem. Simon Hammerskjold was chauffeured through the narrow, serpentine streets of the ancient city in a shiny black consular vehicle that contrasted against its surroundings like a raven against desert sands. Jerusalem looked like dried parchment laid out over an even drier landscape. Modern apartment stacks were bleached to chalk, rising above domes, crenulations and wandering walls that had been bleaching far longer. It was 39C outside, so dry that his sinuses were swelling. Heat shimmered off the vehicle as if it were a rolling barbecue pit. The air coming through the struggling air conditioner smelled like burnt dust. It was mid September, with atmospheric CO2 at 579 parts per million. The Jordan River no longer flowed on the surface.

"What *is* it about Jerusalem?" Simon thought out loud. "Why are they still fighting over...*this*?"

His driver eyed him in the rear view, something resentful in his gaze. Simon looked away.

At the retirement home, Simon was led into a common room. Windows were deeply tinted against the sun, providing a dusky look over a city that hadn't yet reached the noon hour. It was cool though. Blessedly so. He ran a handkerchief over his bald scalp. A male nurse in white scrubs pushed a wheelchair into the room, positioned it next to a window, and then took an at-ease position to the side.

"We'll need to speak privately," said Simon.

"Not a chance," said the nurse.

"It's all right, Yosef," said Dr. Roth. He was a puddle of flesh in the wheelchair, a white and blue blanket over his shoulders. His head lolled forward like a shriveled fruit, his face practically in his lap. His voice sounded like a deep gurgle. "Go outside and pull the door. We won't be long."

The old man managed to lift a gnarled hand from under the blanket. He patted Yosef's hand reassuringly.

"Five minutes," Yosef said challengingly to Simon. "Please do nothing to excite him."

As soon as Yosef had pulled the door Dr. Roth said, "I know why you are here."

Simon tugged a chair over and positioned himself so that their heads were close. There was a roar of noise coming from outside. Simon leaned in even closer to the old physicist, practically at his ear.

"What can you tell me, Dr. Roth?" he asked.

"What is it that you wish to know?"

"Is all of this real? Is time travel possible?"

Dr. Roth's laugh sounded like a spasm, as if his guts were about to come up through his throat.

"Of course time travel is possible," he said sternly. "We are doing it right now, traveling into the future one minute at a time. But then you also have the proof of it in New York. Yosef has given you five minutes, Dr. Hammerskjold. Surely you have questions which are less self evident."

Chastened, Simon gritted his teeth, but then calmed himself. "How?" he asked.

"Simply puncture the space-time continuum with a gravitic probe and dive in. It's when you resurface that my causality equation comes into play. But my equation only yields probabilities so it cannot be used as a predictor, it can only show us trends. I don't think we should expect any grandfather paradoxes, though."

"*Simply*! The *energy* this would require—"

"Yes, the energy. It seems that we will find it though, does it not? Stephen was always dubious."

"Stephen?"

"Hawking."

"Oh, yes of course."

"Stephen thought that if time travel were possible then we should be overrun with tourists from the future, which is why I think you are still asking the wrong question."

His patience ebbing, Simon blurted, "Then what is the *right* question?"

Dr. Roth chuckled in a wet, rolling gurgle. The roar from outside was louder now, chaotic. Simon glanced back and forth between Dr. Roth and the window.

"Don't mind that," said Dr. Roth. "Another protest march of some kind. You get used to it around here. But tell me, how old are you, Dr. Hammerskjold?"

"I'm forty-two."

"Ah, a Millennium child. Raised with smart pads and smart screens and smart lenses and enough visual diversion to distract a lion. We met once, I remember it clearly. I was in better health then. You were just as impatient. Dr. Hammerskjold, I am one hundred and three years old. I have been a time traveler quite a while now, but always moving forward. You have met two time travelers who have moved *backward*. The question you should be asking is: Are these the only two?"

Realization dawned on Simon so suddenly that his breath caught. He felt as if a tremendous weight had just come down on his skull. Words wouldn't form; he mouthed nothings while his mind struggled to come to grips. The question was so obvious! He stood shakily and went to the window, looked down on a throng of women marching through the narrow street. There were Arab women, shrouded from head to toe in the black *abaya*—and in this heat! There were also Western women, Jewish women, young and old, all marching together, chanting something. It sounded like, *Shaw! Shaw! Shaw!* perhaps Hebrew or Arabic. They were pumping their fists in the air. *Shaw! Shaw! Shaw!*

Simon turned away from the window. Dr. Roth gestured toward him with a weak, skeletal hand.

"Find Fischer," Dr. Roth said. "Dr. John Fischer."

Professor Dimitrios Kupolos still smoked cigarettes when he was on a dig. His graduate students disapproved, but at least they were wise enough not to criticize their professor's habit in his presence. "A dig should be an adventure," he lectured them. "Live your follies and excesses now, while we are in the field. Make love, drink ouzo—dance all night. But put these things away at university. There you must have time only for study."

It was late afternoon of an unusually warm September day. The volcanic haze over Nea Kameni scattered the ebbing sunlight into a warm orange glow. Professor Kupolos stood on the cliffs of Fira, looking west over the channel toward the old lava dome, now in sooty silhouette against the blue Aegean. Ships and boats plied the channel in a confusion of crisscrossing wakes. Ferries were departing for the mainland while fishing skiffs were dropping sail and returning to port. A few behemoth cruise ships were pushing away from their berths, bound for their next ports of call: Athens, Alexandria, Constantinople.

Professor Kupolos blew smoke into the wind. There was a tranquil silence in the wind, interrupted now and then by a distant ship's horn or a shouted seaman's command. Gulls cackled with melodious continuity. A woman laughed. A hundred feet or more below him, tourists lounged around a swimming pool. Their resort hotel clung to the cliffs as if defying gravity, steep walkways winding from level to level. The walls were of bleached white limestone, going pink in the lowering light. The pool was a breathless azure, its rippling surface catching the sun and glistening like amber jewels.

As much as he disapproved of the commercialization of this ancient coast, a resort hotel was the reason he was here. Heavy equipment had been brought in to grade a foundation for a new resort, but the giant earth-moving blades hadn't even made a complete pass across the site before they broke through the strata, opening a chamber of some kind. The antiquities department had sent in investigators, who had rappelled into the chamber for the initial survey. It was a dwelling of some kind, buried beneath the ejecta of one of the earlier eruptions. The style, though, wasn't Minoan or Hellene. The style was strange. And so he had been called in with his students to excavate the site.

He heard chants and shouts on the wind, faint but growing louder, sounding from his height no different than the cackles and squawks of the gulls. A crowd came into view, marching north along the Thiras-Megalochonou Road. Another protest. Even here, he thought sourly, on this little island. What was it they were chanting? Had they nothing better to do?

"*Professor K?*"

He spun out of the wind at the voice, startled. His bushy gray beard and eyebrows couldn't hide his disapproval. It wasn't the intrusion he objected to, but the pet name his students had given him. It was Katia who had called him—no, *Kate*, a student from the American continent. The young people from that side of the world were less observant of formalities, and their command of etiquette was limited, bordering on disrespect. He glowered through dark eyes at the girl, who seemed not the least bit discomfited. The young people from the Americas were also insufferably cocksure of themselves.

"Yes, what is it?" he snapped. They were speaking English Standard, something else that annoyed him. How the language of that little island had become the language of science was a mystery to him.

"We're through the archway," Kate informed him, not at all taken aback by his tone. She had wild brown hair and freckles, a plain but confident face, and a smudge of dirt on her nose. "There's another chamber below," she added.

Professor Kupolos had anticipated this, even despite the bizarre architecture.

"No one has gone in?"

"No." Kate shook her head. "As you instructed—*Sir.*"

That last piqued him, but he swallowed back his indignation and let her get by with the veiled barb. It was best to keep the foreign students happy, distasteful as that was. After all, they made up three quarters of his crew.

"Very well then," he said. "Let's go have a look."

He threw a parting glance at the protestors down below.

"Why do they do it?" he mulled out loud. "What does it accomplish?"

Kate looked at him curiously. "You tell *me*," she said.

Sha'raelon did not allow the smile to slip from her face until she was with Pa'ket and well away from the Security Council. They left the building wordlessly, moving briskly, joined the path along the East River and then slowed their pace.

"The reek of the air here," Sha'raelon complained. "Foetid. But I believe it is worse indoors. Their perfumes and colognes make me gag. I can scarcely breathe."

"The interview did not go well." Pa'ket stated flatly.

"These people have minds that compose circular schemes, and then schemes atop schemes within those. It is a trial to peel away their layers. It is exhausting."

She paused to bring long fingers to the bridge of her nose, squeezed her eyes tightly while she massaged at a gathering headache.

"I swear, Pa'ket, I cannot breathe!"

"Calm yourself Mistress. There are people gathering near."

Sha'raelon blinked at her discomfort, raised her face toward the sun.

"The sun is so dirty in this time. It looks weak. I was trained to expect this, but still I romanticized the era, like a holoview play. Knights, chivalry, adventure."

"Mistress," Pa'ket commented dryly. "The era you describe is at least another thousand years behind us. And it was certainly less romantic in the living of it."

"Oh, I know, Pa'ket."

A small bird hummed above them, darting in and out, feathers iridescent in the rusty light.

"A hummingbird," Sha'raelon noted absently. "Are our surveillance countermeasures operating?"

Pa'ket patted a rectangular object under his robe. "Always, Mistress. We can continue to speak freely."

"Who sent it, do you think?"

"There is no way for us to know, Mistress."

"The Americans probably," she speculated. "They are such a paranoid people."

Sha'raelon smiled at the comedy of it, held out her hand for Pa'ket's elbow. The two resumed their stroll.

"This era is marked by nothing," she thought aloud after a moment. She mulled this in silence for a few steps and then said, "I should like to have met Amelia Earhart, or Aung San Suu Kyi, or...or Joan of Arc! There is nothing in this time except distress. Such a waste."

"This is the time of *your* coming, though, Mistress," Pa'ket remarked gently. "Surely you will launch a new era."

"Oh, Pa'ket," she raised a hand affectionately to his face. "Do you not know our history either?"

"No more than you, Mistress."

Sha'raelon felt a pang at that. A cloud passed across the sun, casting them in shadow, masking the darkness in her eyes. Sha'raelon shivered despite the heat. The air was damp and her gown was beginning to cling. She took a deep breath and gazed out over the river, shaking her head.

"They want us to debate," she said.

"Mistress?"

"Mr. Canto and me. They want us to debate during a real-time broadcast. It is undignified and it is unwise. It will only serve to polarize the people. I must speak with Mr. Canto about this. Perhaps we can agree to moderate our responses, minimize the divisiveness."

"His invitation for...coffee?"

"Yes. I think today would be—"

"*There she is!*"

Sha'raelon and Pa'ket spun about to discover a crowd rushing toward them. Pa'ket pushed Sha'raelon behind him and adjusted his stance, bending at the knees, feet toed inward, right foot placed one step back. He thrust the Sha ceremonial baton forward to hold off the crowd.

"No, Pa'ket," Sha'raelon said urgently. "They are not violent, I am sure of it."

"Mistress..."

"No, look," Sha'raelon pointed. "There are young girls among them."

Sha'raelon! Sha'raelon! the crowd chanted.

Soon they were surrounded. A teenaged girl looked up excitedly to meet Sha'raelon's eyes. "You're so beautiful!" the girl exclaimed.

"Well thank you," Sha'raelon blushed. "You are beautiful, too. A beautiful, powerful young woman."

Hands were reaching past Pa'ket, grabbing holds on Sha'raelon's gown.

Sha'raelon! Sha'raelon!

"Enough!" Pa'ket roared in a deep, reverberating voice that sounded as if it were coming down from the sky. The crowd fell immediately silent, either stunned or in awe. "Now back away!" he ordered. "Give the Mistress some space."

The crowd shrank back. Sha'raelon folded her hands delicately at her waist and smiled serenely over the crowd. "I am humbled by your affection," she told them.

Security officers were racing toward them, all men, padded with armor and dressed in black. Jarren Canto was out ahead of them, sprinting along the river in long, loping strides, his dress coat flapping behind him like a black cape, maroon tie streaming over his shoulder. Sha'raelon had time to wonder how he practiced such a powerful stride aboard a ship in space.

"Break it up!" one of the officers shouted on the run. Suddenly the officers were among them, truncheons raised. There were nervous murmurs and cries in the crowd.

"Sirs! Officers! Stop!" Sha'raelon begged. "There is no danger here."

The officers seemed unsure of themselves. Truncheons were lowered haltingly. A cheer went up from the crowd, composed mostly of women, from the aged to the young.

"I am due back inside," Sha'raelon announced, projecting her voice over the crowd. "Let us all walk together, shall we?"

She held out her hands. Girls and young women took hold of her hands and moved with her in a pack along the river. She spoke to them as they walked, beaming smiles, laughing at this or that. Jarren followed closely behind with Pa'ket. The security officers separated from the pack and stood in a group, looking on in confusion.

"She certainly has a way with them," Jarren commented.

"It is why she was chosen," Pa'ket said proudly.

The crowd had grown even larger by the time they reached the steps into the building, with curious men joining in as well. Sha'raelon took two steps, trailing her hand behind as she climbed. She turned to look out over the crowd. She was wearing a peach colored gown today, with bronze strapped sandals and a braided bronze belt. Her hair was unbound, falling to her waist and stirring in the breeze.

"I feel your love," she told them. "And your support. We will journey together into a future of promise and hope. All of us. Together."

The crowd roared at that. Tears tracked down faces young and old, even among some of the men. Sha'raelon sought out the teenaged girl who had held her hand, beamed a motherly smile, and then turned into the building with Pa'ket and Jarren close behind. Pa'ket was deeply pleased. He felt joy welling in his chest even as he maintained his usual reserve. Truly the Mistress had found her voice. Her face was alight, breathless with energy. The pessimism she had felt earlier was gone, forgotten, subsumed by the crowd.

"They have been so without hope," Sha'raelon remarked sadly as they moved further inside. Security had taken up station along the entrance, although no one had followed them in. Pa'ket was at her side, with Jarren trailing behind. "They live such empty lives."

"You had quite an effect on them," said Jarren, somewhat in awe himself.

Sha'raelon turned to him slowly, confused in the moment.

"Why are you here?" she asked candidly. It sounded like a rebuke to Jarren but he didn't show it.

"I saw a crowd swarming toward you and I was concerned. I thought you could use my help."

Sha'raelon's laugh was short but sharp. "*Your* help? Mr. Canto, I assure you that is the least of my needs."

If Jarren was insulted he masked it well.

"Very well then, Mistress Sha," he said with a confident smile and a tip of his head. "I will leave you to your day."

Pa'ket cleared his throat as Jarren walked off. Sha'raelon immediately caught his meaning. "Oh, yes. I had forgotten, Pa'ket." And then she called after Jarren: "Mr. Canto? I meant to ask your opinion of this debate they have requested."

Jarren stopped and turned but did not retrace his steps. "I have no concerns about a debate," he said.

"Oh, I see."

There was that vulnerable sound in her voice again. "Well," Jarren added, "it does seem a sophomoric request to me."

Sha'raelon brightened.

"Would you be willing to discuss it with me?" she asked. "Over...coffee? That is, if your invitation is still open."

"I would be pleased," said Jarren. "When is a good time?"

"Now would be a good time."

Jarren registered surprise at that. Sha'raelon could see that he was thinking quickly. She crossed the few steps that separated them and hovered there as he made up his mind. Again she noted his scent, warm and natural without those nauseating perfumes.

"Very well," he said. The smirk had returned. "Shall we take your limousine?"

"Is it far?"

"Maybe a kilometer."

"Then we should walk. I suddenly find the weather outside to be inspiring."

She had caught him by surprise again.

"I would be equally pleased to walk with you," he said without hesitation. "But dressed as you are you will be recognized. I'm afraid we wouldn't make it far before you drew another crowd."

"You are right, of course," she said. "Very sensible." Her brows knitted in thought. "Where could I possibly find a change of clothing?"

"Have you no change of clothes?"

"All of my clothes are aboard ship."

Pa'ket unbelted his robe and held it open for Sha'raelon. She questioned him with her eyes but then smiled affectionately at the impassive expression on his face. She sighed and slipped into the robe, which fell only as far as her calves, but it was enough of a disguise to allow her to walk freely in public. Once she pulled the hood over her golden hair she became as anonymous as anyone else afoot in New York City. Pa'ket wore a simple white tunic underneath, over loose linen pants, with a wide faux leather belt cinching it all down over his round belly. The belt held compartments of various sizes, their contents a mystery to Jarren. Along with the Sha ceremonial baton hanging from his shoulder, Pa'ket looked strange, but no stranger than many of the people Jarren had seen here, who actually seemed to become invisible in their eccentricity.

"Shall we then?" Jarren smiled smugly, offering his elbow to Sha'raelon, an action that caused Pa'ket visible distress. Pa'ket gathered his composure quickly, though, and nodded his assent. Sha'raelon accepted Jarren's arm and allowed him to lead her out into the city.

Dr. John J. Fischer, as it turned out, was a consultant to the government of the United States, specifically the Department of Defense. Simon Hammerskjold found him at a research lab in Sacramento, California.

"Dr. Fischer," said Simon, wearily offering his hand. He had been airborne for most of the past thirty-six hours. His eyes were grainy red hollows, and the stubble on his face itched. It was a warm morning outside, with a wind up from the south. Dry San Joaquin sand irritated his sinuses the way the dust of Jerusalem had.

"Dr. Hammerskjold, I presume," said Fischer, grinning as they shook hands. "You look like you could use some coffee."

Fischer was in his upper seventies, thin and energetic for his age, with thick, iron gray hair pulled tightly into a ponytail. He had a sharp face, a small mouth, and a diastema that made his teeth look crooked.

Simon's stomach felt like churning acid. "No coffee," he barked. "Where can we talk?"

Fischer was taken aback. "Okeydokey then. Right this way."

They settled in at a long table in a conference room. Simon tossed his briefcase and overcoat onto the table and then walked around the room kicking doors closed.

"Why all the cloak-and-dagger?" asked Fischer. "The whole world knows they're here."

"I have been to see Dr. Roth," Simon said impatiently. "Tell me what you know."

"Ah..." Fischer mouthed. "How is the old man?"

Simon flicked a glance at his watch. "I meet with the president in ten hours, Dr. Fischer. Let's save the small talk."

So Dr. Hammerskjold is one of these self-important types, Fischer thought. Just a kid, really. He could talk circles around the boy if he wanted to, but...funding. It always came down to funding.

"Uh, okay, uh, where to begin?"

"How about at the beginning?"

"It's a long story."

"Condense it where you can."

"Okay, uh—Dr. Roth. It started with him. I had him at Berkeley in the 80s, theoretical physics. There was nothing special about the day. I can't remember what the lecture was. Dr. Roth was writing stuff on the blackboard— we still used chalk then," Fischer gleamed insouciantly at Simon before continuing, "—and then Dr. Roth just froze in front of the blackboard, like he'd forgotten what he was doing. Next thing you know he's erasing figures with his sleeve and scribbling stuff down, chalk dust everywhere. People thought he'd lost it—*I* thought he'd lost it. Books were slamming, students were getting up and leaving, and he ignored us, just kept scribbling.

"And then I saw it. Everyone was gone by then, just me sitting there, and this equation is popping off the blackboard like a neon sign. I didn't understand the half of it, but I could see that there was some real genius going on so I copied it down. And that brings us to 2029."

Fischer paused for effect.

"2029?" Simon asked.

"99942 Apophis, Dr. Hammerskjold. Don't you remember how fun *that* was?"

"But the Apophis asteroid didn't hit—"

"No, it didn't hit the Earth, but it *did* hit a DOD orbital that no one was supposed to know about, and this gave it a wobble that increased the odds of it hitting on the 2036 pass."

"But it didn't hit *then*, either. What has this got to do with time travel?"

"Everything, I think."

Simon was so weary he could barely keep his eyes open, but something in Fischer's tone yanked him alert.

"Our goal," Fischer continued, "was to launch a series of satellites that would keep station along Earth's orbital arc. Think of it as trailing buoys out behind a ship, buoys equipped with radar and communications and armed countermeasures. The idea was to deploy an early warning system. We called it project Orion Shield."

"I've never heard of this—"

"Well, you wouldn't have, would you? We put *nukes* on those things, man, with plutonium reactors. Thank God none of them crashed."

"You mean they're out there now?" Simon asked incredulously.

"Only five of them. We parked the first one at L1 to serve as a permanent near-Earth relay."

"You mean to tell me that we have a *nuclear platform* at Lagrange One?"

"It's nestled right up there next to SOHO," Fischer grinned, the SOlar and Heliospheric Observatory.

Simon winced and lowered his forehead to the table. "Go on," he groaned.

"We had originally planned for ten satellites, but it took so long. The orbital mechanics were...complicated. Anyway," Fischer shook off a stray thought, "by the time we launched Number Five, Apophis had come back around and we knew then that it wasn't going to hit. DOD cut off our funding and the project was cancelled. Oh, but we were gods for a few years there. Poor NASA, we thought, still looking for microbes on Mars while *we* did the real work in space."

"The president has never briefed me on this," Simon moaned while rubbing his temples with his palms. "But I still don't understand what this has to do with time travel."

"Well, that's where Dr. Roth's equation comes in. You see, Numbers Two through Five are not in orbit. In order to accurately track any inbounds, we needed them to keep station in fixed positions in space, that's why we used the plutonium reactors, which means that we would drift away from them over time. We will still be getting telemetry for decades, but I realized that they would mark a point in space where Earth *used* to be. Do you understand? *Used* to be. And I remembered Dr. Roth's causality equation, which pretty much demonstrates the *fact* of time travel if not the means."

Simon raised his forehead from the table with a rising awareness in his eyes. "My God," he said.

"You're getting it, aren't you?" said Fischer. "The problem with fictional time travel is that these characters are always going through the fictional time machine and then popping out in the same place, only a thousand years earlier or something like that. But a thousand years ago *Earth was not located where it is now.* Those fictional time travelers should have materialized in *outer space.*"

"So you—"

"I put neutrino emitters on the satellites as a secondary tasking. It was easy to bury the cost, hell, DOD was throwing money at us hand over fist, and if someday the technology came along then we would already have the means in place to exploit it."

"Dr. Roth said time travel would be possible if you could puncture the space-time continuum with a gravitic probe—"

"Which would leave you sluicing along through the quantum foam. *Unless* there was a beacon to show you where to surface, like a submarine in the ocean homing in on a radio signal."

He had the boy's attention now, Fischer gloated. Simon had come fully alert.

"So," Fischer went on, "we have a satellite at L1 marking our current position in space-time. The other four cover roughly 500-year increments, say birth of Christ to the present. Here's the rub, though: You can only travel backward; there's no going forward, even if we shot satellites into our future arc. Dr. Roth's equation demonstrates this. Which means that your two time travelers are stuck here."

"My God, my God, my God…"

"I think I know how their ships work," Fischer grinned, adding the coup de grace.

"How?" Simon asked, so overawed now that it came out as a hoarse whisper.

"Those rings going around them—they're some kind of a particle accelerator."

"They're using antimatter," said Simon, awed.

"Antimatter," Fischer sighed. "Damn, I wish I was thirty again."

Simon drank scotch during his return flight to D.C., enough scotch to send his mind reeling with the repercussions of what he had learned from Dr. Fischer. Some cold water on his face, a shave, and a clean shirt made him presentable to the president.

"Madam President," Simon greeted his boss as night gathered over the White House. "This is going to take some time."

"You look as if you could use a scotch," said the president.

"It helps," Simon agreed. "Believe me."

Simon was giddy from the scotch as well as his new-found influence. Ever since the Office of Science and Technology Policy had been created in 1976, no science advisor had ever held such importance in an administration. President Carlyle, who usually demanded information from him in quick, digestible bites, leaving him scrambling along behind her as she flitted from meeting to meeting, cancelled her schedule for the evening and gave Simon *hours*.

"What do you think of this city?" Sha'raelon asked Jarren. The sidewalks were crowded, so Jarren had abandoned the formality of leading Sha'raelon along on his elbow. Instead the two walked side by side, Jarren sometimes having to duck in behind her as files of people went by. Pa'ket followed a few paces further back, seeming to be wandering obliviously although his senses remained trained on the way ahead, the way behind, and the conduct of their host. He received a few long looks from people, but no one recognized them.

"It's primitive," Jarren replied, "but it has energy. I have found it not unpleasing to live here."

"But it is so dirty," Sha'raelon complained, "and chaotic—and loud. It is like trying to find order in a hill of angry ants."

"I think that's what I like about this place," said Jarren. "It reminds me of home."

"Of home? I thought you lived in space."

"I do, much of the time, but I know of a few frontier cities that are not much different than this."

"New York City in my time is a jewel." Sha'raelon's eyes seemed to wander to a place far away. "It gleams with translucent domes and glittering spires that pierce the clouds. There are stepped forums, and fountains. Central Park is still there, along with islands of green high above, suspended from glistening threads of walkways like webs. The rivers are clean, and so blue. Salmon run them in a frenzy to spawn—it is a sight to see—and right whales often come in near the shore."

"It sounds beautiful. Is this where you live—in your time?"

"No, I am from Athens. But I received training here."

"Training?"

Sha'raelon fixed him with knowing eyes.

"Oh, *training*," he said. "For this."

"Yes."

"Then you should know your way around the city quite intimately."

"Not at all. As I said, it is very different."

"Does nothing remain from this time, then?"

"A cathedral, library, museums; a few lower buildings and monuments. The Statue of Liberty, of course. The rest of this," she gestured upward toward a skyline jagged with high-rises, "was not structurally sound enough to weather almost six centuries. Most of them did not last two centuries, and none of them could be retrofitted for antigrav lifts anyway. No, today—or in my time—the material that made this city forms coral reefs around the world."

"Humph."

They walked on in silence for a while. Sha'raelon was becoming uncomfortable inside Pa'ket's robe. The afternoon had become warmer yet, and the humidity kept a sheen on her cheeks and forehead. They passed a screen advertising a gossip site. Sha'raelon blanched and stopped to gawk at it.

"Look what they have done!" she exclaimed.

Jarren winced. It was an unflattering image.

"That is a photo of us earlier today," Sha'raelon realized. "On the steps into the United Nations building. What is this?"

She was drawing attention from the passersby. "Let's get away from here," Jarren encouraged her. He guided her by the shoulders, gently pushing her forward. Pa'ket paused at the screen. The disgust he felt was impossible to conceal. He snapped open one of the compartments on his belt, fingered a device inside, and the electronic screen went black.

"I am not *pregnant!*" Sha'raelon complained as they hurried on. "And we are not *aliens.* That is the most hideously undignified thing I have ever seen."

Jarren was laughing.

"What do you find so amusing?" Sha'raelon demanded.

"Well," Jarren sputtered. "The implication is clear—that I am the father of your alien baby."

"Mr. Canto!"

Jarren shook off his laugh and beseeched her with his eyes. "Can you not call me Jarren?"

"That would not be proper."

Jarren's chin fell while Sha'raelon pushed through the steady stream of people. Behind them Pa'ket smiled inwardly.

They came shoulder to shoulder again after a few paces.

"I did ask you once before," Sha'raelon said, "but your answer seemed incomplete. Why is it that *you* were chosen to represent your people?"

His face took on a pained look. "That is a question I have asked myself many times. I truly do not know."

"We looked for you, you know. In my time," she said. "If not you then your father or mother, to—"

"To gain some insight?"

"Yes. But we found nothing of you. Just the background genome."

"We looked for you, too."

"Yes?"

"And we found you—not you, of course, but someone close to you. There is a world in my time called Atheanna. Your descendents, or antecedents—damn it is hard to keep this straight—nevertheless they are there. They are a matriarchal society, fiercely independent. They have warriors, we call them *Amazons*, and we leave them alone. Neither were *we* able to gain any useful information."

Sha'raelon felt a stirring of pride. "You were right," she said contemplatively. "We have diverged much."

"How did this happen, do you think?"

"I think a butterfly flapped its wings."

Jarren rolled his eyes. "Seriously?" he said.

Sha'raelon was grinning at him. Jarren discovered that he liked her this way.

"You see," she smiled. "I can be witty as well."

Jarren returned her smile. "It's a good fit for you," he said.

They crossed a busy street at the light and shouldered their way across.

"It's right up here," Jarren said. "Café Diana."

"Diana?" said Sha'raelon. "I think I will like this place."

They took a table under an awning, looking out over a low rail toward the sidewalk and street beyond. The sun was well behind them now although the tops of the high towers still blazed with afternoon light. Pa'ket stood outside on the sidewalk beyond the rail, yet close enough to be near in case she needed him—and to catch bits of their conversation.

Sha'raelon allowed Jarren to order for her since she had accepted his invitation. Their server was a young woman with dark eyes and straight black hair to her shoulders. She had a compact body and a web of Polynesian tattoos on the left side of her face. She looked at the two curiously for a moment then spun around abruptly to turn in their order.

"We'll have to keep our voices low," Jarren said. The table next to them was empty but there were still plenty of patrons in the place.

"We should discuss this debate," said Sha'raelon.

"What is there really to discuss?" Jarren asked. "We don't live in each other's worlds and therefore know nothing upon which to base an argument. We must simply state our cases and let them decide."

"Do you not fear that the people watching this broadcast will choose sides? This *debate*," she spat the word, "will certainly be watched all over the world. It could cause violence. We should agree not to participate. Neither of us would gain an advantage and neither of us would be harmed."

"I understand your point." Jarren was clicking a fingernail against the table, thinking. "But I believe the people *should* know—everything. Let *them* decide what they want for their future. Let democracy play its part and have this responsibility off of our shoulders."

"Democracy is a foolish exercise," Sha'raelon said firmly under her breath. She had both of her hands flat on the table. Her cheeks were reddening. "Democracy allows the worst to run wild and forces the best to remain silent."

"I would rather be free to make my own mistakes than to have those mistakes made for me." Jarren kept his voice level, even as Sha'raelon glared at him. "Everyone wishes they could change the past, repair mistakes, right wrongs. It's how we learn."

"We are not here to change the *past*," Sha'raelon hissed. "We are here to change the *future*."

"Yes," Jarren said, wincing at her tone, "but the future is just someone else's past."

Sha'raelon opened her mouth to argue but their server arrived just then with their coffees. The silence was potent. Icy green eyes locked with eyes of steel blue, but there was no fierceness in his eyes, only weariness. Or sadness.

Jarren waited until their server had moved well away.

"It would seem that we have been debating," he said. "Debating the debate." He smiled. "You may have a point after all. Can we set this issue aside for now?"

Jarren took a careful sip of his coffee.

"Mmm, this is good."

Sha'raelon returned his smile tenuously, and with that the tension drained from her face. She lifted her own cup and sipped.

"Yes, it *is* very good," she said. "Do you allow your crew to come down to the surface, to enjoy this themselves?"

"I don't have a crew," Jarren answered flatly.

"What?" Sha'raelon settled her cup into its saucer. "No crew? Then you mean...they sent you here *alone*?"

"All by myself."

Suddenly Sha'raelon could feel the ache of the man's loneliness. The cocky swagger—he was compensating, she knew it.

"Then why do you keep your ship in orbit?" she asked.

Jarren had set his cup down. He was absently twirling his earring, gazing vacantly over the rail.

"This will end, you know," he said somberly, his eyes fixed on nothing but memory. "One way or the other.

And regardless, we're trapped. And so when it's over I intend to go home—to the stars. My ship is in orbit where it's safe. Down here...if something happened, if they took it from me, I would be stranded."

"But, but—" Sha'raelon struggled for words. "But there will be no people. It is *empty* out there."

"It's not completely empty."

"But those species will not know you either. You would rather live among them than your own kind?"

Jarren's eyes were glazed, reflecting the traffic on the street.

"Would you please look at me when you speak," Sha'raelon said tersely.

Jarren turned toward her numbly, met her eyes. His face was drawn.

"Your earring is really too large," she commented. "It makes you look vain, and I am learning that you are not a vain man despite the way you present yourself."

"My wife," he said soberly.

"*Your wife?* You are *married?*" And then the realization struck her like a shock. "Oh no, no, no—they made you leave her. How horrible. You wear your wife's earring as a memento. Of course. I had no idea. How awful of me."

"No," Jarren said, his voice weak. He leaned in closer. "This earring *is* my wife."

Sha'raelon sat dumbfounded. Her jaw fell.

"They wanted her so that they could get to me," Jarren continued in a monotone. He lowered his eyes to his hands. "They came at her with three ships, boxed her in. She had no choice but to go superlight in the blind."

Now his eyes were wet.

"She came out right on top of a gas giant, bits of her ship flying off. There was no time. She got off a beacon but she couldn't pull out. She left a trail of debris into the lower atmosphere. The pressure—"

Sha'raelon ached inside.

"—and this is what I found."

She reached across and took his hand. "Jarren—"

"So they took our daughter and made a deal with me."

"You have a *daughter?*"

"It was a simple deal: If I pull this off, she lives; if I don't, she dies."

Jarren sniffed and pulled his hand away from Sha'raelon. He wiped his eyes quickly with his sleeve, sat back and took a sip of his coffee. Their server was edging around them, casting furtive glances. Sha'raelon pulled the hood lower over her forehead.

"But none of this matters," he went on after a minute of reflection. "It's futile, I tell you. We come from but two of multiple realities, and by coming here we have probably spawned an infinity of new ones. Somewhere among them, perhaps in many, my wife and I are together with our daughter and none of this—matters—one—whit."

"I wish we could know that, Jarren." She reached for his hand again. "I fear that time is like the roots of a tree. You can dig down, chop off some of the little roots, change things, yet the main root will grow on."

Jarren smiled tightly and squeezed her hand, the color coming back into his face. He looked into her eyes.

"Well," he said, "since we're on a first-name basis now perhaps you should tell me a little about *your* life."

"Oh!" Sha'raelon snatched her hand away. "I have forgotten myself. These things you have told me are...are deeply moving."

Jarren kept silent while Sha'raelon tipped her head in thought.

"I have not suffered as you," she said after a moment. "And my story is short: I was taken as an infant, revered like a messiah, and spent my entire life being trained for this mission. I carry their names, of course, but I have never been allowed to meet my parents. I have not mated, bonded, or had children. Pa'ket has been with me since I was thirteen. If not for him I, too, would be alone."

"I know that Rae is your name," Jarren said. Sha'raelon reddened at that. "But I don't understand the rest of it."

"I was taught the history of this," she said. "I was taught about *you*. In the telling you were a barbarian from a savage future. I had assumed that you were taught a similar history about me."

"I received only basic information," he said. "I don't know if it was because they didn't want to tell me, or if they didn't know themselves. They told me who you were, or would be, that you came from an entrenched matri-lineal society, and that if I didn't succeed my daughter would—"

"Yes," Sha'raelon cut in quickly. "But 'entrenched' sounds so...so *stagnant*. And we are not that. Far from it."

"And yet you refused to venture outside of the solar system. You have the technology—why won't your culture expand into space?"

"Because there are aliens out there and we deemed it not safe. We chose not to draw attention to ourselves."

Jarren was nodding. "Yeah," he said. "There has been conflict."

"And what of your Earth?" Sha'raelon asked.

Jarren's eyes hooded. "There was a conflict early on. Earth took some hits. It was bad, or so they say."

"So, you see?"

"I see that if you don't find them then they will find you sooner or later."

"We can take care of ourselves," she said menacingly. "And we would not pose a threat to them anyway."

"It's hard for me to imagine not being able to go into space."

"But the solar system is vast," Sha'raelon said emphatically. "There is much to learn and explore. How much time have *you* spent in the solar system?"

"None."

"Well there you have it."

"Okay, okay," Jarren conceded the point while shaking his head. "Still, one could live in a big house and yet wonder what was across the street."

"It is a *really* big house," Sha'raelon said.

Jarren nodded. "And your name? I don't understand it. Is it Sha, is it Rae—?"

Sha'raelon reached across to silence him with the tip of her finger. "The use of the given is for intimates," she said shyly. "Its use is very personal to us, as if we were being...undressed."

Sha'raelon was embarrassed to be speaking about this, but after what he had revealed she felt compelled to satisfy his curiosity. She glanced over her shoulder toward Pa'ket, who was sweeping the street with his eyes. She leaned in close to Jarren and lowered her voice even further.

"In our society we carry both our mother's and father's names. My mother was of the Sha, my father was of the Lon."

"What about Pa'ket, then?"

"Pa'ket is a monk. He serves the Mother, and so carries only Her name."

"Then what would you name *your* children?"

"Their names will be—" Sha'raelon caught herself. Her lips trembled. Jarren noticed. She sipped her coffee before continuing. "*Were* I to have children, I could name them for the Sha and continue that tradition, or if I desired to establish my own line I could name them..." she hesitated before saying it aloud, "...Rae, although this has fallen out of favor. It is considered scandalous. Daughters pass on their mother's line. Sons pass on their father's line."

"Sounds complicated."

"No, it is really very simple."

"Would you consider having children here?" Jarren asked. Sha'raelon looked away.

"I do not wish to discuss that," she said with a trace of anger.

"My apologies," Jarren offered sincerely, but with a note of suspicion in his voice. "It's none of my business."

Their server appeared over Jarren's shoulder, staring down at Sha'raelon, dipping her head to try to see into Sha'raelon's hood.

"It *is* you!" the woman practically shouted. "Sha'raelon. I *knew* it."

"Uh, oh," Jarren moaned. Heads were turning their way. A few people on the sidewalk stopped to stare.

"*Ohmygod!*" the woman exclaimed. "Sha'raelon! Here! There are so many things I want to ask you."

Jarren saw Sha'raelon's hands going for the hood over her head, realized what she was about to do, reached out to stop her but he was too late. Sha'raelon flipped the hood off and tugged out her hair until it spilled over the back of her chair. She smiled at the woman, an affectionate, maternal smile.

"Sit here," Sha'raelon patted the table. "Tell me your name and ask your questions."

"Damn," said Jarren.

The woman was giddy with delight. She tipped up and down on her toes, seemed not to know what to do with her hands, finally clasped them in front of her and sat.

"I'm Bethany," the woman said. She was bouncing on her chair, so excited.

"Bethany," Sha'raelon repeated thoughtfully. "*Be'thany.* A beautiful name. Your tattoos are very distinctive, Be'thany. Tell me what they mean."

Bethany was so enchanted by the exotic way Sha'raelon pronounced her name that she couldn't catch her breath. She held one hand to her chest, waved air onto her face with the other. Sha'raelon sat on, looking amused but not condescending. People were beginning to gather around the table and at the rail.

"Damn. Damn, damn," Jarren muttered. He pushed away from the table, stood, and looked over the growing crowd toward Pa'ket. "Pa'ket," Jarren shouted to be heard. "Call for the limousine. Quickly."

Pa'ket had neither needed nor wanted direction from Jarren Canto. The limousine was already on its way.

Sha'raelon had given her full attention to Bethany. She was patting the woman's hand, lavishing her with praise, listening intently as Bethany poured forth stories of life and pain and desperate want. People were starting to push and shove to catch a glimpse of the Woman From the Future, but Sha'raelon was oblivious.

Sha'raelon! Sha'raelon! the crowd began to chant.

"Where does this devotion *come* from?" Jarren asked out loud, although his voice was lost to the chanting and shrieks all around them.

He was being jostled, pushed aside by a woman who must have been a half meter shorter than him. Other women were shouldering their ways in, displacing him from his position at the table. He lost sight of Sha'raelon through the sea of bobbing heads.

"Now that's enough!" Jarren growled. He pushed through to Sha'raelon's side, took her by the shoulders and lifted her to her feet.

A collective gasp came from the crowd, which had become a mob. Hands began to beat at him. The chant became, *Don't touch her! Don't touch her!* Bethany's eyes were knives. She looked as if she were about to pounce.

"Sha'raelon," he pleaded. "You have got to calm this down."

"*Make way for the Mistress!*" shouted Pa'ket. He had climbed over the rail and was clearing a space by virtue of his girth.

Sha'raelon seemed to have only just become aware of their predicament. Her face worked through levels of astonishment as she looked out over the mob. "Please, everyone. Be calm," she begged them.

No one could hear her.

Jarren began pulling her toward the rail, got her turned around and then pushed her against Pa'ket, who threw a leg over the rail and lifted his Mistress over and onto the sidewalk. Jarren sidled in behind them, shoving with his shoulder, and then he tipped inelegantly over the rail himself. The mob outside the café had become tightly packed, swaying back and forth like one body. Camera flashes were popping off like fireworks. A horn was honking in the street, the limousine creeping through, people out ahead like a bow wave.

"Get in! Get in!" shouted Jarren.

He held the door open with his hip and pulled Sha'raelon while Pa'ket pushed. They all tumbled in.

"Driver! Go!" Jarren ordered. He tugged at the door, but hands were holding it open.

Horn blaring, the limousine inched ahead in jerks and stops. Jarren kicked at fingers, got the door closed at last. With Sha'raelon out of sight behind tinted glass, the mob began to loose its energy. The driver edged up onto the opposite sidewalk, a burst of acceleration, and then they were clear.

Jarren was on the floor, splayed atop Sha'raelon and Pa'ket. He pushed himself up carefully and fell back onto the rear seat. As gently as he could, he pulled Sha'raelon up until she fell back next to him. Pa'ket lifted himself onto hands and knees and then took the forward seat across from them.

"Mistress," Pa'ket said in a pant. "*That* was unwise."

"I do not understand," Sha'raelon mumbled in shock.

"They love you so much they're willing to trample you to death," Jarren cursed.

Their driver made a right turn, which brought them into a canyon of towering buildings. Traffic was stopped ahead at a traffic light.

"You have to understand them," Sha'raelon pleaded. "They want, so much, to *believe*."

"Believe in what?" Jarren shot back. He examined his skinned knuckles. His lower lip was beginning to swell.

Pa'ket watched uneasily as traffic piled up behind them. Jarren strummed his fingers at the traffic light ahead, willing it to turn green and get them moving again.

"*Mistress!*" Pa'ket screamed. He dove toward her, yanked her forcefully to the floor and covered her with his body.

Jarren could barely register Pa'ket's actions before an explosion erupted at the rear of the limousine and he was launched upward into the ceiling. Granules of safety glass shot through like driven snow, and then weightlessness. Something was burning his neck. Rending metal tore at his ears. He heard screams. The air was acrid, gauzy with smoke, and then an impact slammed him onto his head.

The silence, when it came, was relative. There was hissing, and crackling heat. There were screams from outside and moaning from within. Jarren's neck ached. He tested his arms, his legs, found himself splayed across Sha'raelon and Pa'ket again, this time on a crumpled ceiling. Sha'raelon looked unconscious. Pa'ket was growling like an enraged bear.

"Move, Canto!" Pa'ket ordered. "*Move!*"

Jarren crabbed to the side while Pa'ket pulled himself from under his Mistress.

"I must get her out," Pa'ket cried urgently. "Help me."

Pa'ket squeezed his bulk through a shattered door window and then reached in for Sha'raelon's arms. His hair was turning pink above his forehead. One of his cheeks was blistered. He pulled Sha'raelon by her wrists, tugging her ungently through the window. Her robe caught on some twisted metal.

"Canto. Lift her!"

Jarren balanced on his knees and lifted Sha'raelon at the ankles.

"Higher, Canto. Higher."

Without leverage he couldn't lift her much higher, but he got an arm under her knees and stretched as far as he could. Something pulled in his back, but he ignored the pain and shoveled Sha'raelon forward until Pa'ket was able to drag her out onto the street.

"Come now, Mr. Canto," Pa'ket urged, peering low through the window. "Give me your hand."

"The driver," Jarren said, wincing from pain as he turned toward the front of the limousine. "We have to check the driver."

"He is dead, Canto. Leave him."

"We don't know that!"

Jarren flipped onto his back and kicked himself forward. The driver was hanging from his restraints, unconscious. Blood dripped in elongated drops from the tip of the man's nose and from his ear. Jarren checked the man's pulse, which was strong.

"He's alive," shouted Jarren. "I can get him out. Help me, Pa'ket."

"I will not leave the Mistress, Mr. Canto. Come out of there. Leave him to his fate."

Jarren got hold of a buckle and pulled it. The driver fell onto him, smearing blood on Jarren's face. Jarren took the man by the jacket collar and tugged toward the window. He backed out onto the street feet first and then got to his knees, pulling hand over hand at the driver's clothing, bringing an arm through and then a shoulder. Pa'ket had carried Sha'raelon onto the sidewalk and had her propped against a wall. He was ministering her with something from one of his belt compartments. Her eyes rolled open and she lifted her head groggily.

Jarren had the driver's head and shoulders through the window now, and was able to stand and pull the man from under the arms.

"Another comes, Canto! *Beware!*" screamed Pa'ket.

A second explosion crashed, blowing Jarren backward across the sidewalk and into a wall. The limousine lurched upward, crashed down on its side. Jarren staggered to his feet, holding out a hand to ward the heat off of his face. A drone the size of an eagle swooped up from the wreck and hovered, turning wing-tip barrels toward the survivors. Jarren heard a metallic pop—pop, pop, pop—and a line of impacts stitched a diagonal in the wall above his head, showering him with masonry and dust.

"Projectile weapons!" Jarren warned, diving onto his stomach.

A particle beam lanced out from somewhere, slicing the drone cleanly in half. The wreckage of the drone clattered onto a burning yellow taxi. Jarren came woozily to his feet but kept his back pressed against the wall. He took in what he could of the scene through the smoke and his bleary, reddened eyes. Cars were burning, store windows were blown out. Bodies littered the street and sidewalk indiscriminately, some smoldering, some blown apart, walls splattered with gore.

"Here, Mr. Canto," he heard from Pa'ket. "There is an alley here. Too narrow for the drones to maneuver." Pa'ket had gotten Sha'raelon unsteadily to her feet and was hurrying her around a corner. Jarren slipped and staggered after them.

The alley was dank, dusky between towering, grimy walls that admitted only a sliver of light from high above. And it smelled like urine. Jarren caught up to them, shaking his head at the hollowness between his ears.

"Are you injured, Mr. Canto?" Pa'ket asked, gulping breaths.

Jarren patted at himself, searching for wounds. He flicked granules of warm glass out of his collar, wiped at the blood on his face. The blood was cold, not his. "I seem to be okay," he said shakily. "Twisted my back. And Sha'raelon?"

"I am fine now," Sha'raelon answered tightly, leaning on Pa'ket for support.

The three moved deeper into the alley. The screams of the victims were distant now. Sirens were warbling.

"Rest here for a moment," said Sha'raelon. A trickle of blood was drying in her ear, and her face was smudged with soot, but otherwise Jarren thought she looked all right.

"We should keep moving, Mistress," Pa'ket advised.

"This is a defensible position, Pa'ket. We need to assess before we go on."

"I agree with Sha'raelon," Jarren said. Pa'ket scowled at him.

"Very well," the monk sighed. "Sit here, Mistress." He cleared a space on a wooden crate and helped her to sit.

"Who has done this?" Sha'raelon asked acidly. "The Americans?"

"They have the most developed technology," Pa'ket said. "But also the Chinese. That drone—"

"That *drone*," Jarren hissed, "was taken out by a particle beam. And I know they don't have *that* technology."

"Someone else is here," Sha'raelon muttered in exhaustion. "But who? And why?"

Pa'ket and Jarren looked at one another blankly. Sha'raelon stood and shook off her dizziness.

"Everyone is fit?" she asked. "Pa'ket, your head is bleeding."

"A superficial cut, Mistress. Otherwise I am well."

"And you, Mr. Canto? Can you travel?"

"I'm fine," he said.

"Good, then. Let us keep to these alleys and make our way back to the United Nations. No one would dare strike there. Agreed?"

"Agreed, Mistress," said Pa'ket.

"Let's do it," said Jarren.

The alley widened ahead and made a turn to the left. Large metal trash containers were pushed against the walls. It was brighter, and they could hear traffic noise coming from the next block.

"I'll go on ahead and check it," Jarren said. Pa'ket nodded. Sha'raelon was lost in thought, her eyes working at the puzzle of the attack.

A shadow flashed across Jarren's face. He jerked his head upward and saw men rappelling silently down the walls. He counted six of them, all dressed in tight-fitting black, from their feet to the masks over their faces. The men let go their ropes and landed soundlessly ahead. Jarren gawked at them.

"You can't be serious," he exclaimed. "*Ninjas?*"

With that the men began to gyrate into aggressive stances, hooting and shrieking their movements, drawing out edged weapons and holding them menacingly.

"Uh, oh," Jarren mumbled with foreboding. He reached out blindly to his side to draw Sha'raelon behind him, but instead she pulled *him* behind *her.*

Sha'raelon stepped forward, unbelted her robe and let it fall. Pa'ket went into his crouch, held out the Sha ceremonial baton, as if that decorative piece of wood could hold off the danger. And then Pa'ket roared, a rumbling roar that reverberated off the walls. He flicked his wrist and gleaming blades extruded from either end of the baton. There was an attack cry from the masked men, and they leapt. Sha'raelon took two long steps and then she spun, flinging out a bronze-sandaled foot that connected with the head of a masked assassin, who then crumpled in a black heap, not even twitching.

Pa'ket was twirling the baton, spinning it like a propeller. From his crouch he launched himself forward, drove his arms down powerfully, and his blades dripped red. Another attacker fell, clutching at spilling entrails. Jarren stared wide-eyed at the melee. Sha'raelon somersaulted over a man. She kicked him off balance and then Pa'ket took the man's head. Three assassins remained, spinning and shrieking and clashing their steel against Pa'ket's blades. Sha'raelon jumped, ducked, swept with her foot and brought a man down, and then she came down with another foot on the man's neck. Jarren could hear the crack of vertebrae, the finality of that sound.

Jarren had never seen a more incongruous sight. Sha'raelon's gown flared to her hips as she launched roundhouse blows, as if she were a spinning top, her hair whipping like a golden blade. Her legs were muscled but lean, her thighs like solid passion. Her face shone with the ferocity and determination of Leonidas.

And Pa'ket...as agile as a leopard, no assassin had come close to striking him. The monk made his squat body do things Jarren had never imagined let alone seen. The man could leap over an assailant, come down on a knee and then lash out with his blade to slice low at an Achilles tendon, and then sweep around in one fluid movement to impale the next man.

Pa'ket ran the last assassin through and then held the man upright with his blade.

"Who sent you?" Pa'ket boomed.

The assassin gurgled behind his mask. Sha'raelon stepped up forcefully and ripped the mask off. The assassin was Caucasian. Blood trickled from the corners of his mouth. He took panting breaths but did not speak. And then his head drooped and it was over.

"Close your mouth, Mr. Canto," Sha'raelon said wryly with her back to him. She was examining their final assailant closely.

"Wha?"

"I told you we could take care of ourselves."

At a quick nod from Sha'raelon, Pa'ket withdrew his blade and let the dead assassin fall. A flick of his wrist retracted the blades into the baton.

Jarren was still gawking at them. Sha'raelon approached him with a sly smile.

"I trained for twenty years," she said. "What did you *think* they were teaching me?"

"Uh. I'm sorry I called you 'Packet'," Jarren muttered toward the monk.

Pa'ket ignored the apology. He was rummaging through the bodies, snatching off masks.

"One of them is a woman, Mistress," he announced.

Sha'raelon stepped close and leaned over the body. "I took this one," she whispered numbly. The woman's head lay at an odd angle, neck broken. "Asian. She was beautiful."

"Their use of edged weapons," Pa'ket said clinically, "swords, daggers, shurikens...We cannot trace them to a particular technology." He took swabs from a compartment on his belt, ran them across glazing teeth and dabbed them in blood.

"As I am sure was their intention," Sha'raelon remarked.

"We will sequence their DNA aboard ship, Mistress. At least we will be able to determine if they are contemporaries or not."

"Yes, Pa'ket. That knowledge would be of some value."

Pa'ket placed the swabs in specimen envelopes and then tucked the envelopes into a belt compartment.

"I will scout the way ahead," said Sha'raelon.

"No, Mistress," Pa'ket objected. "I will go ahead. Please remain here with our brave ship's captain."

Jarren stiffened at the veiled insult, but then laughed and nodded. "Okay, Pa'ket," he said. "I deserved that. We're even."

"Mistress," said Pa'ket. "There is blood on your face. When we reach the street we will not want to draw attention."

Sha'raelon raised a hand absently to her face and rubbed at a smear on her cheek.

"Yes, of course, Pa'ket," she smiled. "I must do something with this mess."

"I will not be far, Mistress," said the monk, and then he turned the corner toward the street.

Sha'raelon lifted the hem of her gown and used it to wipe her face. Jarren was treated to another view of her legs. Despite himself, he whistled. Sha'raelon looked his way with an amused tilt to her lips.

"Have you never seen a woman's legs, Mr. Canto," she grinned.

"Not legs like yours, Mistress Sha."

Here," Sha'raelon said. She ripped a swath from her gown. "You are bloodied as well, Mr. Canto. Let us attend to that."

Jarren held his head rigid as she wiped at his forehead and cheeks. Her fingers were strong, surprisingly cool, and her scent, adrenaline mingled with femininity, made something tingle in his belly.

"There," she appraised her work. "You look presentable now." She held out her arms to display the pitiable condition of her gown. "Had I anticipated this I would have worn something dark as well."

"We can fix that," Jarren said. He went to retrieve Pa'ket's robe.

High above them, two more assassins had watched silently as their marks below had separated. Now the big man was returning. The two nodded at one another, took hold of their ropes and jumped.

Pa'ket had just rounded the corner when a sword slashed out as if from nowhere. The blade took him in the right shoulder, biting deep enough to sever tendons.

"*Mistress!*" he screamed in warning, throwing his body to the left. The masked assassin landed on sure feet, went into a roll toward Pa'ket, and leapt at the monk with his sword raised high.

"*Pa'ket!*"

Sha'raelon's scream was charged with anguish. Behind her and Jarren the second assassin landed on bent knees and raised his own sword to strike. Sha'raelon's head whipped back and forth between the two assassins, her decision made in less than the tick of a single second. She launched herself forward to rescue Pa'ket.

Jarren backed away from the second assassin, with only fists against shining steel. The assassin lunged. Jarren dodged left, slipped, and slid against one of the bodies from the earlier attack. He scooped up a sword that lay at the fingertips of a dead hand and swung it up to block a slashing blow. The clang of steel rang through his arms as if he had been hit with a pipe. He rolled away from his attacker, kicked to his feet and slammed backward against a trash container. His attacker was on him before Jarren could really gain his footing. Jarren ducked as the blade came down. He spun himself in a squat around the corner of the container and stumbled to his feet. The strike meant for his head scraped along the container instead, a jarring, shrieking sound.

Sha'raelon cut through the air like a razor, left leg forward and extended, arms and right leg tucked in tight.

She caught Pa'ket's attacker in the chest and knocked the man off of his feet, came down on both legs, leapt, and spun. The assassin rolled away as she came down to impale him with her foot, but he had lost his sword. Sha'raelon's eyes glowed with hate as she adjusted her posture to fight hand-to-hand. The assassin did the same. The two rushed at one another, arms flying, hands formed like blades. She parried his hits, he parried hers.

Jarren held up his sword and backed away from the container. His attacker came at him cautiously. An icy finality condensed in Jarren's chest. He could hold his own with his fists, but he had never handled a sword in his life. In less than a harried breath he knew: he could block the first strike; the second one would kill him.

The battle between Sha'raelon and the first assassin moved too quickly to be followed. Arms whipped in tight arcs, were deflected, came in again at new angles. Sha'raelon grunted at the force of the blows while her attacker screeched and hollered his movements, flinging out legs, kicking and sweeping—and then her long arms found their opening and she stabbed with rigid fingers into his trachea. She could feel cartilage collapse but gave no more thought to a dead man who hadn't yet fallen to the ground. In a leaping and rolling motion she snatched up the Sha ceremonial baton, flicked her wrist, and then cast the vicious instrument like a spear.

Jarren blocked the first blow, and in surreal slowness watched his death coming in the arcing sweep of his attacker's arms. He clenched his teeth and awaited the strike of cold steel at his neck, but then of a sudden his attacker frothed bloody foam from his mouth and was driven onto his back, the Sha ceremonial baton buried in his chest.

Time recompressed slowly. Jarren took a breath that felt like years, heard Sha'raelon moaning and crying behind him, but she sounded so far away. He shook his head, numbed, and turned to see Sha'raelon kneeling at Pa'ket's side.

"Sha'raelon!" Jarren shouted.

"Oh, Pa'ket!" Sha'raelon wailed. "No, no, nooo..."

The monk lay flat on his back, blood pooling around his head. His eyes fluttered and he exhaled his last words, "I am...Pa'ket...Pa'ket*lon.*" And then he was gone.

Sha'raelon's face twisted into a cry of anguish that was painful for Jarren to watch. She looked like a wild woman. Her hair was tangled, with bits of debris caught in it. Her gown was torn, stained with grime and with Pa'ket's blood. Tears ran off of her cheeks, splashed into pools at her knees.

"My father?" she wailed. "*You are my father?*"

Her grief let go with anguished cries. She wailed at the sliver of sky above. Jarren looked on unsteadily, his own heart squeezing with the pain of it, but at the same time he scanned the alley, the heights. There could be more of them...

He yanked the Sha ceremonial baton out of his attacker's chest, flicked his wrist as he had seen Pa'ket do, and then looped the baton over his shoulder. He retrieved Pa'ket's robe and held it open.

"Sha'raelon, we must go," he begged her. "*Mistress—*"

She looked up and glared at him with a hate he had never seen, an animal hate that made his blood run cold.

"Stop that," she spat at him. "I do not have such tender sensibilities that I need you to patronize me."

Sha'raelon tugged at Pa'ket's belt, a sob catching in her throat as it came loose. She slung the belt over her shoulder, reached out and took Pa'ket's face in her hands. She kissed his forehead, his cheeks.

"Sha'raelon," Jarren said, gentler this time. "There may be more of them. It's not safe here. Let's be away. I'll come back for him when you are safe."

Sha'raelon stood then and wiped her nose with the back of a hand. Her eyes were puffy and hot but they fixed upon him like ice.

"I do not *require* your help with him," she hissed through clenched teeth.

Jarren flinched at her acid tone but held steady, holding the robe out. Sha'raelon snatched it from him and pulled it on.

"Give me the baton," she ordered, and he did.

She sniffed and studied the alley, looked mournfully upon Pa'ket one last time.

"Let us go," she said, and then she snapped around smartly on her heels and made for the street.

"Who's responsible?" demanded the president. She was in the Situation Room. Simon sat beside her. Milton Phillips, secretary of Homeland Security, was on the screen.

"We don't know, Madam President," Secretary Phillips said. "The attack profile does not match any of our models, and events are still in motion."

"Tell me what we *do* know."

The secretary took a breath before he proceeded. The folds in his aged face seemed to have fallen further, and his eyes looked tired. "It appears that the targets were Jarren Canto and Sha'raelon."

"Oh, no," the president gasped. "Are they dead?"

"We haven't found their bodies. Their UN limousine was struck by one or more drone-launched missiles. Their driver's body was found inside. Theirs were not. But there is a lot of wreckage still burning. We'll know more within the next half hour."

"And casualties?"

"We have recovered eleven bodies. There will certainly be more."

"And what action have we taken?"

"Lower Manhattan has been sealed. We've diverted air traffic, and F-41s are en route to patrol the airspace above Manhattan."

"Very well," said the president. "I need regular updates."

"Yes, Madam President. There is one more item. I hesitate to mention it because our information is anecdotal so far."

"Don't hesitate," barked the president. "Just tell me."

Secretary Phillips shifted uneasily before continuing. He leaned closer to his screen.

"We have unconfirmed reports that an energy weapon was used."

"An energy weapon?"

"Good God!" Simon blurted. "Madam President—"

"What is it, Simon?"

"*Energy weapons?*" There was alarm in his eyes. "We don't *have* that technology."

"Then who does?"

"*Nobody* does."

"Simon," the president tensed. "You're not making sense."

"Canto and Sha'raelon," he said gloomily. "They're not the only ones."

Sha'raelon acted as if she were about to walk boldly into the street. When Jarren reached out to stop her she shot him a look of pure menace.

"You can't just walk out there, Sha'raelon," Jarren pleaded. "You'd be an easy target."

Sha'raelon lowered her gaze. "You are right," she admitted. "Forgive me. You are not the cause of this."

"We'll need to cooperate if we're to survive," he said.

"Yes," she quietly agreed. "Your thinking has been clear. Mine has been...clouded."

The afternoon light came down on them harshly after their journey through the dark alley. Jarren shielded his eyes and scanned the buildings across the street. There were people on the sidewalks but they were hurrying, as if fleeing. Traffic was snarled, horns were honking. There were flashing lights at the south end of the block, uniformed officers directing traffic east toward the river. Jarren couldn't spot any signs of danger.

"Come," he said, holding out his hand. Sha'raelon took it and the two scooted quickly to the left around the corner, heading north toward United Nations Headquarters, hugging the facades of the buildings, crouching low. A few people paused to stare at them warily.

"We need to get over another block," Jarren said.

"I do not see any alleys," Sha'raelon commented uneasily.

"We'll have to cross at the next street. Stay low and let's go between these cars."

Jarren pulled her into the street and then between the cars stuck in traffic. One car bumped forward into the next and closed off their route.

"Damn it!" Jarren cursed. The driver mouthed silent obscenities their way.

Running in a crouch, Jarren and Sha'raelon skirted the side of the car. Pop—pop, pop, pop, pop, pop, pop. The car was suddenly dotted with holes, the cursing driver jerking as impacts ripped through his body in a line ranging on Jarren and Sha'raelon.

"*They've found us*!" Jarren shouted. He pulled Sha'raelon behind the car, ducking low. "We have to keep moving!"

He shoved Sha'raelon ahead of him, almost knocking her off her feet, came up directly behind her like a shield and pushed her on through the next lane of traffic. The clack of impacting bullets was at his back, so close...

"*Down now*!"

Jarren forced Sha'raelon flat on her face, wrapped himself around her and rolled them between a pair of cars and up against the far curb. Struggling to gain his feet, he yanked her bodily across the sidewalk and into the temporary shelter of a doorway. He tried the door. It was locked.

"Damn it! We're trapped!"

Sha'raelon beat at the door glass with the baton, one, two, three times before the safety glass shattered and fell like granular rain. Jarren didn't hesitate.

"Let's go!"

They skidded across the glass and into the carpeted hallway of some kind of office.

"To the end of the hall," Jarren ordered breathlessly. "Emergency exit."

Sha'raelon nodded on the run. They banged through the emergency door and into a service alley. The cross street was only feet away to their left. People were in their cars, oblivious of the gunfire coming from just around the corner. Pedestrians were hurrying past, though, away from the sound of danger. Jarren wasn't sure what to do next.

"It's as if they know our every damned move," he cursed through panting breaths.

Sha'raelon put a hand on his face and turned him to meet her eyes. She was breathing hard as well, but her face was stoic.

"If you think about it, Jarren, they *do* know our every move."

"That's not *possible*."

"It is if we are a part of someone else's history, if something we have done has created a focal point for another timeline."

"That's crazy," Jarren objected. "It's too complex. There would be no escaping it."

"*Someone* saved us from the drone," Sha'raelon argued, "someone who is obviously not from this timeline. *That* is our escape. Someone wants to stop us, but someone *else* wants us to succeed."

Jarren sunk against a wall, ran his fingers through his hair, rubbed at his eyes. Sha'raelon looked left and right nervously, scanned the roofline above.

"We cannot stay here, Jarren."

"I know."

"We have got to keep moving."

"We're dead the moment we step out onto that street."

"We are dead if we stay."

"We've got to find cover." He was beating his head against the wall. "We've got to find...wait a minute."

"What is it?" Sha'raelon asked, concerned.

"I have an idea."

"What?"

"No time. Just go with it..." He fixed her with the desperate look of a trapped animal. "...*Please*."

She nodded warily, eyes going wide as Jarren pulled off her robe and left it lying on the pavement.

"Come on." Jarren tugged her toward the street, away from the safety of the alley walls. They crept to the corner and then Jarren halted. People were scurrying back and forth right in front of them, out in the open.

"Sha'raelon!" Jarren shouted at the passersby. "I have Sha'raelon here!" He could feel Sha'raelon stiffen beside him. "Look," he hollered into the street. "It's Sha'raelon."

He fluffed her hair, worked to undo some of the tangles.

"*It's Sha'raelon!*" he heard a woman exclaim from the street.

People froze on the sidewalk and gawked at them.

"It *is* her," someone said.

Sha'raelon!

People were getting out of their cars now.

Sha'raelon!

Dozens were around them in moments, and then the chanting began, *Sha'raelon! Sha'raelon! Sha'raelon!*

An elegantly dressed woman stepped near. "It *is* you," the woman said reverently. She wore a wide-brimmed hat, black and with gems to match her tight dress and diamonds.

"May I have that hat for the Mistress?" Jarren asked the woman. She beamed her elation at him as he pressed the hat onto Sha'raelon's head.

Sha'raelon! Sha'raelon! Sha'raelon! the chant went on, the crowd growing ever larger.

"To the United Nations!" Jarren shouted over the din. "Let's march to the UN!"

Sha'raelon! Sha'raelon... And then the chant changed, became, *To the UN! To the UN!*

Jarren guided Sha'raelon into the street and allowed the crowd to engulf them and then carry them along. He held Sha'raelon tight, his arm around her shoulders. Fists waved above their heads. *To the UN! To the UN!* Their ranks swelled as they moved up 1st Avenue toward United Nations Plaza, and before long they arrived en masse at the steps between that long line of national flags. Black-uniformed security waded into them and, respectfully this time, ushered Sha'raelon and Jarren up the steps.

Sha'raelon! Sha'raelon! chanted the crowd.

"I must to speak to them," Sha'raelon begged, trying to turn from Jarren's grip.

"No way," he said. "Just keep calm and keep smiling until we're inside."

And then they were through the doors and the chants of the crowd faded away.

"They're safe, Madam President. They walked into UN Headquarters a few minutes ago."

"Thank God," President Carlyle sighed. Secretary Phillips was back on the screen. The Situation Room was now packed with people. Many of them stood along the walls. Individual conversations were low but intense.

"There was another attack on 3rd Avenue," said the secretary.

"Energy weapons?" the president asked with dread.

"No, a conventional assault rifle. One fatality. The death toll from the first attack has risen to twenty-three, including eight members of what appears to be some kind of hit squad; and also the woman Sha'raelon's aide. They put up a hell of a fight. It looks like it was hand-to-hand with swords and knives."

"*Swords and knives?*" the president asked incredulously.

"That's right, Madam President." Secretary Phillips shook his head. "It's crazy."

"Everything's been crazy since they showed up."

Sarah Shields, the president's press secretary, was a hyperactive woman in her thirties. Her bobbed black hair bounced as she was hustled into the room behind Jordan Toomey, President Carlyle's burly chief of staff.

"It's all over the Web, Madam President," Sarah blurted. "And there's some kind of huge protest march going on in Riyadh."

"*Riyadh!*" exclaimed the president. "It must be *midnight* there."

"It's on Al Jazeera," someone cut in.

Sarah fingered a remote and Al Jazeera English popped up on a monitor. A nervous male reporter, no older than twenty-five, stood in the glare of camera lights as a mob of black-robed women holding candles moved through the street behind him like a dark tide. *Sha! Sha! Sha!* the women were chanting. Shrill ululations warbled in the night.

"*This is an extraordinary event for the kingdom,*" said the reporter, "*a completely spontaneous uprising by women of all ages. There has been no violence so far. Police forces are continuing to show restraint. It seems to have started when news broke that Sha'raelon, the woman from the future, had been attacked in New York City and had gone missing. We now have word that she arrived safely at UN headquarters some minutes ago, but have no further information about her condition at this time...*"

President Carlyle waved her hand and the monitor was shut off. "The king's not going to like this," she said smugly. "Better get the ambassador on the phone, see if we can head off any violence."

"We have our own march going on in Manhattan right now," someone offered.

"What is this...this *effect* she has on women?" quizzed the president.

A few suspicious glances fell on her but then flicked away.

"She certainly doesn't have that effect on *me*," President Carlyle added, perhaps defensively, "but for everyone else it seems that if she wakes up with a headache women take to the streets. I don't understand it."

"I think that's the least of our concerns right now," Simon interjected. "Mr. Secretary, do we have any further information on the energy weapon?"

"None. So far we can't corroborate the initial reports."

"So maybe this energy weapon doesn't exist," said the president, looking at Simon speculatively, "and our hearts are in our throats for no reason."

Simon smiled uncomfortably. Every scenario he could possibly envision ended badly.

Sha'raelon's bathwater had turned pink, with a disgusting grimy sheen on the surface, compelling her to lift herself painfully out of the comforting warmth to rinse and refill the tub. It was worth the effort, though. The hot water and bath salts soothed her aching muscles, her scrapes and bruises. She had not been hit in the face, fortunately, but her arms, abdomen, thighs and shins were mottled with blue-black welts. She moaned with relief and eased in up to her chin. Her hair fanned around her face like a golden Sargasso Sea.

And then she cried silently. *Pa'ket...* Jarren was in the next room. She fought for control, splashed away her tears. There was a knock at the door.

"Sha'raelon?" Jarren asked tentatively through the door.

Sha'raelon squeezed the water out of her eyes, took a breath and sighed. "You may use my given name now, Jarren," she said, cheeks flushing.

"Really? Does that mean—"

"It *means*," Sha'raelon cut in before he could say something inappropriate, "that we have been forced closely together, and therefore formality has become burdensome. But," she added with emphasis, "*never* use my given name in public."

"I understand...*Rae*. I have been given some clothing for you. The Greeks, it seems, have not worn gowns like yours for a couple thousand years," he smiled and shook his head, "but the Indian, French, and Turkish ambassadors have all donated items. We have a crimson sarong, a gray business suit, and a white scarf, the Turks called it a *shayla*. Shall I make more calls?"

"No, Jarren. Thank you. I believe I can work with what you have."

"Good. Oh, one more thing—the media are all over the Plaza. We're going to have to make a statement. And fairly soon."

"Very well," Sha'raelon sighed. "I will be along."

She gave herself a few more minutes before reluctantly climbing out of the tub.

Jarren looked up expectantly as Sha'raelon padded barefoot into the room. She wore a white terry bathrobe, with her hair wrapped in a matching towel atop her head. She sighed and folded her tall form into a plush chair. Jarren's anteroom was spacious. Wide windows looked out on the East River and Roosevelt Island. It was evening now. Lights glittered along FDR Drive and traced gossamer lines across the 59th Street Bridge. Clouds had come in low, and shone gray with reflected city light. Jarren tossed back a bourbon, neat from a crystal tumbler, rose from his sofa and crossed to a liquor cabinet for a refill.

"Would you like one?" he asked.

Sha'raelon shook her head. "No, no—I do not drink alcohol."

"Never?"

She looked away, but then brought her eyes back around. Jarren was dressed for the evening in a white jacket and shirt, with black slacks and a black tie. A bandage wound around the knuckles of his right hand.

"How is your hand?" she asked.

"Just scrapes, the least of the aches I feel right now." He downed his second drink while standing at the liquor cabinet, clinked glass as he poured another.

"Perhaps you have some water?" Sha'raelon asked.

Jarren smiled soberly and poured club soda into a tumbler. He carried it to her and then fell back on the sofa, kicked off his shoes, propped his feet on the coffee table and exhaled with weariness.

Sha'raelon sipped her water thoughtfully. Her lips began to tremble. She covered this with another sip.

"The Americans also called," Jarren said hesitantly. "They retrieved Pa'ket's body."

"Yes," she acknowledged darkly, eyes downcast. "I shall have him taken aboard my ship."

"I probably shouldn't mention it," Jarren said, rolling his tumbler between his palms, "but I was growing fond of Pa'ket. He had this subtle humor to go along with his... skills. I wish I had known him better. He was very proud of you, I could tell."

Sha'raelon tipped her tumbler and finished it off. Her mind seemed to float. She said quietly after some moments, "I had him for most of my life, but I did not know..."

"*He* knew."

"I *loved* him like a father, though. The Lon should know of his sacrifice. They *must* know." She squeezed her eyes closed and whispered, "*They will know.*"

There was something about her words. Jarren regarded her contemplatively, vague suspicions tugging at his mind. Sha'raelon lifted her eyes beyond him, gazed blankly at the city lights through the window. Her empty tumbler dangled from her fingers.

"I think he was devoted to you, not fame," Jarren said reassuringly after a few moments.

"Your wife..." Sha'raelon trailed off before continuing. She lowered her eyes numbly to meet his. "...I believe I can now understand your grief. I am sorry that you have been involved in this."

"I am no less involved than you," Jarren said earnestly, his eyes glistening.

Sha'raelon was shaking her head. She had been trained all her life to face this man, but he had come to be a bystander in her mind, an innocent man caught up in a centuries-long scheme. These were disturbing thoughts.

"We shall have to perform this debate, I suppose," she said, changing the subject.

"I think we must. Is it not recorded in your history?"

"Not that which was revealed to me."

"We are to meet them in the morning, at eight."

"So early?"

"They told me this would gain the widest worldwide audience."

Sha'raelon scowled.

"But first," she said wearily, unfolding herself from the chair, "we must compose ourselves and make a public statement. Will you show me to this clothing?"

Jarren led her into a dressing room. The donated clothing hung from hooks next to a mirrored wall.

"I'll wait for you out front," Jarren said. "We're to meet with the media somewhere in the lobby. You should know that we have been given Secret Service protection by the Americans. They seem like competent people. For safety reasons they will not allow us to meet with the media outside of the building."

"They will not *allow* us—"

"Please, Rae. They're only doing their jobs. There's a huge crowd outside. They can't guarantee our safety. Representatives from several media outlets have been chosen by lottery. Afterward they want you to remain here and not return to your ship. I think that makes sense."

Sha'raelon moved to object, but then caught herself. She selected the gray French business suit, held it to her chest and examined herself in a mirror.

"They are right," she said wistfully, closing the door with her hip. "I will not be long."

The debate was to be held in the General Assembly Hall, where Sha'raelon and Jarren had delivered their addresses just days before. Jarren waited in the wings as the hall filled. He felt squeamish, not about his upcoming debate performance but about whether or not he would or should voice the suspicions that had been coalescing in his thoughts. Twenty-four hours ago he wouldn't have hesitated, but now that he and Rae had faced death together...

Jarren leaned against a wall and sipped coffee from a paper cup as members filed past him to their seats. Riggers were drawing cable, setting up lights and cameras. No one noticed him particularly. He wore a conservative gray collarless jacket this time, in contemporary fashion, with matching slacks and a white collarless shirt. His feet were wedged into black patent leather shoes that squeaked when he walked. He chuckled, sloshed his coffee and had to step aside quickly to keep from staining his suit. He laughed because he knew that if Rae were here everyone would stop and mob them. She was the one they wanted, not him. He doubted that there was anything he could do in this timeline to save his daughter, but at the same time he doubted that he would be able to take the chance that he couldn't.

"Come to the podium, Mr. Canto," Secretary Chen said, gesturing from inside the hall. "Mistress Sha will enter from the other side."

Jarren slugged down the rest of his coffee and dropped the cup in a bin. "Here we go," he mumbled.

Secretary Chen walked ahead, leading Jarren up the dais and to the podium. The assembly was uneasily reserved as Jarren climbed the steps. All knew the details of what had happened yesterday. Once Jarren took position at his end of the podium, though, there came scattered clapping that grew into a raucous wave rolling through the hall. Jarren acknowledged the applause with a tight smile and a bow.

"Thank you," he mouthed at the microphone. "Thank you."

Jarren shined with guilty satisfaction at the adulation directed toward him, but when *she* stepped forward the assembly came to its feet. The applause Sha'raelon received was overwhelming, numbing, so loud that Jarren had to struggle not to cover his ears. He bit back his frustration and joined the applause. How could he not? Sha'raelon was beautiful as always, vibrant. She beamed as she swept up the steps, hand resting on Secretary Chen's elbow. She paused before she stepped behind the podium, and she curtsied—*curtsied*—the assembly.

Jarren had to smile. Sha'raelon was shrewd, a true warrior, not the waif she had appeared to be at last night's press conference. The world knew her as the indomitable Goddess in the Golden Gown, but she had stood shyly before the cameras during the press conference, wincing at the lights and glare. Dressed in the French business suit, uncomfortable in another woman's clothes, she had looked fragile, orphaned in time, and the media had fawned over her as if out to rescue her with their hearts. If *they* had seen her do the things *he* had seen her do then they would know that their concerns for her wellbeing were misplaced.

She was dressed this morning in an eclectic combination of the clothing Jarren had gathered for her last night. The sarong from the Indian ambassador, the color of arterial blood, tapered chastely from her waist to her ankles, draping above her bronze sandals, which she had somehow managed to clean and shine during those few hours between last night's press conference and this morning's debate. From the French suit she wore a white blouse under the gray jacket. She had wrapped the pure white Turkish scarf, the *shayla*, loosely around her face and also draped lightly over her shoulders. She had pushed the scarf back on her forehead, letting some golden curls show, and also away from her cheeks, which glowed with healthy innocence. The Sha ceremonial baton, darkened with Pa'ket's blood, hung over her shoulder. All of this was calculated to appeal to the sympathies of the assembly, Jarren was sure of it.

Secretary Chen brought the two together to shake hands. Sha'raelon's hand was warm and soft. Jarren was amazed. He had seen her use this very hand like a deadly blade. He saw that her knuckles were bruised, though, so was careful not to squeeze too tight. Sha'raelon smiled confidently, looked knowingly into his eyes. Jarren gave her a sardonic smile and a wink in return, which drew a perfect white grin.

"Ladies and gentlemen," Secretary Chen announced into the microphone, "if we may come to order."

The applause went on unabated, although a few people began taking their seats. Jarren scanned the floor ahead of the dais. The fifteen members of the Security Council sat stonily at tables ahead of the dais. None of *them* were clapping or heaping adoration on Rae. Jarren had personally met with the ambassadors of the five major powers. They were an elusive bunch, but Jarren had received impressions from the American, British, and Russian ambassadors that seemed favorable to his cause. The Chinese and French had been harder to read.

"Ladies and gentlemen," Secretary Chen waved for silence. "By unanimous vote the Security Council has called for a debate between these two ambassadors, so that you might with greater knowledge choose the destiny of mankind."

That set off another roar of applause, which Chen quickly waved back to silence.

"All are aware," he continued, "of the violent and horrifying events of yesterday. It is with my deepest personal thanks that Mistress Sha and Mr. Canto have agreed to appear before us despite the traumas they have suffered."

Chen turned his thin eyes to Sha'raelon.

"And please accept my personal condolences for your loss," he told her in a somber voice. Murmurs of compassion filtered through the assembly.

"With only seven days remaining to us for a decision," he went on, "it was crucial that we proceed as scheduled, otherwise we would certainly have postponed this event.

"All know our dilemma: We know that there is a bright future ahead for the human race, regardless our decision. Already the seeds of hope are growing within our worst conflicts. We see it all around the world. Combatants are laying down their weapons. Food and aid are reaching people whom, only weeks or even days ago, were isolated by violence. Fewer suffer every day. Soon, none will suffer."

The applause started up again, faces beaming with messianic fervor—except, Jarren noted, for the members of the Security Council. They were unmoved. Some looked on with stern expressions, especially the American and the Russian. The Arab in the flowing white robes—Jarren couldn't recall which nation he represented—was actually glowering at Rae. If she noticed him she didn't show it. She was looking out over the assembly, her face ebullient.

"And this," Secretary Chen continued, "is perhaps the greatest tragedy before us, for this future of hope comes to us at so little a cost—the mere scheduling of a satellite launch. None can say why this particular, mundane event leads to such dynamically different futures, and so your decision is all the more poignant, for while we know that the human race will prosper, one of these two ambassadors will lose all they have known."

Jarren reacted to that with a tightening in his face, although his smile remained rigid.

"Moving on to the format of this debate," said Chen. "The Security Council will direct questions toward each of the ambassadors. If the ambassadors wish to rebut one another they may do so. I will serve as moderator. I will also present questions collated from the General Assembly if these questions are not addressed by the Security Council. Are there any objections?"

Chen scanned the assembly and the council for objections. There were none. He then turned to Jarren, who met the secretary-general's unreadable expression with a quick nod of assent; and then to Sha'raelon, who also nodded her approval.

"Very well then." Chen's eyes hovered on Sha'raelon. His voice had taken on a paternal quality. Sha'raelon looked away demurely while Jarren gnashed his teeth in irritation. Secretary Chen left Sha'raelon's side, reluctantly it seemed, and took a seat off the dais. "We will now proceed with the first question," he said once he had settled in, "from the ambassador of France for Mistress Sha."

The French ambassador was a prim woman with an angular face and silver hair. She wore old fashioned rectangular reading glasses, and a gray suit identical to the one Sha'raelon had worn last night. Sha'raelon smiled her appreciation, which the ambassador acknowledged with a tip of her head.

"Ambassador Sha let me first say," the woman's accent was thick, "how sorrowful we are for your loss."

"*Merci beaucoup, l'ambassadeur. J'apprécie vos mots gentils*," said Sha'raelon in lyrical French. The French ambassador caught her breath and smiled her approval. Jarren looked on with incredulity.

"Your French is very good, Ambassador Sha. Is French still spoken widely in your time?"

"*Oui!*" Sha'raelon chirped. "*Le français est parlé et est enseigné à travers le système solaire.*" French is spoken and taught throughout the solar system.

The French ambassador's pleasure at that was undisguisable. She pulled off her reading glasses and let them dangle by their gold chains, clasped her hands and leaned forward on her elbows. "Tell us where you live," she asked.

"I live in Athens," said Sha'raelon fondly, "in apartments that look out toward the Acropolis. The Parthenon still stands proudly in my time." There was a hoot and a cheer from somewhere in the General Assembly.

"Then you are Greek?" asked the French woman.

"Not in the sense of contemporary times," Sha'raelon said, drawing a puzzled look from the ambassador. "Although many of us are descended from the Hellenes, I am Sha."

"What does this mean?"

"Sha is my family, my line. I am of the Sha."

"Then this is your clan?"

"No," Sha'raelon answered patiently, "it is not that at all. It is rather—"

"Perhaps we can move this along," Derrick Albertson, the American ambassador, interrupted rudely. His expression was sour. "Madam Sha, what is your governing system?"

Sha'raelon shifted her attention to the American, who was dressed in a dark suit. He reminded her of Jarren, except that this man had receding hair and a stern face. She kept her smile firmly in place as she answered, "We are a republic."

"Humph."

"Mistress?" asked the Chinese, a delicate woman with translucent skin, "How is it that your culture was able to so quickly populate the solar system?"

"Oh," Sha'raelon took a breath. Her face beamed proudly. "Once we found water on Mars it seemed that we then found water *everywhere*: on the moon, Ceres, Europa."

"*There's water on the moon!*" someone exclaimed from the assembly. "I *knew* it."

Sha'raelon smiled sincerely at the interruption and then continued: "And so with water in plentiful supply, to support our bases and for use as reaction mass, colonization followed quickly, in less than four generations."

Jarren strummed his fingers on the podium. It took an effort of will to keep his smile locked in place. Sha'raelon made the colonization of the solar system sound like some kind of monumental event, while *his* culture had colonized a sizeable portion of the Orion Arm during a similar period of time.

"Ambassador Sha?" asked the Russian in a gravelly voice. "Who was the first to land on Mars?"

Sha'raelon shook her head. "I am sorry, I do not know her name."

Her name? Jarren's brows dipped. He studied Sha'raelon skeptically. She was beaming at the assembly with breathless exhilaration, a portrait of hope and beauty.

"What *nation?*" the Russian barked.

Sha'raelon didn't even flinch, came right back at the Russian with: "That is a part of our history that was not revealed to me." Her look was as if to assuage his disappointment—to *mother* him. "This was to prevent me from accidentally unleashing competitions among you. I am so sorry."

Jarren was tapping his foot now, irritation rising. Why weren't they asking *him* any questions?

"Madam Sha?" asked the British ambassador. He was an athletic man, erect and poised, gray at the temples. His accent was charming, his elocution precise. "If you would, please inform me of the status of the Crown in your time."

Sha'raelon smiled warmly at the Brit. "I am proud to inform you and your people that descendants of your king carry on to this day—" she caught herself mid breath and flashed her prettiest smile, "—or I should rather say, *will still be* carrying on in the British Isles in my time."

The British ambassador's relief was so heartfelt that his eyes were misting.

Jarren was now squeezing the podium, his knuckles white.

"Mistress Sha?" asked the Brazilian ambassador. He was a handsome man with a rakish face and ruffled salt-and-pepper hair. There was a pleasant lilt to his accent. "Please describe to us the ecological condition of the Amazon in your time."

The Brazilian ambassador's cheeks took on a rapturous flush as Sha'raelon turned her eyes to him and gave him her warm, intimate smile. Jarren wasn't smiling now, though.

"The ecosystem of the Amazon Basin, as well as the other damaged areas of Earth," Sha'raelon scanned the assembly, her face like light, "including the Dead Sea, the Aral Sea, the Australian Outback, the Kalahari—"

"*Mistress Sha!*" Jarren blurted, the growl in his voice reverberating harshly through the enraptured hall. There were some gasps in the assembly, and then silence descended like tangible weight. Secretary Chen squirmed in his chair, pressing palms to the table as if to stand. The Brazilian ambassador had balled his fists, looked as if he were about to climb the dais. Sha'raelon turned to Jarren with a shocked expression. Jarren cleared his throat nervously and began again.

"Mistress Sha?" he asked, levelly this time. "What *kind* of republic?"

Sha'raelon's eyes narrowed and her smile became a tight line.

"*Mr. Canto!*" Secretary Chen objected, coming to his feet.

"I was told I would be allowed to rebut," Jarren argued forcefully, his eyes locked on Sha'raelon.

Chen fell back into his chair in resignation. "You are correct, Mr. Canto," he admitted grudgingly. "Please proceed with your question."

Jarren arched his brows. "Well?" he asked Sha'raelon quietly.

Her mind was working, he could see the indecision in her eyes. The silence in the hall had gone hollow, every small sound magnified. Finally Sha'raelon turned to the assembly.

"We are a *matriarchal* republic," she answered firmly.

"Matriarchal?" Ambassador Albertson called out. "What does *that* mean?"

Sha'raelon returned to her training, of the barbarian she had been destined to face since long before she was born, and of the cynical politicians she had to sway to her cause. It was crucial that her governing system appear to be compatible with contemporary systems.

"We have a chief matriarch," she said after a moment of pause, "elected by an upper house of matriarchs, much as if the president of the United States were elected by the Senate, or the prime minister of Great Britain by the House of Lords."

"Uh, huh," said Albertson dubiously. "And who makes up your lower house?"

"The men are represented there," she answered, working to keep her voice level. "And so all the people have representation. All are equal."

"It seems that some are more equal than others," Ambassador Albertson grumbled.

There came uncomfortable murmurs and rumbles from the assembly.

"I know this sounds novel to you," Sha'raelon continued smoothly, "but all governing systems evolve. And remember, it is *you* who will eventually design the system that I was born to."

"Will they?" Jarren interjected. "Or will *you*?"
Sha'raelon's lashes fluttered.

"How is it that our two timelines could have diverged so far in only five hundred years?" he asked her in an accusing tone. Sha'raelon shot eyes his way.

"The events of the Focal Point will determine that, Mr. Canto," she answered him righteously.

"I think not, Mistress Sha," Jarren said with skepticism. He could see concern knit into her brows. She *knew*, he thought. Damn if she didn't. Jarren felt a pang of pity for her—to have to *live* with that knowledge. Her history was not as nebulous as she claimed, and he could tell from the worried look in her eyes that she was realizing just now that he had worked it out for himself.

"You have quite a following, Mistress Sha," he went on. "We see it everywhere." Sha'raelon turned away from him with indignation. "What will you and your followers do once we cross the Focal Point? Launch a revolution?"

"That is absurd," Sha'raelon spat, turning on him with scorn.

"Your own children will carry your legacy forward—"

"I *have* no children."

"Not yet you don't, but you will—and when you do you will give birth *to your own line.*"

Ambassador Albertson sat gaping at the two sparring on the dais. He turned his face to a camera and seemed to be looking incomprehensibly out of the monitor at President Carlyle.

"Do you get this, Simon?" the president asked with an incomprehension that rivaled the ambassador's. She was at her desk in the Oval Office. Simon was sitting on a sofa alongside Jordan Toomey. Joaquin Merida and Secretary of State Tiber Long sat across from them.

"I think..." Simon tapped his lip, "...I think he is describing a loop in time. Dr. Roth said there would be no grandfather paradoxes, but this is similar. Damn."

"Grandfather paradoxes?"

"Yeah, the idea that if you went back in time and killed your grandfather when he was a boy then you would never have been born, so how could you kill your grandfather if you never existed?"

"You can't be serious."

"The only way we can get around this paradox is to assume that there are multiple universes, or timelines, bifurcating at focal points, which is where Sha'raelon and Canto seem to have come from—it's why they're here—but Canto is claiming that her children's children's children will eventually give birth to *her*, which means she's caught in a self-fulfilling loop...*inside* a timeline. I don't know *how* you would sort that out."

"I think I'm getting a headache," said the president.

Jarren's guts were twisting. He hadn't wanted to attack her, not like this. There were some looks of revulsion in the assembly, but most looked dumbfounded, unable to grasp what they were hearing. Members were tapping their headphones in frustration, questioning their interpreters. The women who had gathered outside in the plaza were stunned to silence by what they had just witnessed on their screens. Jarren turned to Sha'raelon with sympathy, expected to find betrayal written in her eyes, but instead she met his gaze fiercely. He swallowed hard and pressed his advantage, even as guilt made his belly tremble; even though he felt as if he were plunging a knife into her back.

"The fact is, Mistress Sha," Jarren said numbly, "your culture is stagnant, lacking in inspiration, cocooned within the solar system where you hide in fear."

Sha'raelon's tight lips lifted at the corners. Her emerald eyes looked devious, darkening like evergreens in winter. He had seen that look before, in the alley, where she had taken lives as indiscriminately as an enraged tiger. His spine tingled.

"We are neither stagnant nor fearful," she said casually, never breaking eye contact with him. "We simply wanted to avoid encounters with the aliens."

"*Aliens!*"

The hall erupted.

"*What kind of aliens?*"

"*Where?*"

"*Are they dangerous?*"

"*Aliens*, Simon?" President Carlyle asked with disbelief.

"There were bound to be, Madam President," Simon shrugged his shoulders, "somewhere. Carl Sagan, the brilliant twentieth-century astrophysicist, said that in the vastness of the cosmos there must be other civilizations far older and more advanced than ours."

"And now these *people* have brought them to our doorstep," Joaquin said acidly. "How do we defend ourselves against...against *aliens?*"

President Carlyle pushed a button on her comm. "Ron," she spoke at the comm. "Would you send for Secretary of Defense Channing, please?"

"Yes, Madam President."

Back at the United Nations, the uproar had settled enough for Sha'raelon to continue.

"Yes, there are aliens," she said calmly to the assembly. And then accusingly to Jarren, "How many wars have you fought with them, Mr. Canto?"

"*Wars?* Did she say *wars?*" President Carlyle asked, growing more and more alarmed.

"I would not describe them as wars," Jarren answered hesitantly. "More like conflicts."

Sha'raelon's face was as sinister as anything Jarren had ever seen. *Of course*, he thought. *Of course* she knew what his arguments would be. *Of course* she knew how to deflect them.

"And yet Earth *was* bombed, correct?" she said as flatly as if she were citing dry history.

"*Bombed!*" President Carlyle exclaimed. She pushed anotherbuttononhercomm. "Assemblethejointchiefs," she ordered.

"That was a long time ago," Jarren said firmly. He straightened his posture, clenched his stomach tight. He would never, *ever*, underestimate this woman again. "We fought one near-Earth battle but we gained the galaxy. The technology transfer of that battle was *worth* the cost. It allowed mankind to—"

"A long time ago?" Sha'raelon interrupted with a laugh. "Mr. Canto, 'a long time ago' for you is *today* for them."

"Okay, that tears it," President Carlyle said with chilling finality. She activated her comm. "Take us to DEFCON 2."

"*Madam President,*" pleaded Secretary Long. He was a tall man in his sixties, lean and fit, with a full head of white hair. He had been a litigator before he joined the administration. He used those skills now. "We have no evidence of an impending attack."

"We didn't have any evidence of these time travelers either," the president shot back. "I can't take the chance. I *won't* take the chance."

"We must protect ourselves," Joaquin Merida advised with cool calculation. "Preemptively if necessary."

"Madam President," said Simon, as aghast as Secretary Long. "We are dealing with a science that is not understood. Timelines are being created constantly, and the uncertainty principle cannot be disregarded." The president's eyes seemed to have glazed at that. Simon went on, suddenly less sure of himself. "I mean," he said, "in an infinite universe *anything* could happen. These two timelines may not even be relevant anymore; or...or even our actions *now*—they could be the very thing that sets these events in motion rather than UNCOMMSAT. We should think carefully before—"

Secretary of Defense Channing charged into the Oval Office, trailing staffers like a procession.

"That will be all, Simon," President Carlyle said dismissively.

Simon hesitated a moment, meeting eyes throughout the room that now looked upon him with disdain. "Yes, Madam President," he swallowed, and then he walked alone out of the Oval Office, straightening his jacket and tie as he went. A Secret Service agent pulled the door closed behind him.

There was something sticky on the bar. Jarren wiped his hand distastefully on his pant leg, knocked back his whiskey and held up a finger for another. He was alone at the bar, in what was called a *pub* by the contemporaries, a strange name that sounded more like a particle field bubble than a place for him to remain quietly anonymous. But the pub was intimate and dark, which suited his mood, and the bartender who had come on at sunset was not chatty, which also suited his mood.

The bartender carried a bottle over but hesitated before pouring. She was a woman in her thirties, with stringy blond hair, a rough complexion, and a large gold stud in her tongue. The thing bobbed like a glob of phlegm whenever she spoke. Jarren's stomach turned.

"It's gonna be a long night," she said. She had a husky voice to go with her looks. "You might wanna start taking it easy."

Jarren averted his eyes. "I'm okay," he told her. At least he wasn't slurring yet. He could feel her eyes on him, like two points of heat.

"Do I know you?" she asked.

Jarren looked up out of reflex but then quickly away. "No," he said to his hands. "We've never met."

"Hmmm," she said. "You look familiar for some reason."

She topped off his glass without further comment and then returned to the end of the bar. The screen was tuned to a dull twenty-four-hour news feed, images flashing, the volume too low to follow. The front door creaked open behind him, letting the street noise intrude before the door slammed closed with a rattle of glass. Footsteps crossed to the barstool next to him.

"Mind if I join you?" someone asked.

Jarren looked up heavily at a trim, smartly dressed man with a tanned bald head. Jarren sighed at the intrusion but said nothing. He returned his eyes to his hands.

The man slapped a briefcase on the bar. "Scotch rocks for me," he said toward the bartender, and then he settled onto the stool next to Jarren.

"I'm Dr. Simon Hammerskjold," the man announced. "And you must be Jarren Canto."

"Shhh." Jarren raised a finger to his lips. "Unlike *her* I am comfortably anonymous—and I want to keep it that way."

"Yes," Simon mused. "She does draw a crowd. It's one of the things I wanted to speak with you about."

"Forget it," Jarren said, annoyed. He looked around the pub woozily. "I've got Secret Service guys here somewhere."

"I'm the science advisor to the president of the United States, Mr. Canto. I have clearance to speak with you."

Jarren rubbed his temples, ran his fingers through his hair. "It's Jarren," he mumbled. "Just Jarren."

"Very well...Jarren."

Jarren lowered his eyes as the bartender brought a glass and poured Simon's scotch.

"Run a tab?" the woman asked Simon. That thing would be bobbing in her mouth. Jarren couldn't get the nauseating image out of his mind.

"Sure," said Simon.

"Mr. Hammer...? Hammers—" Jarren stuttered once the bartender had moved off.

"It's *Dr.* Hammerskjold, but please call me Simon."

"Okay, uh, Simon." Jarren fixed eyes on the man. "What do you want?"

"I want to know how this ends."

"I don't *know* how it ends." Jarren banged the bar with his fist, drawing a reproachful look from the bartender.

He covered his face with his hands, elbows propped on the bar. "I'm a merchant captain, not a fortune teller," he said hollowly into his palms.

"Jarren," Simon smiled impatiently, "your timeline has a history. Tell me about that history."

"I told the secretary-general," Jarren hissed, reaching for his whiskey, "and I told the Security Council—I don't know much about it."

"Then tell me what you *do* know."

Jarren downed his whiskey in one shot and then hurried a napkin to his mouth. His stomach felt unsettled, sour. He needed a moment before he could speak.

"You want to know when you're going to die, right?" he asked sarcastically.

Simon was startled.

"You *know*?"

"Of course I don't know," Jarren spat. "How would I know that?"

"Jarren—"

"Look, Simon. We all knew a story, a time travel story. It made for good fiction, you know? It was a good drinking story—a story about time travelers who went back to change our future. That's it, just a story."

"And yet here you are," said Simon. "Apparently the story was about you."

"Yeah, and now I'm trapped in this Jack-forsaken time. Ironic, isn't it?"

"Surely there's something of this time period that you can appreciate," Simon said with a defensive edge.

"I really appreciate Jack Daniels whiskey." Jarren held up his glass, frowned that it was empty. "Oh, and I appreciate hamburgers, especially the big ones cooked on actual fire. So rustic."

Simon let that rest. He sipped his own scotch whisky in silence for a minute or two, and then:

"What about the aliens?"

Jarren jumped, startled, but then shook his head and laughed. "Yeah, who knew you people would be so xenophobic? Does anybody remember anything *else* about that damned debate? You people are obsessed with aliens."

"We're not obsessed, Jarren, just concerned."

"You should be more concerned about *her.*"

"When do they attack?"

"It wasn't like that."

"Then what *was* it like?"

"All right, look," Jarren took a deep breath, puffed out his cheeks as he exhaled, "I don't know the year, but it can't be too long from now. They followed your radio and video emissions in. Earth must have been the brightest thing in the Orion Arm in your time. Not real smart." He gave Simon the same condescending look that Simon might give a medieval alchemist. "I'm not even sure they came to fight," Jarren continued after a pause, "but somebody shot a nuke at them and then it was on. Earth took a few hits until somebody captured one of their ships and reverse engineered it. It wasn't long before humans were out there taking the fight to the aliens. Later, we ran into other species, some advanced, some not. We imposed treaties. The aliens stay within their boundaries and we leave them alone. That's it. That's all there is to the aliens."

Simon mulled that for a moment, and then: "How long has your culture had time travel?"

Jarren rolled his eyes.

"I didn't even *know* we could until they came and got me," he answered testily.

Simon pressed on without pause. "Tell me what you know about particle weapons."

Jarren stiffened. "What is this?" he complained irritably. "An interrogation?"

Simon ignored that.

"Do you have particle weapons on your ship?" he asked.

Jarren exhaled in resignation, fiddled with his empty glass. "Every ship has them," he said at last, "but not for offensive purposes—not even as weapons, really. We use them to deflect obstacles like small asteroids, comets and space junk—and they're used for mining."

"But someone fired one at you."

"They didn't fire at *me*, they fired at the *drone* that was firing at me."

"So someone else has come back?"

"Yeah, it looks that way."

"Any idea who?"

"I have no idea."

"Has anyone approached you, anyone you suspect might be from the future?"

"You mean besides Sha'raelon and...well—" his eyes hooded, "—Pa'ket? No. No one."

"Then what do you think is going on?"

"You're the scientist, you tell me."

"I have no evidence, but if I had to guess I would say that someone from another timeline is trying to take you out; and someone else from yours or Sha'raelon's timeline is trying to protect you."

"Gives you a headache, doesn't it."

"It *is* complex."

"Oh, look!" exclaimed the bartender. She stumbled for a remote, thumbed it urgently with both hands, bringing the volume up on the screen. Jarren glanced up at the screen and groaned.

"It's Sha'raelon!" the bartender went on ecstatically.

"Where is she?" Simon asked no one in particular.

"Somewhere in the East," Jarren mumbled, his words finally beginning to slur.

"She's on a goodwill tour with the United Nations," explained the bartender. "She's so beautiful."

Jarren thumped his forehead onto the bar.

There was a split image on the screen, a close-up of Sha'raelon, and a view from further away of women marching into a large plaza between towering minarets. Sha'raelon was dressed in a white gown, her golden curls coming loose from her scarf. She stood out vividly against waves of women shrouded in black. The secretary-general was at her side as she smiled and moved fluidly through the adoring crowd. Women clung to her open arms, enthralled by her touch. Soldiers with guns looked on from atop stone walls and low roof tops.

"It's a damned cult," Jarren grumbled, raising bloodshot eyes toward the screen.

"This must be from yesterday," the bartender said. "The king of Saudi Arabia gave in. He emancipated their women." Her eyes glistened. She wiped them with the back of her hand. Exhilaration colored her cheeks, making her face almost pretty. "They have full rights now," she added with pride. "*Full rights.*"

"They may regret that," Simon muttered under his breath.

Professor Kupolos looked out through the excavated archway toward the Aegean. The sun was just rising behind the site, and his view west was lit softly in shades of red and purple. From this angle he could see none of the resort hotels or roadways below. But for the fishing boats heading out for the day's catch, and the small village of Thirasia across the channel, the view would be little different than it had been when this dwelling was built.

The site had been dated stratigraphically to three thousand years, plus or minus five hundred years. So far they had found no artifacts to refine that date, which was odd. A lot of history had occurred in the Aegean during that time frame, a lot of opposing forces and overlapping cultures, which could account for the unusual architecture: the straight lines and sharp angles, the lack of columns. He had a theory, one he kept to himself for now, that a rich Persian or Carthaginian had built this place as a picturesque getaway, a place to woo mistresses or consort with concubines far away from wives and matters of court. Considering the dearth of artifacts, the site certainly held no other significance.

Sunlight began to spill through a circular roof vent behind him, warming his back. This would have been a bright, airy room, he thought. He had mentally dubbed it The Sunroom. The walls had been whitewashed with lime, and most of this was still intact. There were places where the lime had flaked off or where soot had smudged the walls, but the room still glowed as the sun came up, as it would have then. There were vents elsewhere, in the roof and in the walls, which would have channeled light throughout the day.

The room, with its open view, would have been beautiful, even romantic, but there were no decorations on the walls; no tattered tapestries or fading murals—and no broken pottery. No sign at all that the inhabitants had departed quickly, as from invasion, eruption or disease.

"*Professor K?*"

He squeezed his eyes tight and swallowed. *Patience,* he thought. *Give me patience.* He turned. It was a male student, the German, Andreas was his name. The boy was as ungainly as an ox, with dirty blond hair and dark blue eyes, but he was smart, even brilliant. He wore old fashioned eyeglasses with thick black frames. He had a sheaf of papers in his hand.

"Yes, Andreas," Professor Kupolos sighed.

"I have," sounded like *haf,* "some findings here you must see—"

Andreas seemed hesitant to proceed.

"Yes? Get on with it," the professor demanded impatiently, despite himself.

"Uh-uh," the boy stammered. Professor Kupolos ground his teeth. "As you know, sir," the boy finally got out, "I am studying for two degrees, archeology and geology."

"Yes?"

Andreas pushed his glasses nervously up his nose.

"Well," *vell,* "for my geology dissertation I made to study the stratigraphy of this cliffs. I run a spectrographic analysis of the layers and I discover this..." Andreas was reluctant to say it out loud. Instead he handed the papers to the professor.

Professor Kupolos snatched the papers and scanned them. He tugged at his beard as he read, and then his hand froze, eyes locked on a graph. Andreas was already blanching in anticipation.

"This is not possible," the professor objected strongly. "You corrupted your samples."

"No *sir*," Andreas countered, finding his voice. "I run three tests on three samples. It is iridium layer."

"But this strata is no more than a few thousand years old, well within recorded history. There have been no meteorite impacts during this time."

"I have no explanation for the presence, sir. Only this results."

Professor Kupolos had gotten his color up. Andreas was backing timidly away. Guilt stabbed at the professor. He relaxed and smiled faintly.

"I'm sorry, Andreas. You are not responsible for what you have found. It's just that it's so—shocking." The boy looked relieved. The professor felt another stab of guilt. "I would say, though, that you will need to form a hypothesis before you release these findings, yes?"

"Yes, Professor K—ah—*Kupolos*."

The boy flinched. Professor Kupolos just smiled steadily. "You will keep me aware of your findings, though, yes?"

"Yes, Professor," the boy brightened. "I will do that."

"Very good then," said the professor. He turned his attention to a darkened chamber that opened at the rear of the sunroom.

"*We're almost ready*," he heard as an echo. Students were tugging cables into the chamber. A generator hummed somewhere outside. "*That's it!*" someone yelled. "*Switch it on!*"

Klieg lights came on with a burst of white that cast the professor's shadow across the orange pool of sunlight coming from above. Professor Kupolos stepped down into the cooling chill of the chamber, careful not to get caught in the cables. These walls were also whitewashed, were also flaking, but the chamber had been sealed off from the ravages of time and so was in better condition than the sunroom. Two gray slabs were positioned in the middle of the room. Their texture was like clay, but they were unadorned, no markings of any kind.

"They must have been sleeping platforms," one of the students commented under his breath.

A reasonable hypothesis, thought the professor. There were also no obvious seams, which ruled out his initial hypothesis, that these were sarcophagi. He had already sent for ultrasound equipment. In a few more days they would all find out if the slabs were hollow. The chamber had been purposefully sealed by someone in ancient times, as if it were a tomb. They had all been excited when they first broke through, anticipating the trappings of a wealthy burial chamber. What they discovered instead, during their first survey with flashlights, was a simple bare chamber. There was no art; there were no artifacts. No one with the wealth these people must have possessed would have had themselves entombed in such a plain room. No, it couldn't be a burial chamber. It had to be something else. But what?

"Professor," someone hollered. "Look here."

"What is it?" asked the professor.

"Some kind of shelf."

It *was* some kind of shelf, carved cleanly out of the stone, and running the length of the far wall just below the ceiling. The shelf was tall enough and deep enough, perhaps, to display modern hardcover books. It had been lost in the shadows during their survey with flashlights.

Professor Kupolos' heart quickened. There was something on the shelf! "Bring stepladders," he ordered. "Quickly!"

Several students scrambled out of the chamber. They returned a few minutes later with two aluminum stepladders, and busied about setting them up under the shelf. Professor Kupolos was climbing even before the students had finished folding out the legs. Kate climbed the other ladder, and the two peered expectantly over the shelf ledge. They were both holding their breaths, not in anticipation, but to keep from inhaling millennia-old dust.

"What *is* that, Professor?" Kate asked.

Professor Kupolos felt his heart fall. It was nothing but scraps of something, perhaps animal hide, and all of this was in a pile going to dust. Something within caught the light, though. His hopes rose. He turned away to speak so as not to disturb the dust.

"Bring a camera at once."

"Professor," Kate said excitedly. "Step up a little higher and look at this."

The professor raised himself until his head bumped the ceiling. Looking steeply down from that angle he could see some kind of emblem or art. Dust covered most of it.

"What is that?" he mumbled.

"An infinity symbol, maybe?" she speculated. "Point to point deltas?"

"An infinity symbol is a good guess," he offered. "It would be contemporaneous with the age of the site. And a mathematician in that era would have been wealthy."

"And look at this," she added, pointing.

"Don't touch!" he blurted. His breath stirred up the dust.

Kate turned away quickly and held her nose to keep from sneezing. "I wasn't going to *touch* it," she hissed. The other students looked up at the two nervously.

"I'm sorry, Kate." The professor kept his voice low. "Show me what you've found."

Kate paused for a sneeze that wouldn't come, and then turned back to the shelf. "This here—" she pointed again, glanced accusingly at the professor—"*I'm not going to touch it.* Just look."

Professor Kupolos craned over to see. Protruding from the rear of the pile of scraps was the end of some kind of cylinder. It looked like a document tube. The material could have been wood or stone, perhaps even bronze, he couldn't tell through the layers of dust. There were engravings on it, possibly classical Greek letters, elaborately stylized.

"Your thoughts, Kate," he asked, chastened by her tone. It was well past time for him to be her mentor, not her tormentor.

"It looks like a document cylinder to me. Bronze I bet."

There was an excitement of discovery in her voice. The professor smiled in agreement. His students needed to have their moment. He vowed to let them.

"Very well then," he said, stepping down the ladder. "Kate, you lead this. All of you," he swept his finger before the gathered students; there were about ten of them crowded together in the chamber, and others leaning in through the opening, "I want all of you to participate. Be careful, touch nothing, but photograph everything in this chamber. Document every detail." He looked up. Kate was still hunched against the ceiling, intently examining their find. "And Kate," he added. She turned to him confidently, a sparkle in her eyes. "I want you to photograph that art and that cylinder. High resolution. Get as much as you can without moving them. Put the images on the Network. Let's see if anyone out there recognizes them."

"Right away, Professor K," she smiled.

He chuckled, shook his head, and pushed his way out of the chamber and into the morning sun.

Sha'raelon stood on a dry promontory overlooking the city of Alexandria in Arachosia, known as Kandahar to the contemporaries. The sun was rising beyond the city, molten orange tinged with streaks of red and purple in the hazy desert air, shimmering where it touched the horizon. Her skin glowed preternaturally bronze in the early light. Her eyes shone like Greek fire. She wore a blue gown, as pale as the desert sky. Pa'ket's belt and the Sha ceremonial baton crossed her chest like bandoliers, emphasizing her breasts. The white *shayla* covered her head and shoulders, billowing in the light, chilling wind coming across the city. The wind brought with it the pungent smells of dust, wood smoke and manure, as well as the distant chants of the women filling the narrow streets below.

Sha! Sha! Sha!

Sha'raelon shivered and pulled the *shayla* tighter around her face. She could make out a few bodies, like piles of dirty rags thrown across stone walls or else abandoned in dusty corners, turbans coming unwound and trailing in the wind, long black beards rigid with dried blood. *These women are fierce*, Sha'raelon thought proudly, *fiercer than Alexander, fiercer than the grizzled, black-turbaned men from the mountains.* Most of the women wore the dour black *abaya*, but many wore the ghostly blue *burka.* These weaved through the monochromatic throng like wraiths, their wrath hidden behind layers of linen.

There would be a reckoning, Sha'raelon knew. This was the first time lives had been lost. She hadn't wanted that, had entreated the women against it, but the repression they had been suffering for centuries was destined to explode into violence eventually. The secretary-general was down there somewhere, with a team of blue-helmeted soldiers—all men—attempting to hold back the seething anger. She already knew their efforts would be futile.

She couldn't hear the missile coming in. It trailed its sound well behind in successive sonic waves, like the knotted tail of a kite. Perhaps it was a premonition, perhaps it was the strange electric quiver coursing along her arms, but something caused her to look into the sun, where she saw a black spot growing larger, and a ragged contrail that formed a descending arc toward the city.

"No," she moaned.

Jarren turned disgustedly away from the screen. Even separated by half the globe he still couldn't avoid the woman. And he'd had enough of Simon's questions. He was just pushing away from the bar when an explosion tore into the front of the pub, peeling the façade cleanly off of the place. In an instant the pub was opened incongruously to the night, exposing the interior as if it were a theater stage of smoldering debris and shattered glass. Jarren found himself on the floor at the foot of the bar.

He could hear the bartender whimpering on the other side. Simon was on the floor as well, to Jarren's left, dazed, bleeding from a cut on his head, but conscious.

Sha'raelon dove for cover into the lee of a rocky outcropping. An otherworldly blue-white light flashed across the sky, followed by a deafening *crack*, like a close lightening strike. She covered her ears, squeezed her eyes tight and pressed herself against the sheltering rocks. Superheated air swept the promontory, scouring off every particle of dust and sand. The *shayla* came loose, was caught by the wind and whipped away.

The event was over in less than a minute. Sha'raelon stood shakily and wiped the tangled hair from her eyes. She gasped as she peered over the rocks at what remained of Kandahar. Her heart rose in her throat, aching with each beat, each breath. Her eyes filled. Tears sketched clean tracks down her dusty cheeks. She could make out an irregular black line along the foot of the promontory, like the flotsam of a receding tide, a black line speckled with blue—

—The heaped remains of thousands of brave women.

Jarren rose unsteadily to his feet. Car alarms were flashing and honking down the block. Water was splashing somewhere, a broken pipe maybe. A few screams from shattered windows across the street sounded distant and hollow. He tried to shake the numbness out of his ears, but no success.

Simon hauled himself up. His face was white, shocky. He kept the weight off of his right leg. "Are you okay?" he managed to ask.

"Yeah, I think so," Jarren answered without conviction.

A steady breeze was quickly clearing the air. Jarren noticed a pair of legs protruding at the knees from a pile of debris out on the sidewalk. Black pants and shoes...one of the Secret Service men, maybe both of them.

"You check on the bartender," Jarren said numbly to Simon. "I'll see if anyone's alive out there."

Simon lifted a white handkerchief to the cut on his head. "Yeah, sure," he said.

Jarren worked his jaw to open his ears as he made his way toward the debris pile. He knelt at the black shoes and searched a cooling ankle for a pulse. The man was obviously dead.

"Is anyone alive?" Jarren hollered. "Does anyone need help?"

There was a crunch of glass behind him. He turned on his heels and then rose slowly, jaw dropping. Two men were moving toward him, dressed completely in black.

"Who *are* you people?" Jarren uttered in disbelief.

The ninjas advanced, swords raised high over their heads.

President Carlyle was working alone at her desk when her comm chimed. It was late and her eyes were weary. She rubbed them and exhaled before she answered the comm. She was achy. The stress of the past few days...

She pushed a button. "Yes, Ron," she said, struggling to keep her voice firm.

"Madam President," Ron announced anxiously. "There's been a detonation..."

Sha'raelon was surprised at how clear the air had become, and that so few fires were burning below. The sun was well above the horizon now, shining yellow in the blast-cleaned air. Light plumes of gray smoke rose here and there, like camp fires rather than infernos. Kandahar's taller buildings looked as if their tops had been torn off, like jagged stone stumps, while minarets lay broken on their sides like ancient Roman columns. But the lower buildings were intact. There would be survivors.

The explosion had been too powerful to have come from a conventional device. Sha'raelon took a small meter from a compartment on Pa'ket's belt, held it out and read the scale. No radiation, which could only mean—

—Antimatter.

She dropped to her knees with gut-wrenching realization and sobbed into her hands. "*The damned waste of it!*" she swore through her tears. "*This was not supposed to happen. This* did not *happen. All of those women. So many women...*"

Something moved behind her. In the space of a single heartbeat she flicked her wrist and spun around into the Swan, arms out like avenging wings, knees bent, blades glinting wickedly in the low light. A squad of soldiers dressed in desert cammo came at her tightly, laser sights dancing on her chest. She didn't think. She didn't need to. She took a deep breath through her nose, her muscles coiling like springs. Her eyes were pure hate. She spun her blades and prepared to leap—

"*Wait!*" someone cried. "*Guns down! Guns down!* We're Americans—*Americans.*"

A harried soldier ripped open a Velcro flap on his shoulder and urgently displayed the American flag underneath.

"Special Forces, ma'am," he said breathlessly. "On patrol. The explosion...we came to investigate."

Sha'raelon allowed some tension to ease from her muscles, although she remained warily on guard. The soldier exhaled in relief.

"I know who you are," he went on. "We can take you out of here, ma'am—if you want."

At a flick of her wrist Sha'raelon's blades snapped back into the baton. One of the soldiers jumped at the unexpected sound, while another one laughed and thumped him on the back of the helmet. With perfect grace Sha'raelon flowed from the Swan into a casual, non-threatening posture.

"Yes, I will go with you," she said softly, sadly.

Jarren backed away from the ninjas. They were approaching slowly, cautiously, fully aware, no doubt, of what had happened last time. And then, from somewhere behind the ninjas, Jarren heard the unmistakable screeching whine of a particle generator charging up...

It's ugly what a particle weapon does to the human body. Blood and other fluids, concentrated mostly in the cranium, chest and abdominal cavities, boil instantly, exploding in a pink froth. Scraps of flesh are flung out like wet rags, while what remains—naked ribs, cracked bones and oily gristle—collapses in a disarticulated heap that will steam in cooler air.

The ninjas froze at the sound, and then one of them just—exploded. Jarren was sprayed with warm foam. A scrap of flesh shot over his shoulder and slapped the wall. And then the second ninja exploded. Jarren fell onto his stomach, scuttled around the back side of the debris pile for cover. He searched the darkened street in a panic. Brownstones fronted either side of the street, nowhere for an assailant to hide. The particle generator wound down and Jarren followed the sound to a third-storey window across the way. The window was dark but he could make out an even darker shape inside, a human shape. The shape hovered there, as if meeting his eyes.

"Jarren! My God!"

Simon limped out of the pub, glanced back and forth queasily between Jarren, ghoulishly flecked with red spots that were beginning to run, and the two abominable steaming piles. A black SUV screeched to a stop in front of the pub, Jarren's other Secret Service agent at the wheel. Jensen. His name was Jensen.

"Mr. Canto, Dr. Hammerskjold—*get in*!" Jensen yelled.

Simon yanked open a door. "Come on, Jarren."

Jarren's eyes were fixed on the window. The shape watched him. If there were only more light...

"Dr. Hammerskjold," Jensen pleaded, "we need to be *leaving*!"

"Damn it, Jarren, *come on*!" Simon screamed in a panic. He crossed in three painful, wincing steps, took Jarren by the shoulders and pulled him to the SUV. The shape in the window vanished. Simon pushed Jarren inside and slammed the door. The SUV lurched ahead, spinning tires on damp pavement.

It was 1:37 a.m. when the black SUV idled up to the southwest gate of the White House, its batteries humming in concert with the quiet throb of its fuel cell. Streetlamps cast garish, rose-hued circles around the gate, while the hedges and fencerows were shadowed in murky gray. The air was cool but humid. Moths flapped around the streetlamps, otherwise the city was quiet, just the urban hum. No traffic. A sharply creased Marine sentry logged the time—*zero one three seven hours*. Two more Marines stood behind the gate, wearing full kit and serious expressions, their rifles at port arms.

Simon stepped out of the SUV, slammed the door, and limped through the glare toward the sentry. He flashed his I.D., whispered something in the sentry's ear, and then he shuffled over to a darkened personnel gate. Jensen remained at the wheel. Jarren lay in the rear seat, in and out of a fetid, fitful sleep. He awoke with a start at the slam of the door. He felt sticky. His mouth was gauzy, tasted like iron and whiskey.

A few minutes later, a silhouette materialized from the darkness beyond the gate.

"Simon," Joaquin Merida said quietly through the black iron bars. "You shouldn't be here."

"You have to get me in, Joe. Believe me—the president *needs* the advice of a scientist right now."

"No way, Simon," Joaquin said hotly. "Things are too tense around here." He looked nervously over his shoulders before continuing, lowered his voice. "Look—I shouldn't be telling you this but it will be out soon enough. There's been a detonation in Afghanistan. The president doesn't have time for scientific theories right now."

"A detonation?" Simon blurted.

"Shhh! Damn it, keep your voice down."

"What *kind* of detonation?" Simon asked, quieter.

"We're still investigating."

"Radiation?"

"Everything looks clean so far."

Simon gave that some thought, and then his eyes widened. "Joe, you *really* need me in there. More than you know."

Joaquin clenched his teeth. "Let it go, Simon," he demanded. "If the president wants you in the loop she'll call." He began to turn away.

"*Wait—*" Simon pleaded, and then quickly, "I've got Canto."

Joaquin paused. "You've got Jarren Canto? Where?"

"Over there in the car."

"*What?* Are you *insane?* Someone's shooting ray guns at the guy and you bring him to the *White House?* We're at DEFCON 2 for Christ's sake!"

Muscles throbbed in Simon's jaw as he bit back the humiliation of being dressed down as if he were an undergraduate.

"We couldn't get a secure line," he explained in a trembling voice. "The Secret Service ordered us to stay on the move and not broadcast our destination. We even had to toss our comms. Where the hell were we *supposed* to go?"

"*Anywhere* but here."

"Think about it, Joe. *Think.* If we've got Canto then we've also got his ship. Particle weapons—your ray guns. Get it?"

Joaquin was two beats from brushing the raving scientist off when those last words hit home. He returned to the gate, deep in thought, pressed his face against the bars and spoke in a whisper.

"Okay," he said. "Good play. You've got Canto and we've got Sha'raelon—"

"You've got *Sha'raelon? How?*"

"She was at the detonation. Rangers picked her up. She's airborne now and should be on the ground in about twelve hours." Joaquin paused again to think. "I'll tell you what to do. Take Canto up to the Naval Observatory. The vice president is at a secure location with her family, so the residence is empty. It'll be quiet. *And discreet.*"

"Okay. Okay," Simon nodded.

"I'll get word over there; clear the way. Just sit tight. When the president gets up I'll brief her. She can decide what to do. Fair enough?"

"That's good, Joe. Thanks."

"Don't thank me," Joaquin said as he turned to leave. "She's liable to rip your head off for this stunt."

Simon returned to the SUV. He explained the plan to Jensen, who nodded with what looked like relief. Driving through empty streets, it didn't take long to reach the Naval Observatory. The three weary men pulled up out front of the opulent Queen Anne-style residence at Number One Observatory Circle and were met by a pair of Secret Service agents. One ushered them inside while the other took off in the SUV.

Jarren's clothes were stiff with dried blood. He could barely stand to breathe his own rank odor. "I need a bath, stat," he announced impatiently.

"Of course, Mr. Canto," his new agent said. Jensen had slipped away somewhere. Simon was sprawled on a wingback chair, fighting to keep his eyes open. "I'll show you to your suite. This way please."

The two men walked through a wainscoted hallway and then up a flight of stairs, pausing at an elegant door with polished brass knobs.

"It's right through here, Mr. Canto," the agent said. "You have full use of the facilities, but we *are* in lockdown. So please do not try to leave the premises or contact anyone outside."

Jarren was too weary to protest. "It's a luxurious jail," he commented under his breath.

"Not at all, sir," said the agent professionally. "It's for your protection. We'll know more in the morning. Good night."

Jarren ran the bath and flung off his blood-soiled clothes. He swore to have them burned. The steaming bathwater turned pink as he lowered himself into its enveloping warmth. He meant to drain and refill the tub but he fell asleep before he finished the thought.

It was early afternoon of the same day, although to Jarren it seemed as if the surreal events of last night had come from a different life, a different world—something he had dreamed. He was sitting in the solarium, sipping coffee and breakfasting on dry toast, the only things he could keep down. His stomach was still weak and uneasy. His right temple throbbed with sporadic jolts of pain. The Secret Service had provided him with clothing: black slacks, black jacket and tie, white shirt—if he were wearing dark sunglasses and had a comm in his ear he could pass for one of them. He scanned the news on a pad. The big story, of course, was that the United Nations had voted to launch UNCOMMSAT on schedule, tomorrow morning at 9:52 a.m. Eastern Daylight Time. It would be Friday, September 19, 2042 by the old calendar; 1.001:0001 Standard Galactic Rotation to Jarren; Focal 1 to Sha'raelon's lost timeline.

He had won, but he felt no satisfaction. He felt nothing at all.

There was other news: the media were scrambling for interviews with Canto and Sha'raelon but neither could be located; there had been a terrorist explosion in a place called Afghanistan; the Chinese had deployed tanks against a mass protest by women in something called Tiananmen Square; in Rome, Swiss Guards had fired on a crowd of women who had forced their way into the Vatican; people known as Kurds were resettling in the northwest of the former Iran now that radiation levels were falling, although the levels were still considered to be unsafe; people called *Occupiers* were gathering in Titusville, Florida in protest of tomorrow's launch. NASA was threatening to close the causeway...

He tapped the pad off and pushed it aside. This chaotic terrestrial news made his head pound worse. A Secret Service agent entered and scanned the room quickly yet thoroughly. Apparently satisfied, the agent took position next to the door.

"*Jarren!*"

Jarren glanced up with incomprehension and then leapt to his feet.

"*Rae?*"

She ran to him and wrapped him tightly in her arms. Jarren stood stiffly, arms out, but he gradually relented. Sha'raelon's embrace was—strangely comforting. He returned her embrace lightly and then pushed back to look at her. She was wearing a flight jacket over a wrinkled blue gown that was soiled at the knees, the hem tattered. She smelled of sweat and dust and diesel. Her hair was tangled and dirty.

"Rae, what happened to you?" Jarren asked with concern. There was a peculiar fluttering going on in his chest.

Sha'raelon's eyes were wet, but she smiled. A sad smile.

"I am so sorry," she moaned.

"No, I'm sorry," he said, although that's not what she meant. "I'm sorry I attacked you in the debate."

Sha'raelon sniffed and wiped her eyes. "No," she said, "we attacked each other, not because we wanted to but because we were compelled to, and all of this—" she threw up her hands, searched for words, "—all of this *havoc* just to make us do or not do something in this timeline. I am so weary of it."

"Have you heard?" he asked with a note of remorse.

"Yes," she lowered her eyes, "and they all died—for nothing."

Jarren was puzzled.

"What do you mean, Rae? What's happened?"

She gave him another of those sad smiles. "Later," she said. "I am filthy and I am barely on my feet. After a bath and some rest we can speak."

She patted him lightly on the chest.

"Michael?" she said then.

"Yes, Mistress Sha," the Secret Service agent replied. Jarren's eyes went up at that. Sha'raelon laughed.

"Michael is my bodyguard," she explained. "My protection." She gave Jarren a wry wink. "And I truly appreciate his courtesy and respect."

Michael's face was a professional mask, but Jarren was certain the man was beaming inwardly from the praise. Michael was Jarren's height and of similar build. He looked to be in his forties. He had a solid, square jaw, blond eyebrows, and hair cropped like a stiff brush. His eyes were piercingly blue.

"If you will show me to my quarters then, Michael, I will see about making myself presentable," Sha'raelon said.

"Certainly," said Michael. He presented his elbow and led Sha'raelon out of the room. Jarren shook his head and laughed, returned to his coffee and toast.

The sun was setting through a graying sky by the time Sha'raelon returned. Jarren had been napping on the solarium sofa. He awoke as the door opened, sat up with effort, rubbing his eyes, and then—he just goggled at Sha'raelon as she came into the room. He slowly rose, stupefied. Sha'raelon was wearing a gray sweatshirt emblazoned with the Navy globe and anchor, and she was wearing matching gray...*shorts*. Her legs were—stunning; muscular but perfectly proportioned, smooth and healthily bronzed; and her *thighs*— Jarren felt an awkward stirring.

"Uh," he said.

"They have sent for clothes," Sha'raelon explained without apology. "This is all they had."

Her hair was wet. She had it tied back in a high ponytail that made her look like a school athlete fresh from the showers. She was tapping the parquet floor with her bare toes. She seemed not the least bit self conscious.

Jarren was fidgeting like a teenager. Sha'raelon looked at him quizzically. "Is something the matter, Jarren?"

"Uh, uh—no, not at all." Jarren found his voice. "Have you eaten?"

"Yes, a snack. It is much too early for the evening meal." She scanned the room, gestured toward a wet bar. "Is that wine?"

"I—I believe it is," he answered unevenly.

"Let us have some then."

"But I thought—"

"I'll be right outside, Mistress," Michael interrupted with amusement. He pulled the door and left them alone.

"—never mind," said Jarren.

He uncorked a bottle of Madeira and poured for both of them. Sha'raelon dropped her baton and Pa'ket's belt on a chair, and then she snuggled onto the sofa, folding her legs, tucking her feet. The sofa was still warm from Jarren's nap. Jarren handed her a glass and took the adjoining chair.

"Well this is a surprise," he said after a moment.

"Why do you say that?"

He left the answer hanging, instead asked, "What will you do now?"

Sha'raelon took a sip of her wine, grimaced, but then followed it with another. She gazed out at the darkening sky. Traces of rain were beginning to dot the windows. Finally: "I know what I was supposed to do, what I could still do, but now I am not sure."

"What do you mean?"

"You were right about me, you know. I never lied, though. I held back some things, things people would have difficulty accepting, but it is true that I am, like you, mostly unaware of Focal history—except for my role in it."

She paused to sip her wine, used a finger to move a loose curl away from her eyes. Her gaze went distant again. Silence gathered, and then she straightened her shoulders and continued with unexpected candor.

"I *am* the founding matriarch of my line."

Even though he had suspected as much, Jarren was still startled by her admission.

"Why are you telling me this?" he asked.

"Because you were brought into this against your will," she said. "But *I* was trained for this. I have been training for this all my life, to do my duty. I was destined to succeed. Do you understand? *Destined.* And now..."

She tipped back her glass and then held it out to Jarren for a refill. His eyebrows went up in surprise, but he took her glass, padded silently to the bar and poured. The rain had become a patter now, and the sun had fully set. When he returned he asked, "Rae, what has happened to you?"

Sha'raelon's eyes were unfocused.

"I wish you could see my world," she said dreamily. "It is beautiful."

"But Rae—"

"We have balance; we have *harmony.*" She shook off those thoughts, faced him squarely. "But it is as you said at the café. Do you remember?"

"Vaguely. A lot happened that day."

"Yes...Pa'ket," she said, almost a whisper. "*My father,*" lower still.

Jarren leaned in closer. "Rae, what are you trying to tell me?"

"I am trying to *explain.*" She turned on him, cheeks flushing. "This is difficult."

Jarren pulled back at the rebuke. "Yes, it must be," he said. "I'm sorry. Please go on."

Sha'raelon considered him for a moment, and then: "You said all of this was futile, that we are from but two of many realities; that we cannot change anything without creating even more realities. Do you truly believe this?"

"Yes, I do."

"So your daughter...?"

Jarren stopped her with his eyes. "Lost," he said, voice cracking.

"As always, how can we really know?" she said. "And yet I have come to believe that I am caught up in something else entirely, something...different. I lead—*did lead*—these women into their future. I bonded with a man—I know his name—I had children—I know their names, too." And then soberly, "I know when I died—"

"Dear Jack!" Jarren exclaimed. "And you've had to *live* with this—"

"—and when I will be born," she went on, as if he hadn't spoken. "In essence, I give birth to myself. This timeline is how I come to be. I would not be alive otherwise. How can you explain that?"

"I can't."

"Of course you cannot, nor can I. I would give my life for one breath that I knew with certainty I had never breathed before, something that you take for granted every waking minute."

"Rae, I, uh—I don't know what to say."

"There is one theory," she went on absently, "similar to what you believe. It was revealed to me by a monk many years ago as a possibility; only as a possibility. I think he was sincerely trying to expand my mind." Her eyes went soft at some memory. "Pa'ket was furious with that monk. Now I know why. But that theory always seemed too fantastic to me, too improbable, so I spent no time dwelling on it. Now, though...I wonder."

Jarren leaned closer again, intrigued. "What is this theory?"

She wouldn't meet his eyes. A single heavy tear fell. She sniffed and said, "That I am cycling through realities."

"Huh?"

"By going back in time," she explained, staring through smeared windows at the gathering rain, "I create a new reality. I live, I die, and then I am born, only to go back and create *another* reality—*infinitely.*"

Jarren felt a headache coming on that had nothing to do with last night's whiskey, this and a soul-emptying despair for Sha'raelon.

"So—" she finished off her second glass of wine, examined it vacantly. "No more of this for me. My head is swimming."

"Rae, I'm...staggered, but I still don't understand why you're telling me these things."

"Because only you can understand."

The loneliness in her voice was wrenching.

Sha'raelon twirled her glass in her fingers. She said, "I was in Arachosia yesterday, as I knew I would be, gathering the women, thousands of them—*thousands.* There was a bomb. They are all dead now. It was an antimatter bomb—you know what that means." Not a question.

Jarren snapped to attention.

"Who?" he asked.

"How can we know? And what could it change if we did? It is my fault that those women are dead. It will be my fault if it happens again."

Sha'raelon stretched out on the sofa, closed her eyes and brought a hand to her forehead. Heavy rain pelted the windows in a constant, hollow roar.

"I do not know what to do," she said.

The Situation Room was tense, all eyes on the monitors. Sweat beaded at Joaquin Merida's temples. A young staffer was biting her nails.

"T minus five, Madam President," said the director of NASA.

That seemed to focus everyone even more intently.

"Lighten up, people," said President Carlyle. "This isn't the Super Bowl after all, just a routine launch."

She smiled faintly and hoped it was enough. There was some feeble laughter around the room, but attentions were quickly returned to the monitors. The venerable Atlas V launch vehicle stood tethered to the gantry. Coolant steamed from its base, and its long shadow fell away from the morning sun. The Florida coast was perfectly clear. An armada of boats speckled the waters off shore like flocks of sea birds, held back by a pair of Coast Guard cutters tacking diligently parallel to the coast, laying perfectly straight wakes. Thousands were protesting on the mainland. The causeways had been closed from Titusville to Cocoa. Boat traffic was prohibited in the Intracoastal north of Merritt Island.

There would be hell to pay for this, President Carlyle thought sourly, not to mention the political capital she had spent at the United Nations to have the launch go off as scheduled. She mused that it just *had* to be NASA, and *had* to be a Canaveral launch, rather than a launch from Vandenberg or the New Mexico Spaceport, further away from protesters and prying eyes. But NASA had been semi-privatized in the 20s, and had outbid Space X and Virgin for the launch of UNCOMMSAT. And so all of this had landed in *her* lap, what would have been a routine launch, unnoticed by anyone, had *they* not come.

"T minus four, Madam President."

Sha'raelon picked listlessly at her breakfast of cubed fruit. Her eyes looked glazed. Her hair had lost its luster, hanging dull and lifeless over her shoulders. She was dressed in a white blouse, navy blue skirt, and black pumps. She wore white stockings. Her clothing was some kind of regulation dress for Navy women. She didn't look like herself. Jarren ached for her.

He sat across the small breakfast table from her, sipping coffee, dressed as he had been last night except that this morning he had left off the tie. The rain had moved out overnight, and the day had dawned warm and clear. The sun shone through the windows, flickering through trees that swayed in a light easterly breeze. The wall screen showed a tall chemical rocket. A digital launch counter ticked down in a sidebar. Sha'raelon had her back to the screen, so Jarren had both her and the rocket in his view. He focused on one and then the other, back and forth, worried about Sha'raelon, ambivalent about the launch.

"It's soon now, Rae," he said gently.

She lifted defeated eyes to meet his. A wave of sorrow passed through him, a penetrating sense of loss. This could not be the indomitable Sha'raelon, he thought. Not

Mistress Sha. Jarren felt weak, lost. Sha'raelon seemed to sense this. She dropped eyes to her lap, folded her hands there. She sat very still. Jarren could hear her breaths.

Michael stood careful watch next to the door, in obvious distress at Sha'raelon's condition. He was rigidly upright as always, his face professionally unreadable, but his eyes were pained, Jarren could tell.

Simon sat on the sofa, petulantly sipping a Bloody Mary. He pulled out the celery stalk and flung it into a waste bin, not caring that a few red drops had splotched the vice president's sofa. He was singularly unimpressed with Sha'raelon, now that he had finally met her. Certainly she was a pretty woman, but she was also distant and emotionally cold. Why had everyone gone on so about her?

"What will you do after, Madam Sha?" Simon ventured through the heavy, uncomfortable silence in the room. Jarren heard Sha'raelon exhale with annoyance.

"We must wait to see what will transpire, Dr. Hammerskjold," she answered in a biting tone, eyes never leaving her hands.

"You may call me Simon," he said with a weak smile.

She looked up then, fixed Simon with a withering stare.

"Certainly not," she said acidly.

Jarren perked up his ears, leaned in close and asked in a whisper, "Do you know something you haven't told me, Rae?"

She answered with a despondent look that rushed guilt across his face. Suddenly his coffee tasted bitter. He pushed the mug away.

"T minus one, Madam President."

"And you, Jarren?" asked Simon. "What will you do?"

"I've made no secret that I will return to space."

"But—but you can't do that," Simon sputtered. "There is so much you can teach us."

Jarren avoided the man's desperate eyes, said crossly, "I *can* do it, and I think I've taught you too much already."

"Thirty seconds..."

"Shouldn't you be with your president right now, Simon?" Jarren asked then. Simon's presence was intrusive. Sha'raelon needed the quiet comfort of a friend, not the stumbling of a bureaucrat.

"Yes, I should," Simon answered tensely, face reddening. "Perhaps later I will be called." His tone and posture didn't make that outcome seem likely.

Jarren sighed, looked to Michael, who answered with a commiserating expression. Jarren tipped his head toward the door, reached across for Sha'raelon's hand. Michael nodded once in agreement, a discreet dip of his chin. Sha'raelon needed a smooth exit from the stuffy room, a quiet place to gather herself once the rocket was off the ground.

"*...eight, seven, six, five, four, three, two, one... lift off! We have lift off of UNCOMMSAT on a sunny Florida morning, blasting into high Earth orbit on a mission to improve communication between nations.*"

President Carlyle had been holding her breath without realizing it. She exhaled in relief. Cheers filled the

Situation Room. That last little bit from NASA had a nice, altruistic ring to it. Left unsaid and unalluded, though, was the planet-wide chaos that would now have to be managed. And also what to do about Sha'raelon...

Sha'raelon had her face in her hands. Tears leaked between her fingers.

"Go at throttle up."

President Carlyle slapped Joaquin on the back, stood with a grin and shook hands around the table.

"Gentlemen," she said, gesturing with her hands as if wiping them clean. "Now that we have *that* over with we can get back to the business of the *real* world."

Someone hooted. Someone whistled. The very air seemed lighter. Staff were standing, gathering papers, moving toward the door, but then—

"Bogey! Bogey! Bogey!"

President Carlyle whipped up at the screen in confusion. Wide white grins dropped into foreboding frowns. Silence fell like a weighted curtain.

The compact timeship flared out of subspace at an altitude of thirty thousand feet over the Atlantic Ocean, just six nautical miles downrange of Cape Canaveral. The energy discharge raked the ocean with lightening, flash steaming the surface into a boiling fog. Fish by the thousands floated to the surface, rolling with the swells in an oily mat. The ship jinked into a course correction that should have stewed its crew, should have flung off bits of hull along its previous vector. Enveloped in inertial fields, though, that didn't happen. Instead a generator shrieked, and a focused beam lanced out from the prow. The Atlas V carrying UNCOMMSAT exploded, raining an umbrella of smoke-trailing debris.

"*What's happening, damn it?*" President Carlyle screamed. Alarms were shrieking. The screens were going dark or else dropping to gray static.

"The Atlas has exploded, Madam President!"

"*Confirm Missile launch! Do we have missile launch?*"

"Wait—!"

"It's too late, Ma'am," said Joaquin anxiously.

Missiles arced into the sky, ground based as well as sea based. Contrails traced chalky lines against pastel blue, all angling toward the timeship. The ship swept smoothly through the atmosphere in a long turn that carried it over the landmass of central Florida, stern down, prow pointed at the stars. The missiles were converging. Seconds now. Gravitic fields flexed on either side of the ship, like lungs taking air, and then the ship stretched out in a smear of light from Earth to space.

There is a reason why it is mortally taboo throughout Human Space to go superlight inside a gravity well.

It might actually have looked beautiful from space, as if God's own hand were sculpting and reshaping Florida. Fields rippled and folded the air between the timeship and the surface, pulling at the landmass as if it were elastic. Eastern Florida wrinkled, like a wad of paper. A mountain was tugged out of this roiling cataclysm, drawn toward the firmament, the source. Fingers of blue crept across the new surface like spilled ink, forming fjords and tumbling waterfalls, lakes and straits. It may have looked beautiful from space, but on the ground, of course, it was apocalyptic. Much of central Florida was remade into a mountainous archipelago. Diffuse gray clouds of debris—cars, trucks, buildings, trees, alligators—people—fell like rain. Scientists would later determine that no higher life forms had survived between latitudes thirty degrees and twenty-eight degrees north; and also that Earth's rotation had measurably slowed.

"Florida has gone black, Madam President!"

"What the hell does that mean? How can Florida go *black*?"

President Carlyle was out of her chair, palms pressed flat on the table. A surge of fear tingled along her spine. The Situation Room was chaos. Joaquin Merida was hastily pushing staffers and nonessential personnel out the door. All of the screens showed gray static. Secretary of Defense Channing was barking into a comm, a hand cupped over his ear against the piercing alarms.

"Shut off the damned—"

The alarms fell silent

"Thank God! Now somebody talk to me, damn it!" President Carlyle slammed her fist on the table.

"We have an image, Madam President," Secretary Channing shouted. He was a black man with a bull dog's body and a prize fighter's face. He had retired from the Army with the rank of lieutenant general, so he knew how to handle tension and stress. Still, he had a harried look in his eyes. "Coming up on the screen...now!"

Everyone froze in that moment and stared. A grainy image flickered on the screen, grainy but unmistakable. It was a ship, shaped roughly like an arrowhead and encircled by a pulsing ring.

"What is this?" demanded the president. "One of their ships?"

"This is video just prior to the explosion. That ship fired on the Atlas."

"Those bastards," she seethed. "Detain Sha'raelon and Canto! Seize her ship!"

"*Madam President,*" Secretary of State Long pleaded. "They're *ambassadors*. They have *immunity*."

"*Like hell they do!*" she spat back. "That's nothing but Chen's gimmick. He was besotted with that woman, the poor bastard. *We're under attack!* Do it! *Do it now!*"

A missile boomed into the stratosphere over the North Atlantic, dropped supersonic to two thousand feet and then went hypersonic, plowing a shock wake across the ocean, hurtling so fast that radar operators thought their screens were glitched. It flashed across Long Beach and Inwood quicker than an eye could blink, homed in on Sha'raelon's ship at JFK Airport, and impacted cleanly in the center of the ring.

Fortunately for the Northeastern United States, although not for those in the immediate vicinity of Sha'raelon's ship, the missile was only an unarmed kinetic device.

"Are you telling me that after everything we've been through, the damn thing just *explodes?*" Jarren exclaimed with equal parts anger and disgust. Their screen had gone gray with static. He walked to it, rapped it a few times. No change. He threw up his hands in frustration and turned to a window, gazed vacantly at his reflection in the glass.

Sha'raelon had come fully alert when the Atlas exploded. She was sitting upright now, wary and observant. Simon was pacing nervously, checking his comm every few steps. Michael maintained a rigid position next to the door, but his eyes were in constant motion, scanning, assessing.

"The light outside is strange," Jarren thought out loud. He pulled the curtains for a better view. The sky was pale, as if washed of color. Wispy rings of high cloud were flattening toward the north.

"Damn them!" Simon cursed suddenly. He flung his comm side-armed at the sofa. It bounced, hit the floor and shattered. Both Michael and Sha'raelon turned reflexively toward Simon. Michael's eyes hardened with disapproval; Sha'raelon's were dismissive. Jarren was still standing at the window, staring up at the sky.

Simon was red in the face, the color rising like a rash into scarlet patches on his bald head. He caught the look in Sha'raelon's eyes and reddened even deeper.

"What are you staring at?" he shouted. He crossed to Sha'raelon threateningly, fists opening and closing. Sha'raelon only smiled; an infuriating, mysterious smile. "This is your doing!" he spat, hovering over her. Michael somehow materialized between them. The agent never said a word, just pushed the scientist away from Sha'raelon. A second push sent Simon flopping backward onto the sofa. Throughout it all, Sha'raelon didn't even flinch.

"What the hell's going on?" Jarren demanded to know, spinning away from the window. He looked at Simon accusingly. "What's the *matter* with you?"

Shame had replaced anger on Simon's face. He looked away.

"Will I be having any more problems with you, Dr. Hammerskjold?" Michael asked with professional detachment.

"No," Simon muttered, embarrassed and humiliated.

"Very good then, sir," said Michael. He returned to his place by the door.

Jarren shook his head in disbelief. He returned to the table and sat next to Sha'raelon.

"Rae?" he whispered. "Are you all—"

A beeping sounded from a compartment on Pa'ket's belt, which was lying across Sha'raelon's lap, three piercing beeps, then a trilling sound followed by three more beeps. Sha'raelon stiffened.

"What's happening?" Jarren asked. "What's that sound?"

Sha'raelon was stonily calm as she met his eyes and said, "It would seem that my ship has been destroyed."

It took a moment for her words to register, but Jarren jumped to his feet when they did, an alarmed, cornered look on his face. Michael was pressing fingers to the comm in his ear, listening intently to something. He inhaled sharply and nodded, dropped his hands and came up behind Sha'raelon.

Sha'raelon could sense his presence at her back, the warmth coming off of him, the astringent smell of his aftershave. Jarren looked at the man in confusion.

"Mistress Sha?" Michael said, taking her arm.

"Yes, Michael," Sha'raelon answered grimly. His fingers were tightening on her arm. She closed her eyes against a wave of remorse. Michael was a good man, an honest man. He had talked about his family: a wife, two daughters and a son...

"Please, Mistress," he said regretfully, squeezing tighter. "I need you to come with me."

Just then another Secret Service agent burst into the room.

"Jarren Canto? Come with me please," the man ordered, sweeping the room with his eyes, discounting Simon, who was still flopped on the sofa.

"What?" Jarren blurted. "Why?"

"I have orders to escort you to a secure detention facility immediately, sir," the agent said firmly.

Sha'raelon twisted abruptly and lashed out with the blade of her hand. Even as Michael was falling unconscious into her arms she was using his body as a pivot to launch her legs at the second agent. The man was going for his shoulder holster as she scissored his neck between her calves and flipped him onto his back. A punishing strike with her heel to his solar plexus finished the agent off.

Jarren hadn't moved, not so much as a quiver. He stood as if mired in mud, his jaw hanging practically to his chest. Simon was on his feet now, as equally astonished as Jarren.

Sha'raelon lowered Michael gently to the floor. She gazed at his face sadly, brushed his cheek. "I am sorry my friend," she whispered. She felt his neck for a pulse, exhaled with relief when she found it. Michael would live, his daughters would prosper. "Teach your daughters well," she said, and then she was away, slinging Pa'ket's belt over her shoulder, clutching her baton as she banged through leaded-glass doors into the pale morning sunlight.

After a quick, confounded glance at Simon, Jarren sprinted after her, rolling up his left sleeve while on the run. He caught up to her across a bricked patio, where he found her crouching behind a hedge. Beyond the hedge was a broad, manicured lawn bordered by a thicket of trees. Jarren knelt beside her.

"Impressive as always, Mistress Sha," he commented dryly.

"I did not want to do that," Sha'raelon admitted in a pained voice.

"I know you didn't, Rae," he said. "What's your plan?"

"My plan is to get away." She glanced curiously at his arm. "What is that?"

There was what looked like a small keyboard tattooed in indigo blue on the back of Jarren's left forearm. Jarren tapped at some of the keys and the tattoo began to glow in a neon outline.

"I have a better plan," Jarren said. His fingers worked speedily at the tattoo. Sha'raelon noticed other features. There were scales with luminous points that Jarren could move by sliding his finger, and a subcutaneous digital display that began to flash through a sequence of numbers.

Five hundred kilometers above them, Jarren's time-ship broke orbit and began its descent.

"Help's on the way," Jarren said. "And this lawn is more than large enough."

"Large enough for what?"

"For my ship."

"*Ah*," Sha'raelon mouthed with dawning awareness. "That device—your tattoo—it controls your ship?"

"Yeah. Most spacers have them. It helps us prevent being—oh—let's say *accidentally* separated from our ships."

"I had thought that you must have used a shuttle to come to the surface."

"Naw, waste of mass."

Sha'raelon returned her attention to the lawn. All was quiet, too quiet, not even the chirping of birds. The sky *did* look strange. Colors were flat, and she was able to look directly into the pale sun without discomfort.

"How long?" she asked.

"Minutes, but it's coming in hot. I'll have to brake and cool the bow wave before I bring it in too close. Over the ocean, I think. That'll make a good heat sink. Call it fifteen minutes. If we can just sit tight—"

Simon shuffled up behind them, stooped and panting. He caught his breath and asked, "Who are we hiding from?"

"Go away, Dr. Hammerskjold," Sha'raelon said dismissively.

"No way," he shook his head. "I'm staying with both of you until I know what's going on."

"You're liable to get yourself hurt," said Jarren.

"Who would want to hurt *me*?"

"Enough of this," Sha'raelon snapped. "We do not have fifteen minutes, Jarren. We will be discovered long before then."

Jarren thought quickly. "How about those trees? They'll give us cover and freedom of movement. The ship will come in between us and the house."

"That is our best course," Sha'raelon agreed.

"What ship?" asked Simon.

"Do you see anyone out there, Rae?" Jarren asked.

"I have seen no one. I believe it is clear."

"What about security cameras?"

"We need not be concerned about that," she said with certainty, patting a compartment on Pa'ket's belt.

"I have *got* to get one of those belts," said Jarren earnestly.

"What ship?" asked Simon.

Sha'raelon worked quickly to tie up her hair. "Are you ready, Jarren?"

"Let's do it...*go!*"

The two jumped from the cover of the hedge and raced across the lawn. Simon stood with a bewildered look but then kicked after them. A shadow swept across the lawn ahead of him. He stopped to look up, shielding his eyes. A silhouette passed before the sun, wheeled around and dove like a bird of prey.

"What is *that?*" Simon asked himself. And then he jumped at the popping of rapid-fire guns.

Twin lines plowed across the lawn, from the trees directly toward Sha'raelon and Jarren. The lawn was still wet from last night's rain. Jarren's feet slipped out from under him as he pulled up short. He fell onto his back with a jolt, but still managed to roll out of the line of fire.

Sha'raelon dove to her left just as the thumping impacts reached her. Simon flailed his arms in indecision, looked left, right, left, took a step back, tripped and fell into the hedge. He was struggling to untangle himself as the drone broke off and wheeled above him for another pass.

The lawn had been churned to mud. Sha'raelon slipped to her knees as she made her way to Jarren. She got arms around him and they pushed up together, unsteadily. The drone completed its turn and swooped in for the kill. They wasted no time, but ran hand in hand for the trees. Impacts thumped behind them, clods of grass and soil flinging into the air.

Jarren could feel the impact vibrations through the soles of his shoes. Close, too close. They weren't going to make it. He lowered his shoulder, prepared to shove Sha'raelon forcefully out of the line of fire. Grass and mud were splattering the back of his neck... *Now!* He shouldered into her too hard, spinning her off her feet but at least away from the strafing. He gritted his teeth, the impacts were at his heels, and then—a familiar screeching whine from somewhere ahead. An ice-white beam of light slashed upward at a steep angle, cleaving a wing off of the drone. The drone spun away to Jarren's right and crashed into the trees like a tossed can.

Jarren slid to a stop, his chest heaving. He focused on the tree line, tried to recall where the beam had come from. Sha'raelon was up and moving toward him. Her stockings and elbows were muddied, along with the palms of her hands, but she was uninjured.

"Jarren, what *was* that?" she asked, flicking mud from her fingers.

"It was a particle weapon," answered Simon, coming up behind them. There was a note of vindication in his voice, that and satisfaction.

Jarren was oblivious of them. He was transfixed on the trees. He could make out a form within the leafy shadows. He tipped his head one way and then the other for a better view. The form stepped out from the trees and into the light. Jarren's face went ashen. He fell to his knees.

"*Sulea!*" he cried.

Sha'raelon couldn't make any sense of the scene before her. Jarren was on his knees, tears dripping off his cheeks. A woman had come out of the trees, an exotic looking woman wearing a sleeveless dark gray flight suit. The woman was of compact build, the taught lines of her body emphasized by her tight suit. She had copper skin, dark almond eyes, and smooth black hair that feathered above her brows and ears. She hefted an industrial looking piece of equipment with her right arm, gray metal with a long clear barrel, and this was tethered by a white tube to a shiny metal box that she carried by a handle with her left hand. Her right arm... Sha'raelon's breath caught in her throat. The woman's right arm bore a tattoo identical to Jarren's!

"*Sulea!*" Jarren cried again. He staggered to his feet. "*How?*"

The woman called Sulea heaved the device she was carrying to the ground and let the box slip from her fingers. She moved toward Jarren, trepidly at first but then with gathering joy, arms opening. Her eyes were wet. "*Jarren!*" she cried in return.

The two rushed into an embrace. Jarren was calling out her name, "*Sulea, Sulea,*" kissing her neck, dripping tears onto her shoulder. "*Oh, Sulea. My love—my* wife."

Sha'raelon froze in place, eyes going wide. *Wife?*

"*Sulea, Sulea, Sulea,*" Jarren murmured, mouth pressed to her ear. It was her, impossibly, but it was her. He had been so long without her. She looked different; she *felt* different. Her body was more athletic than he remembered. Her hair was shorter. And she smelled—different.

Jarren pushed back and gazed into her soulful brown eyes. "Laurel?" he asked, his voice trembling.

Sulea looked down at her feet. "She is safe and well."

"Oh blessed Jack!" Jarren cried with relief.

Sha'raelon edged in close to the couple. Simon stood a ways back, looking around nervously, at the trees, up at the sky.

Sulea turned eyes on Sha'raelon. "I am Sulea," she said.

There was something about the look Sulea gave her that put Sha'raelon on edge. And the woman's accent was odd, a hardened, frontier-like drawl.

"*Su'lea,*" Sha'raelon mused aloud.

Sulea's eyes went flinty. "No, it's *Sulea*. And I know who *you* are. You're the cause of all of this."

Caught off guard, Sha'raelon snapped back, "I am the *cause* of nothing!"

"Sulea...?" Jarren questioned her with his eyes.

"You can tell, can't you my love." She smiled softly and stroked his face.

"What—?"

"I am not your Sulea, and you are not my Jarren." Her eyes began to glisten. "My Jarren is uptime with Laurel."

"I—I don't understand."

"Oh, of course you do, my love. I can see the doubt in your eyes. Tell me about us—" Sulea had to pause to keep her voice from breaking"—in your timeline."

Jarren's face contorted with grief.

"Oh..." Sulea understood. "Oh, my poor Jarren," and she embraced him again.

"You're not from my timeline?" he asked, gently swaying, face pressed into her hair.

"No, my love." Her voice was a whisper of sorrow.

"Then you came here to...to protect me?"

Sulea hardened in his arms. Suddenly she spun out of his embrace and faced Sha'raelon.

"Not exactly," she answered with a sinister smile.

What happened next was too quick for Jarren to follow. Sulea whipped a long, wicked knife from her boot while Sha'raelon flicked her wrist, baton already spinning. The two women launched themselves at one another without warning. Metal clanged. The fight was vicious and close. Sha'raelon towered over Sulea, but the spacer had the body of a gymnast. Sulea back-flipped away from Sha'raelon's spinning blades, came down low like a cat and swept around with her knife, aiming for the back of Sha'raelon's knee. Sha'raelon leapt instinctively, grasped her baton for a savage downward thrust.

"Stop this! Stop!" Jarren screamed.

Simon was backing away, glancing over his shoulder as if preparing to run.

The women ignored Jarren, or rather, were too engaged to take notice of him. Sulea did something like a horizontal cartwheel, which flung her into a low stance, left arm forward for balance, right arm wide and ready to slash. Sha'raelon's blade impaled the ground where Sulea had been an eye-blink before, and this gave Sulea the opening she needed. She tumbled toward Sha'raelon, went into a roll, and at the last minute leapt, her knife's edge angled for Sha'raelon's neck.

There was no time to think, but Sha'raelon intuitively knew she had opened herself to a counter strike, and from which direction it would come. No time to pull the baton out of the soil; no time to lift it, spin it and parry. No time. She side-stepped and whirled about, levered the baton like a staff, its free blade positioned where she instinctively knew her assailant would be...

...and then Jarren was there, screaming at them, one blade slanting downward, the other slanting upward, Jarren in between...

Sha'raelon gasped and checked her blade. Sulea froze in mid strike. She was up on her toes, as rigid as an arrow, grasping her knife back-handed, ready to cut.

The fight ended as abruptly as it had begun. The lawn was utterly quiet. Simon had been about to turn and flee for the house, but now he held himself as immobile as the two fighters, either from shock or from morbid curiosity. Jarren didn't flinch, didn't blink, but used his peripheral vision to confirm how close he had come to death. Sha'raelon's blade was at his neck while Sulea's blade was at his throat. He swallowed hard, and delicately pushed the two women away. His knees were trembling.

It took him a moment to gather himself. The two women glowered past him at one another.

"Sulea," he said weakly. "What is this?"

Sulea gave an ironic laugh, reached down and sheathed her knife. At that Sha'raelon flicked her wrist, retracting her blades. Sha'raelon stepped up behind Jarren, just stood there and coolly observed his doppelganger wife. Sulea looked from one to the other, puzzled at first but then she had it and she smiled bitterly.

"You've bonded with this woman, haven't you, Jarren?"

"I have not!" Jarren protested. Sha'raelon's cheeks flushed.

"Ah," Sulea said coyly, pacing loosely before him, "but you want to. Yeah?"

"Sulea, I—"

"There's no need to explain, my love. I know you too well. Trapped here in the past...she's a beautiful woman."

"Sulea," Sha'raelon stepped forward. "Your husband and I have not—"

"*He's not my husband!*" Sulea screamed. "*My* husband is in *my* time, with *my* daughter, and if I let you live then *they* die." She kicked at the ground. "It should have been *so* simple, but every time I had you in my sights somebody started shooting at *him*." Shaking with rage, she thrust a finger toward Jarren. "*He's* not my husband," softer, "but he *is* my love." She turned to Jarren, eyes begging. "Darling, what was I supposed to do? I couldn't let *them* kill you, but now *I've* killed you. And Laurel..."

"No, no, Sulea." Jarren's eyes filled. He went to embrace her but she pushed him back.

"Keep away from me," she hissed. She was pacing back and forth as if caged. Her eyes were conflicted, moving from hate to indecision and then back again at each turn. She tugged at a fistful of her hair, beat her head with her palms. Finally she settled on Sha'raelon. Sulea's eyes were hard, hateful. It ached Jarren to see her this way.

"I can't let you kill her," he said in a wavering voice.

Sha'raelon tensed, was about to protest that she needed no one's protection, but then thought better of it and held her tongue.

Sulea seemed to wilt. She stopped her pacing, faced Jarren and searched his eyes.

"You would really try to stop me?" she asked. "For *her*?" A tear pattered onto her cheek. "This woman means that much to you?"

The betrayal in her face crushed Jarren's heart.

"Yes, that," he said uncertainly, "but also because I know *you*. You're not a murderer. I won't let them force you to become one."

Sulea threw up her arms and then sat back on her heels, face in her hands. After a moment she sniffed and wiped her eyes. "Still my chivalrous Jarren," she said ironically, "my captain; my white knight." But then her eyes went somber. She stared at the ground. "Not anymore, though," she whispered.

Simon observed all of this, fascinated. He imagined a point in his mind, a focal point, and from that point sprouted Jarren and Sha'raelon and Sulea, truly like the branches of a tree. He labeled them time vectors A, B, and C. But then, who bombed Kandahar? Label that one time vector D. And there were certainly more operating here in the present...

The diagram in his mind became a complex fan, points bifurcating and then bifurcating again. His central question then became: Could the time vectors ever intersect? Would it be possible to cross from one to another? And exactly *why* couldn't these people return to the future?— ah! *That's how one crosses over!* Damn, he wished Roth were here. But Roth's causality equation wouldn't help, it only provided future infinities...unrealized potentialities. *Of course!* It would be virtually impossible to navigate through the infinities uptime. You would *never* find your way back to your own time. Instead you would cross unpredictably into *another time stream!*

Simon stepped forward, his mind whirling. "Er, uh, Mrs. Canto?"

Sulea looked up at him scornfully.

"Who are you?" she asked derisively, as if offended by his very presence if not also his archaic greeting. *Mrs. Canto?*

"This is Dr. Hammerskjold," Jarren offered. "Uh, an American contemporary."

To Jarren, frostily, "What's his part in this?"

Simon took another halting step toward Sulea. "No part, ma'am," he answered before Jarren could. "I'm just a bystander who seems to have gotten caught up in your little drama."

Sulea snorted. "Paranoid Americans." She shook her head, laughing darkly. "I *blame* her," she pointed a finger accusingly at Sha'raelon, "but really it's *you* people who did this."

Simon saw only the time diagram in his mind. He saw it objectively, professionally—breathlessly. He took another step forward, more confident.

"Please tell me what you know of this focal point," he said with quiet authority. Jarren gave him a reappraising look. Sulea took note of his seriousness as well. She dropped the scornful look, answered him frankly.

"It was the attack on the satellite—"

"*Attacked,* you say."

"—and that bomb that missed *her.*" Sulea stabbed another finger at Sha'raelon.

Sha'raelon tensed. There was cold malice in her eyes. "Was that your doing?" she asked menacingly.

Sulea returned the challenge with an equally menacing stare. "No," she answered, eyes unyielding.

"Time vector D," Simon pondered quietly, but loud enough to catch Sha'raelon's attention.

"Who was responsible for Arachosia, Dr. Hammerskjold?" she demanded.

"I don't know. I don't know that it matters," and then to Sulea, "please continue."

Sulea's eyes drifted from Sha'raelon to Simon. "You Americans had your missiles cocked and ready, and you kept them that way. There were no threats—there was nothing to shoot at—but no, you wouldn't stand down. And then the aliens came. Somebody panicked and you started a war...then you captured their ship."

"My God," said Simon. "*Of course.*"

"What?" asked Jarren.

"UNCOMMSAT. It's so obvious." Sha'raelon and Jarren looked at one another in confusion. "If Sha'raelon had succeeded in rescheduling the launch then there wouldn't have been an attack. The vectors would have bifurcated at different points. We wouldn't have stayed at DEFCON 2 and we wouldn't have fired at the aliens—"

Awareness rushed into Sha'raelon like a drowning breath.

"And you wouldn't have gotten their ship!" she exclaimed. "Jarren's timeline would never have been created and I would have been able to—"

A jet roared overhead, low enough to shake the ground. Jarren covered his ears and ducked, they all did, and then the jet shot beyond the trees, out of view. They followed the roar of its engines, fading in a harsh rumble.

"Were we seen?" asked Sha'raelon.

Everyone looked at Simon, who shrugged his shoulders.

"Surely they wouldn't send *aircraft* after us," Jarren said in a daze.

"Paranoid Americans," Sulea commented, shaking her head.

"Call your ship, Jarren," said Sha'raelon. "We must go."

"Sulea," said Jarren quickly. "Where's your ship?"

"On a sports field beyond these trees."

"We should go; we should go now," he said. He rushed to her side, tapping at his tattoo.

"I'm flying a scout class ship, Jarren. Only room for two."

"Rae can take my ship," he said bluntly.

Something flickered in Sha'raelon's eyes—hurt, vulnerability, a naive innocence that was painful to witness—only for an instant but Sulea saw it for what it was. Surprisingly though, she took no satisfaction from it.

"No," Sulea said firmly. "You take the *mistress* with you."

"Sulea?"

She took him by the shoulders, looked deeply into him. "I am gone in your timeline, yeah?" she said, low so the others couldn't hear. Jarren had to look away "You've grieved for me, haven't you? You've sent me into a star."

Jarren couldn't answer. He tugged absently at his earring.

"I am not your wife," Sulea continued. "I will not be the ghost of your wife."

"But Sulea," he pleaded with tortured eyes, "we can be together—"

"No, my love." She silenced him with a finger to his lips. "You see, you are also not my husband. When I look at you I will see him, and when you look at me you will see her. Over time we would both notice the little things, the little differences, to remind us of who we are not. No, we would grow to hate one another. I can't bear the thought of it. You look at her," she nodded toward Sha'raelon, "they way you once looked at me. You've moved on. Keep moving now. Call your ship," and she brushed past him toward Sha'raelon.

Sha'raelon was uncertain what had just transpired, but she could make a good guess. Sulea confronted her.

"He's the love of my life," Sulea told her. "Could you possibly know how that feels?" Sha'raelon didn't answer, refused to answer. "Do you really believe you're the woman he needs?" Sulea went on.

"I will not to be bartered like chattel," Sha'raelon hissed with indignation.

"Oh, do shut up!" Sulea blurted, exasperated. "There's a world in my time called Atheanna. It's full of women like you. They deny themselves the most natural things.

What gets into your heads? What's *wrong* with you people?"

The verbal slap stung. That vulnerability was showing through again.

"Nothing; there is nothing wrong—" Sha'raelon looked up, searched the sky for an answer, finally, "I do not know if I am the woman he needs, but he is the man *I* need."

"Good. Good." Sulea moved as if to comfort the woman, caught herself and stepped back.

A cracking boom sounded from the east. Jarren's ship soared in just above the trees, settled gracefully onto the lawn, fields rippling the air. A gust of baking heat washed over them, but this dissipated quickly. Jarren's ship was a bit smaller than Sha'raelon's had been. It was about the size of a private jet with clipped wings, but it had the same delta shape and encircling ring. And while Sha'raelon's ship had gleamed with polished metal, Jarren's was painted white. An emblem on the forward fuselage showed a galaxy being strained through an hourglass.

"All right, then," said Sulea. "We won't have much time before that air breather is back. Jarren, fly well." These were her final words to him. She turned for the trees.

"What about me?" Simon asked her as she went by.

Sulea paused, turned back. "What about you?"

"Take me with you."

"What in Jack's name for?"

"I'm a scientist. You can use me."

Sulea was about to dismiss him out of hand, but then her lips lifted into a coquettish smile. Dr. Hammerskjold *was* a handsome man, after all, even if somewhat inept.

"Sure, why not," she said nonchalantly as she snapped around and made for the trees. Jarren stood rock still, dumbstruck, and followed with wet eyes as Sulea walked away.

"Come, Jarren," Sha'raelon urged him. "We must go now."

Jarren turned numbly, nodded his stunned assent and then moved heavily toward her.

Simon gave Jarren a hesitant glance and then hurried after Sulea. "What about your particle weapon?" he called after her. Sulea had almost vanished into the thick growth.

"The fuel cell's depleted," she shouted back. "I can't recharge it with contemporary technology."

"But—"

"You want to be of use? *You* carry it."

Simon was gripped by indecision. Sulea was now out of view; she might leave him behind. He needed to catch up with her, and quickly, but the technology...he had to study it; he felt driven to study it. He had to *know*. He couldn't just leave it lying there for someone else to discover. He hefted the weapon reverently. The thing was as heavy as it looked. Behind him, Jarren and Sha'raelon were climbing the ramp into Jarren's ship. Simon adjusted the weight of the weapon, took up the tethered fuel cell, and then plunged into the trees.

He emerged onto a golf course and there it was. Sulea's ship was tiny compared to Jarren's ship, somewhat larger than a government SUV, but still shaped like an arrowhead and encircled by the accelerator ring. The ship was sky blue, with no insignia or markings.

"Oh, so you *did* bring it," Sulea hollered mirthfully. "Hurry then. I have to reinstall it before we lift off, and I think we can expect company soon."

Simon waddled over, straining under the weight. Sulea took the weapon from him and hefted it with practiced ease. She carried it to the pointed prow, tugging Simon along by the fuel cell's umbilical. There was a hollow in the nose of the craft, some attaching rings. Sulea jostled the weapon into the hollow until she felt it click into place. She pushed the fuel cell into a rectangular slot, wound the umbilical into a compartment and then slapped an access panel closed.

"All right, then," she said, slapping dirt off of her hands. "This is a scout class ship, so we don't have the amenities of the explorer class ships. The entry hatch is under here."

The ship rested on three stubby landing struts. Sulea ducked underneath the hull, reached up through a small circular hatch, and pulled herself expertly into the craft. Simon stooped after her, indecision nagging at him again. He shook that off at once. This opportunity was too exceptional to be thwarted by last-minute nerves. He stood upright with his shoulders through the hatch and then pulled himself gracelessly inside. A hatch panel slid out of the hull the moment his feet cleared. Servo motors whined as the panel expanded into a flush fit.

Simon found himself in a cramped cockpit. The air was sour with body odor. He cupped a hand over his nose.

"You'll get used to that," Sulea said off hand. She sniffed at herself and winced. "Yeah, it's bad. Scout class ships are small, but they're Jack-all maneuverable." She grinned at him then, humor lighting her eyes. "The head is here." She pointed to an open compartment in the rear bulkhead. Simon gulped immodestly. "Water and food packs are in these cabinets." Simon gulped again. The head was also the kitchen. "And we sleep in our control couches."

The nose of the craft was transparent, although from the outside it had appeared to be solid metal. Two padded couches sat side by side behind a bank of screens and controls. Their center armrests were joined.

"The right couch is yours."

Sulea bounced onto the left couch as if she were mounting a balance beam. She snuggled herself in, positioned her right arm in the concave armrest, controls at her fingertips. Her left hand was on a joystick. There were no belts or harnesses.

"Say something, Dr. Hammerskjold." She was looking at him sharply over her shoulder. She was grinning as much with her eyes as with her teeth.

"Uh," he said. "Call me Simon?"

"All right, Simon. Saddle up and let's get off this rock."

Simon clumsily kicked her arm while mounting his couch. He was still muttering apologies as the ship lifted into the air. Simon watched the ground fall away, dizzyingly so, and yet he felt no change in inertia.

"Amazing," he said in awe.

Jarren's ship was a utilitarian design, spacious, but lacking the accoutrements and colors that had given Sha'raelon's ship its regal feel. They passed through a narrow companionway onto the bridge, more of a tight, buzzing control center than the open, softly aesthetic bridges she was accustomed to. Colors were metal gray. The bulkheads and panels brimmed with screens, gauges and switches. Two command-and-control couches were positioned side by side, deep into the vee of the nose. There was auxiliary seating along the bulkheads behind the couches. Sha'raelon dropped her baton and Pa'ket's belt onto one of these.

"The left couch is yours," said Jarren. "Take a seat."

He went to a panel and flipped switches, tapped at his tattoo. The dull gray nose cone lit up with the exterior image such that the couches seemed to be suspended in air. Sha'raelon saw churned lawn beneath her feet, the hedge and house ahead, pale sky above.

"Incredible," she said in awe. "Our ships use flat screens."

"Well, they told me this was a new design," Jarren said. He took her hand and helped lower her onto her couch. Both their hands were filthy with dried mud. Sha'raelon's white stockings were also filthy, along with the back of her skirt. She had a finger-streak of mud across her forehead. Jarren brushed lightly at it. "Once we clear orbit," he said, "I'll show you to your cabin. It won't be long."

"Jarren?" She squeezed his hand as he was about to pull away. "Where will we go?"

"I don't know," he answered darkly. "As soon as we're safe," he glanced at her legs and smiled, "*and clean*, we can decide. All right?"

Sha'raelon nodded.

Jarren settled onto his couch. His tattooed left arm lay in the concave hollow of the armrest, fingers resting on a track ball. With his right hand he tapped at a keyboard that had a small joystick within reach of his middle fingers. With a catch of breath, Sha'raelon realized that if she were Sulea then her tattooed right arm would rest side by side with Jarren's tattooed left, a functional pair, in harmony...

Of once Sha'raelon felt inadequate. It was a disturbing feeling. She subtly clenched her teeth and looked soberly toward Jarren. He was immersed in his flight preparations, looking away from her toward some screens, his fingers working like a pianist's at keys and switches. She hesitantly slid her right arm onto the armrest, let it lay side by side with his. Jarren's tattoo was glowing, she could feel the warmth of it. Their arms were almost exactly the same length, elbows and wrists aligned. There was symmetry in that at least, harmony.

"Perhaps I can help navigate?" she asked, almost timidly.

Jarren caught the fragile quality in her voice but he didn't let on. "Yes," he replied casually, "I'll need you for that. There's a screen above your left hand." He turned to her, their faces practically touching. His breaths were warm on her face. "Monitor here," he pointed. "Call out anything you see."

Sha'raelon smiled with renewed confidence.

"All right, this is it," he said. He toggled back on the joystick and the ship lifted breathlessly into the sky.

A warning alarm sounded at ten thousand feet. Sha'raelon's screen began to blink with vectors. She was focused in an instant, calling upon her training, the endless drills.

"Multiple inbounds," she announced expertly. "Five, check, *six* SAMs; bearing two seven zero; two two zero; three one zero..."

Jarren was already reacting to the threat. The horizon tilted steeply as he banked the craft out over the ocean. Choppy cobalt waves seemed to hang over their heads. Inertial fields dampened all sense of motion, but Sha'raelon's eyes betrayed her and she became dizzy. She had been trained on flat screens, which provided a sense of objectivity, but this three hundred sixty-degree immersion was disorienting. She refocused on her screen and the dizziness passed.

"There is a naval vessel along our flight path," she announced next, and then suddenly, "*Missile launch!*"

"Oh, for the love of Jack!" Jarren cursed. "Enough of this! Accelerating to escape velocity."

Jarren banked the ship again until their view was only of pale blue sky. He eased back on the joystick but Sha'raelon warned him off before he could engage. "*Contact! Aircraft high. Dive! Dive! Dive!*"

The sky seemed to spill around them as Jarren wrenched them onto a new course, banking sharply away until the ocean came at them laterally. Diving on them from above, a pair of F-41 fighter jets fired a spread of AMRAAMs at the fleeing ship.

"*Missile lock! Missile lock!*"

Jarren swiped his left hand across the track ball, spinning his ship as a SAM flashed past. Another SAM was coming at them from below. The AMRAAMs were streaking in. There were now too many threats for Sha'raelon to call out. The sky around them was full of tangled contrails, missiles sweeping around to reacquire. In a rush they were back over land, rectangles of cultivation and wooded lots ripping beneath them.

"Countermeasures, Jarren," Sha'raelon urged him. Threat points were no longer vectors on her screen, but roiling confusion. Jarren was weaving between them, around them, under them; dodging and banking.

"This isn't a fighter, Rae," he said, not in a panic but edged with danger. Sweat was beading on his forehead. His eyes were set and focused ahead. "We don't *have* countermeasures."

"We are being herded," Sha'raelon thought out loud, and then to Jarren, "What about your particle gun?"

"That's only for relative obstacles. We can't aim it in this...chaos."

"We can aim it manually."

"Like *hell* we can."

"*We do not have a choice.* Where is the access hatch?"

A missile got in close and detonated. The ship rocked. Shrapnel spanged along the hull. Although the beams and stern were protected by drive fields, the ventral and dorsal lines, as well as the prow, were vulnerable during atmospheric flight. The power flickered, and for a moment g-forces pressed them against their couches. The inertial fields immediately reestablished themselves, but both Sha'raelon and Jarren would have been turned into paste if even that brief interruption had occurred during full acceleration.

"Damn it! If any of that hits the ring—" Jarren thought fast, made up his mind. "All right then. It's on the deck behind us." He dared not take his eyes off the screen to point the way.

Sha'raelon spun off of her couch, located an indented ring on the deck and gave it a pull. The hatch opened on a narrow access tube. She dove in without hesitation and shimmied forward on her elbows.

"Screens, Jarren," she yelled, and at that the tube seemed to go transparent. She clenched her eyes against vertigo as she appeared to be falling through the sky, contrails twining all around her. Popping her eyes open, she focused on the gun, which seemed to be dangling unattached in the air. She gave a push in the tight, transparent tube and got hands on the controls.

"I am in place—"

"Be careful, Rae," Jarren cut in. "If you fire below the arc of the horizon and you miss, the beam will hit the surface. Innocent people could die."

"*Charging now!*"

The shriek of the generator was deafening in that confined space. Sha'raelon was stretched out, flat on her stomach. She tested the rotational range of the gun, which she was able to manipulate with two d-ring handles on a servo console. She sighted in on a missile coming at them head on.

"*Firing!*"

The electric buzz of the discharge made the hair stand up on her arms. Ahead, the missile disintegrated in a flare and a puff of smoke.

"Great shot, Rae!"

"*Charging!*"

She pushed up on the d-rings and this dropped the barrel of the gun. Another missile was coming in from below. She tracked it in closer. This was the moment Jarren had warned her about. If she missed, the beam would boil something on the surface, now some thirty-odd thousand feet below them.

"*Firing!*"

Another silent flash and puff.

"Pulling up into an inside loop," Jarren shouted. The sky whirled.

"*Charging!*"

"Coming to bear."

"I see it. *Firing!*"

She fired too soon, but their trajectory carried the beam across the missile like a slashing blade. They had thankfully been above the horizon. The premature pulse of that discharge was now racing through space at nearly 299,792,458 meters per second. Sha'raelon didn't have time to count her good luck, though.

"There's another!"

"*Charging!*"

Jarren adjusted course to give Sha'raelon a direct line of fire.

"*Firing!*"

"You *got* it!"

Jarren accelerated through the gap Sha'raelon had just made, and prepared to go to full atmospheric power, which would leave all of these chemical missiles behind like the archaic technology that they were.

"Whoa!" this from Jarren.

"What?"

"A timeship just jumped in."

"Into the *atmosphere*? Is it Sulea?"

"I don't think so. Sulea would never do that."

Jarren banked for a better view. Sha'raelon could see it now, a fiery hole in the sky, the corona flickering with lightening. They were over the ocean again, fortunate for those below. Boiling steam was billowing across darkening waves as if the ocean were a stormy sky.

"I see the ship, Jarren."

"It's coming right for us."

"Is it hostile?"

"I don't know."

Sha'raelon felt a cold, nagging anxiety in the pit of her stomach.

"*Charging!*" she yelled.

"They haven't fired."

"Look at them, Jarren. They are maneuvering evasively."

Sha'raelon was right. The ship was skewing side to side, presenting its drive fields as if to prevent a direct line of fire. Jarren magnified the image. It was an explorer class ship, but it was painted a dull military gray. There were no markings or insignia. And then it fired...

Sha'raelon screamed. The flash was blinding, but the beam hit the port-side field and was bent harmlessly away.

"*Jarren...*"

Sha'raelon blinked rapidly at the painful afterimage on her retinas. The sky was spinning as Jarren went through evasive maneuvers, spinning so fast that her mind wasn't quick enough to make any sense of up or down. She braced herself against the sides of the tube. This wasn't necessary, but it gave her a sense of solidity and focus. The ship leveled off into the sun. Sha'raelon could see the ocean far below, cobalt waves glowing in a violet streak of reflected sunlight. Jarren began to yaw and pitch the ship.

"He's on our tail," Jarren announced then. The yaw and pitch were to keep their impenetrable drive fields between them and the hostile. "He's overhauling us."

They were hypersonic now, shooting east over the ocean. Sha'raelon couldn't guess their altitude.

"If I break high or low he'll have us."

"You have got to come about and give me a chance to fire," Sha'raelon begged him, feeling helpless.

"We'd never make it."

"Jarren, we are not *going* to make it." Sha'raelon squeezed her eyes guiltily and said, "You have to go superlight."

"*No!*" Jarren objected angrily. "Not in a gravity well. I can't do that. I can't have that on my—"

"*I thought you were a real pilot. Why did you let that guy get on your tail like that?*"

It was a woman's voice over the comm, laced with humor. Sha'raelon looked out in surprise.

"*Sulea!*" Jarren exclaimed. "Where are you?"

"*Coming at you out of the sun, love. Your bad guy can't see me. Just fly straight until I say 'break,' and then break right. Two seconds...break!*"

Sulea's tiny blue ship hurtled past so quickly that Sha'raelon could only catch it as a fleeting speck out the corner of her eye, and then the horizon was swinging wildly again. A short breath later, Sulea reversed the polarity of her port field. Air rippled and folded, and as she passed the hostile the two ships were knocked apart like billiard balls.

"*You're clear, Jarren,*" they heard over the comm. "*Climb! Climb!*"

Jarren pulled up and went to full atmospheric power. Somewhere below and behind him, Sulea regained control of her tumbling ship and pulled up hard as well. Sha'raelon watched as the sky around her went violet with icy points of light, and then black with a canopy of stars.

Aboard Sulea's ship, Simon had observed the whole thing, enthralled. He hadn't screamed; he hadn't covered his eyes. Sulea regarded him with new-found respect.

"My God," Simon stammered. "The physics of this... fantastic!"

Sulea had a cocky smile on her face. "Pretty good, huh. Who needs guns?"

"Can you teach me?"

"There's a lot I can teach you, *Dr.* Hammerskjold, the least of which is the operation of this ship."

They had just cleared the stratosphere. The sky was black and full of stars. Simon was too absorbed to notice the playful lewdness in Sulea's voice, but not too absorbed to be startled by the sudden trilling of a proximity alarm.

"Uh, oh," said Sulea.

"What is it?"

Sulea ignored him. "Jarren," she spoke anxiously into her comm. "They're on me."

Jarren came back fast. "Where are you? Ping me."

Sulea tapped at her tattoo. Simon looked on with a dumbfounded expression.

"I'm coming," said Jarren. "Pitch and yaw, girl. Pitch and yaw." And then to Sha'raelon, "Rae, are you charged?"

"Yes. What is happening?"

"The hostile's on Sulea. I'm taking us in. Be ready."

Sha'raelon grasped the d-rings and focused ahead. The sky was black, velvety. The stars wheeled as Jarren banked the ship. They were in the mesosphere now. Red sprites lit around them, some stretching into halos of ethereal light.

"Can you see them, Rae?"

The hostile was a shooting star, Sulea's ship hidden beyond its rippling fields.

"I see them. Closer—*Firing!*"

The screech and discharge vibrated through the tube. The beam struck the hostile's drive field obliquely and bent away, as light through water.

"You missed."

"Get above them, Jarren."

"I'm *trying.*"

"*Charging!*"

The hostile began to pitch and yaw, which made it virtually impossible for Sha'raelon to target a vulnerable area, but it also made it impossible for the hostile to do the same to Sulea. As if in proof, an icy beam pulsed from the prow of the hostile and disappeared harmlessly into the blackness of space.

Jarren pitched his ship above and below the hostile's stern, trying to get an angle on the vulnerable dorsal and ventral lines, but the jockeying back and forth gave Sha'raelon no clear shot.

"Sulea," Jarren practically screamed into his comm. "We can't get a targeting solution. Go superlight. Go now!"

"*I can't do that, love. You're in my wake.*"

"But if I break off he'll have you."

"*No choice. I have to tunnel...*"

"Sulea, *no!*" Jarren felt as if a cold knife had just pierced his heart. "*You'll be lost!*"

But even as he screamed these last words to her, focused gravitic probes lanced out from the prow of Sulea's ship. As enraptured as he was by the fantastic physics he was witnessing, Simon still edged up the back of his couch in terror at the sight of the churning black maw forming ahead. A gurgle rose in his throat and he screamed as his atoms were stretched across the event horizon into temporal infinity.

Sulea was gone, lost somewhere in the foamy substrata of time. Despite the cold knot in his chest, Jarren didn't hesitate. He deflected his course by a few degrees, stabbed at a keyboard and went superlight. The hostile saw nothing but a brief streak and a flare of discharge.

Sulea had tunneled out, Jarren was silent, and the ship was banking away from the hostile. Sha'raelon felt naked and exposed, crushed by the enveloping blackness of space. Stars wheeled around her, but they provided no scale, only timelessness. A cold ring of light formed ahead, bristling with electron discharge. There was no sound except her own breaths, but she imagined the crackling of that discharge, felt hairs rising on her arms, but only for an instant. The transition through the ring was so instantaneous that she couldn't recall it with her senses, no matter how hard she concentrated. Now she was bathed in ghostly wisps of milky white light from the folded tracks of photons that as yet followed straight paths in normal space.

Jarren held course for exactly thirty seconds before he disengaged and flared back into normal space. He tapped at keys, altered course by another few degrees, and went superlight again.

Wheeling stars, another bright ring, and then the eerie wisps of folded luminescence. Jarren was making short jumps to confuse any pursuers. Of course. Sha'raelon squeezed her eyes tight against the disorientation, exhaled with a sigh, and then pushed out of the tube with her elbows. She shielded her eyes as she rose through the hatch.

"Please Jarren," she said, wincing, "opaque the screens. My head is splitting."

Jarren raked fingers across switches. The nose cone returned to dull gray. He leapt from his couch, worry in his eyes, and hurried to Sha'raelon.

"Are you all right?" he asked, fumbling boyishly with his hands, but then he just scooped her off her feet and pulled her to his chest.

"I will be fine," she said. She looped her arms around his neck and pressed her forehead to his shoulder. "I just need to rest. My head aches; my *eyes* ache." She looked at him then. Her eyes were haggard and bloodshot. "Are we safe?"

"For the moment. I made three jumps. Right now we're in normal space, parked in Mars' shadow. I doubt anyone could find us."

"That is good." She patted the back of his head. "Now take me where I can rest."

Jarren carried her off the bridge and down the narrow companionway to a starboard cabin. Sha'raelon felt light in his arms. Despite all they had gone through during the past hour or so her scent was still alluring. He felt that tingle in his belly again.

"Here you go," he said.

He lowered her to her feet and drew her through the tight door into her cabin. The cabin was small, with a narrow bed along the hull, screens shaped like portholes above, a desk with comm and screen in one bulkhead, drawers and a thin closet in the other. Colors were varying shades of gray. Light came down from glazed rectangular panels in the ceiling.

"It's not much," Jarren said in apology.

"It is fine," Sha'raelon smiled sweetly.

"There's a sonic shower further astern, and a galley. As for clothing, though—"

Sha'raelon's brows lifted in weary amusement.

"—uh, it's either a man's suit like what I'm wearing or else coveralls."

"Thank you, Jarren," she said wanly. "I will manage."

She pecked his cheek and patted him out the door. Jarren hovered in the companionway for a time, his belly stirring, and then he returned to the bridge.

Sonic showers can't provide the languid relief of a steaming hot bath, but Sha'raelon still came out feeling clean and tingly. She dozed for an hour, naked beneath sheets that were gratifyingly smooth and warm for such a utilitarian vessel. When she awoke it felt like a new day.

She slipped into the baggy gray coveralls she had found in the closet, zipped them to just above her breasts, and pulled on a pair of matching gray deck shoes. She found tea bags in the galley, filled two composite cups from the straw-sized tap, dropped in the bags and pulled the heat strings to brew the tea. These she carried to the bridge. Jarren was napping on his couch. The screens were off and the lighting had been dimmed.

"Oh!" he said, coming awake. He wiped at his eyes.

"Tea?" Sha'raelon asked.

"Love some."

She handed him a cup, and then she curled up on her couch, head toward the prow. She sipped thoughtfully, met his eyes across the way.

"What are you thinking?" he asked.

She sat her cup on a console. She felt luxuriously mellow in the dim light, on the warm couch with Jarren lying across from her. He had kicked off his shoes and had unbuttoned his collar. His jacket was draped across the back of his couch. She reached up to a panel and flipped switches. The bridge went dark, all except the telltale lights of the instruments. She flipped another series of switches and the exterior view enveloped them, a panorama of stars and the mottled, maroon orb of Mars. Jarren recognized that vulnerability in her again, some fragile quality in the set of her face.

Slowly, perhaps timidly, perhaps seductively, Sha'raelon pulled the zipper and let her coveralls fall open.

By Standard Galactic Rotation, Jarren informed her, it was 0800 hours, or eight o'clock in the morning. To her it felt as if it were late evening. They were in the galley. Jarren sipped his coffee and winced.

"Oh, that's horrible," he grimaced. "I've been spoiled by contemporary coffee."

Sha'raelon sipped her own coffee, which was tepid and weak, but she smiled anyway and said, "No, it is not bad."

Jarren pulled plates from the warmer, set them on the small table, and the two sat for breakfast. He was wearing black slacks and a white shirt with the tails out. Both needed laundering. His sleeves were down but the cuffs were unbuttoned. His hair was mussed. He looked sloppy. She was wearing the only clothing available that she was willing to wear, gray coveralls, emblazoned with the ship's emblem above the left breast: a galaxy being strained through an hourglass. Sha'raelon picked at her food, cubes of protein and carbohydrates, and a starchy equivalent of bread. She didn't mind the bland fare, she simply wasn't hungry.

"What is it?" Jarren asked.

Sha'raelon pushed away her plate, sat back and crossed her legs. Jarren recognized *that* look. Days ago he had moved them away from Mars and into the asteroid belt, where they had become an insignificant speck of matter among countless other insignificant specks. They were safe, he was perfectly content, but Sha'raelon was restless. She wanted him to make a decision.

"Rae, listen," he pushed his plate aside as well, "I understand how you feel, I really do. But, but—"

"There is nothing *for* you out there, Jarren," she said with an edge in her voice and a hardness in her eyes. He felt as if they were debating at the United Nations again. "Your dream of returning to the stars is pointless."

"There are worlds, Rae—"

"*Alien* worlds. Not human worlds. Would you have us spend our lives as refugees? I will not bear children who could never find their own happiness."

That softened him.

"You're asking me to strand myself—"

"I am *asking* you to be *with* me."

"On a small planet."

"On a vast new world."

"But in your shadow."

"Never."

"Then what?"

"Would it not be thrilling to pilot a ship at sea, Jarren, to let the wind and waves carry you to unexplored lands? Imagine the adventure, the skill—the freedom. It is a virtually unexplored world. It is all there for you."

Jarren rubbed his stubbled face and sighed. Sha'raelon sensed an opening and pressed on.

"Superlight ships have altered your sense of time and space, but sailing before the *wind*—oh, I think you would discover that the world is endless."

"I've underestimated you again, haven't I?" Jarren said. A vein in his forehead was throbbing. "I swore I wouldn't let that happen twice."

"Oh, Jarren." Sha'raelon stood and cradled his head against her stomach. "I have lived my entire life for a purpose that was presented to me as history; not that which I might build for myself, but that which was *destined* to be built, over and over again. I must break the cycle."

"It's a crazy idea, Rae."

"It is possible."

"But still crazy."

"It is the only way that I can live anew; the only way that we can have a life together—and the only way that we can be truly safe."

Her face was breaking, eyes glistening. Jarren stood and held her, marveled at the nature of a woman who could be at once deadly yet vulnerable, hard yet fragile. He looked up at the ceiling, focusing on nothing. His own eyes were conflicted, reddening. There was really only one choice.

"When?" he asked, resigned.

Sha'raelon took a breath like a quickening, as if she were new born. She pulled his face to hers. Her cheeks were wet, and her sweetly innocent smile reached into his heart. She sprinkled him with kisses, but then he took her and pressed his lips to hers. They rocked gently together, fitting together as one, warm and centered.

Sha'raelon turned to meet his eyes, to look into him. His eyes were soft, those fine lines lifting with his lips. "Now," she whispered. "Now."

Sha'raelon was already seated on her control couch when Jarren came onto the bridge. The screens were on. Asteroids hung in the space around the ship like a field of scattered, dimpled potatoes. She glanced at him over her shoulder and then did a double take, her brows arching in surprise. He was wearing a standard spacer flight suit, dark gray, sleeveless—deliciously tight. She had never seen him dressed as anything other than a contemporary, in business suits that had concealed his true figure, his true nature. He looked taller. He was clean shaven, his hair combed forward into a point over his brows. His posture was erect and formal. His tattoo glowed warmly.

"Well *captain*. It is so good to fly with you again." She let slip some sarcasm, but she meant this seriously.

Jarren gave her a wink and a tight smile and moved professionally to his control couch. Sha'raelon followed him with glittering eyes and a perfect grin. He settled in, slid his left arm into place, and tapped at a navigational computer.

"Pinging One," he announced without preamble. His eyes were on his screens. "Pinging Two."

Sha'raelon felt giddy. There was a ticklish flutter in her stomach.

"Pinging Three..."

There were more preparations. Jarren's hands moved like a maestro's, tapping at keyboards and control panels. Calculations had to be precise. After some minutes Jarren's right hand paused over a keyboard. The fingers of his left hand rested lightly on the track ball.

"Are you ready?" he asked.

"Yes," she answered eagerly.

Jarren tapped a key and they went superlight.

Sha'raelon was ready when they flared back into normal space.

"*Charging,*" she called out. Targeting rings aligned on her screen. "*Firing.*"

No sooner had she discharged her weapon than Jarren tapped a key and they were gone with a streak and a flash.

They re-emerged into normal space...

"*...Charging...Firing...*"

...and then they were gone again.

They repeated this maneuver twice more before they flared in on their final target. Sha'raelon took a deep breath. Jarren ground his teeth.

"This is it," he said.

"I know," she said with all the love and affection two syllables can convey. Her face was glowing with a girlish exhilaration and innocence that touched Jarren's heart.

"All right," he said. "Timing..."

"Yes. *Charging.*"

His fingers were like dancers on his keyboard. The shriek of the particle generator merged with the pulsing thrum of the ring.

"*Tunneling!*" He shouted this.

"*Firing!*"

"*Engaging!*"

A black maw formed out ahead of the ship. Sha'raelon had seen this twice before, and yet now she felt a terrifying uncertainty, an uncertainty that she had, truly, never felt before. They were pulled across the event horizon and into a formless gray slush of eddies and currents. Jarren was fixed on his screens.

"Watch the meters," he warned. "If we miss..."

They were moving against the current, downtime. If they missed then they would have to come about—into uptime infinity.

Sha'raelon pointed excitedly at the screen. "I see lensing!"

Eddies were bending into polarized bands.

"I've got field interference patterns," Jarren announced calmly.

"Gravity well!" Sha'raelon shouted. "There it is!"

"Just a little further..."

"No, Jarren! Tunnel now!"

"A little further..."

"You are going to lose it!"

"A little further..."

"*Jarren!*"

"Tunneling...*now!*"

Gravitic probes twisted gray eddies into a roiling black maw. They were through quicker than they could sense the transition, their screens erupting with stars. Sha'raelon's face fell in despair.

"Oh, no," she moaned.

She saw only cold pinpoints of infinity, blackness and space.

"Jarren, where *are* we?"

Jarren looked at her smugly.

"Faith?" he asked.

He spun his track ball and the ship came about... and there was Earth, a shining blue jewel on black velvet. Europe and Africa were in the full light of noon. The northern pole was pure and white.

Sha'raelon gasped with a sudden breath that made Jarren smile. "When?" she asked, wonder gleaming in her eyes.

Jarren consulted his navigation screen, ran off numbers in Standard Galactic that made absolutely no sense to her.

"Convert that," she demanded impatiently.

He gave her a wry look and tapped away some more.

"Converting to the archaic calendar, it is Thursday, June 3, 331 BCE, uh, 1223 Zulu."

"Oh," she brightened. "Even better! I did not think we could go back further than year one or thereabouts."

"I pushed it that last bit."

"Yes you did!" she rounded on him with mock fury. Jarren laughed.

"We're here," he said.

"Yes we are," she said, barely a whisper.

Sha'raelon rose dreamily from her couch. Earth filled their screens with majestic beauty. She pointed at the screens, native pride coloring her cheeks. "This is called the Mediterranean Sea." Her eyes were as bright as a high mountain meadow in the full light of the sun. She pointed to a jagged peninsula. "And this is where I was born. This sea here is called the Aegean. We will live on an island in this sea, a beautiful island." She spun around to him. Her face was ebullient. "And you will have ships and you can explore the world for a lifetime."

Jarren rose and took her into his arms. She clung to him as Earth turned over their shoulders.

"You're safe now," he breathed, kissing her cheek. "You can live your life. Without temporal buoys to ping no one else can come here." Jarren's voice broke. "It's yours, Rae. A new focal point. This timeline cannot be altered."

"And you will destroy this ship as you promised?" She said this lightly against his cheek, afraid to meet his eyes.

Jarren hedged his answer with a long sigh.

"Jarren!" she looked up at him in a panic, "you *promised.* It is the only way we can know for certain—"

"Yes," he answered finally. There was sorrow in his voice, but also love. "There's no need to do it right away, though, is there? At least until we know that everything will be all right?"

Her eyes filled. She stroked his cheek. "Agreed," she said.

Sha'raelon turned to the screen, blinking back tears.

"Think of it." Her voice was as wondrous as a child's, touching the core of him. Her face was so pure his lips trembled. "We do not know what will happen. We can *live*."

Jarren stood at her side, gazing at the beautiful world.

"This is our time now," she cried. "We are free."

Three of Professor Kupolos' students were working at a line of tables in the shade of a long canvas tent. The day was unbearably hot, so the sides of the tent had been rolled up. Kate blew a damp strand of hair out of her eyes and paused to look out on the blue Aegean. They were set up near the cliffs in order to take advantage of the sea breeze, which gave some relief but it was still stifling under the tent. Professor Kupolos stood behind her and observed as she continued her work. Wearing white latex gloves, she carefully and patiently brushed dust out of the engravings on the cylinder.

"Those *are* letters," he said over her shoulder.

"Yes," she agreed, concentrating on the cylinder. A bead of sweat rolled down her nose, which she caught with a shrug of her shoulder before it could drip onto the artifact. "It looks like sigma alpha upsilon to me. The stylizing is ornate. I have no idea what it means."

"We've had no response from the Net. I have no idea what these characters signify either," said the professor.

"And look here," Kate rolled the cylinder gently, "soldiers, swords, scenes of personal combat. And on this side," she rolled the cylinder again, "it looks like a court scene, a queen or noblewoman and her entourage. This figure is kneeling and holding something up to her. It's too short to be a sword. It could be a scepter maybe, or—"

"It looks as if it could be this very cylinder," the professor said, intrigued. "Have you found a way to open it?"

"Not yet. I cleaned the ends first, looking for seams. I didn't find any so now I'm doing the middle to see if it pulls apart."

He patted her on the shoulder appreciatively. His mood had improved, he noticed, now that they had something to work on. His students had noticed as well.

"Let me know the moment you find something," he said before moving on to the next table, where a young man was working on the emblem.

The young man was also from the Americas. His name was, incongruously, Johnson Johns. He was tall and lean, with sandy hair, handsome. Something about his name amused the American girls. They would call out to him, "Hey Johns, bring your Johnson over here," and then they would laugh libidinously. Their humor was lost on professor Kupolos.

"How is this coming, Johnson?" the professor asked. Johnson was so tall that he had to stoop to work. He turned his head and looked up at the professor, excitement in his otherwise serious brown eyes.

"Well, I think it *is* some kind of plaque," the boy said, "but there are no attachment holes, see?"

Professor Kupolos stretched to peer over the boy's shoulder. "Yes, I see."

The plaque was perfectly round, about the size of a dinner plate. It was made of metal, dull gray. The paint was severely faded.

"That can't be pewter," said the professor. "Not during that era."

"Naw, the weight's too light," said Johnson. "I think it's bronze, but the graying...I don't know yet."

"At least the image is coming out."

Johnson was using a solution to clean away centuries of accumulated grime. The image was faded, but colors were beginning to show through.

"I think your initial opinion is correct, though," said Johnson. "It's an infinity symbol."

Professor Kupolos gazed at the plaque, tipping his head from side to side. "Turn it this way," he said. Johnson rotated the plaque. "Now *that*," the professor said, "looks like an hourglass. See, it even has sand in it."

"Hmmm, could be."

"There might be an inscription on the back. We'll know soon enough. Good work."

"Thanks, Professor K," Johnson said, smiling proudly.

Professor Kupolos didn't sigh, just closed his eyes for a moment before moving on.

"*Professor Kupolos?*" someone called from behind him. The professor turned and saw Andreas jogging toward the tent. "Professor Kupolos," Andreas pulled up, panting, "I have some more findings for you."

"Yes, Andreas, what have you found?"

Professor Kupolos took the German by the arm and walked him out into the sun.

"I took samples," Andreas paused to catch his breath, "from Therasia across the channel, and also from the east side of this island. I found iridium on Therasia but not on the eastern cliffs."

The ramifications were obvious. Professor Kupolos stiffened. Both men gazed out across the channel to the lava dome of Nea Kameni, with the island of Therasia beyond.

"This," *ziss*, "means that the volcano eruption brought the iridium!" exclaimed Andreas.

"Not possible. Not possible." Professor Kupolos was shaking his head. "Iridium is too heavy to come up with magma. You mustn't publish that, Andreas. They will laugh at you. There *has* to be another explanation, some kind of impact or explosion at the volcano. A meteorite *must* have hit. But there were no tsunami. How could this not be recorded?"

"I must have samples from the dome to complete my research, but I am not able to get the permissions."

Professor Kupolos nodded in understanding, patted the boy on the back. "I'll see what I can do for you," he said.

"*Danke*, ah, thank you, professor," said Andreas, and then he sprinted away.

Professor Kupolos mulled Andreas' findings for a moment and then stepped back into the shade of the tent. One of his Greek students was working on the pile of scraps. Alesia was her name. She was a full figured girl, with wavy black hair, a studious face, and soft brown eyes. She wore a white gingham dress with pink, blue, and green floral patterns, black tennis shoes, and white socks rising up her calves. Unlike the others, Alesia did not come from money.

"Have you determined what it is?" the professor asked her. She was using long tweezers to probe the pile. A couple of dull gray metallic objects sat in a tray to her right.

"I cannot say for certain," she said in the native Greek accent that the professor was most comfortable with. "Perhaps livery; a harness of some kind."

"And what are those?" Professor Kupolos pointed at the two metallic objects.

"Unknown," Alesia answered him. "There are more in here. I want to inventory them all before I proceed with the cleaning."

"Good. Good. Excellent work, Alesia.

Two black SUVs crunched along the gravel and pulled up between the tent and the entrance to the site. Their black paint rippled the air with heat. Professor Kupolos frowned. He stepped toward the SUVs. He couldn't see through their darkened windows.

"What is this?" he demanded, hands on hips.

Kate, Johnson, and Alesia all turned to see what the commotion was. Doors sprung open on the SUVs and gray-uniformed women piled out. There were ten of them. They had serious expressions on their faces. They had *guns.*

"What the..."

"Do not interfere, Professor Kupolos," one of them said.

Before he could voice an objection they were in the tent, corralling his students and marching them away. Kate tried to fight them off, but her hands were caught and wrenched behind her back. Johnson was cursing with those colorful American epithets, struggling, but his hands, too, were pinned behind his back. Alesia just held up the flats of her hands and followed reluctantly.

This was over in seconds. Professor Kupolos stood, alone in the tent, his jaw on his chest. A front door opened and a woman stepped out. She was young, late twenties, no older, and she was tall enough to play that American game, basketball it was called. Her hair was a long fall of golden curls, and her eyes were the greenest he had ever seen. She wore a tight black dress that began just above her breasts and ended just above her knees. Her shoes were black stiletto heels. Professor Kupolos gawked, he couldn't help it. The woman was beautiful.

She walked toward him lithely, a feline deviousness in her eyes. "Professor Kupolos," she said. Her voice was rich, deeper than he would have expected. "My name is Shah Jeanne Kahn." She pronounced this with a French inflection, softened consonants, and spoke the syllables so quickly that her name sounded oriental.

"Wha—?"

"I apologize for this intrusion," she continued, oblivious of his stupefied expression, "but it was necessary."

"Wha—what do you want?"

"These things, of course." She pointed at the tables.

Behind her he could see the gray slabs being brought out of the site. The women—Guards? Soldiers?—were like pall bearers aside each slab. They loaded the slabs into the backs of the SUVs.

"What are you doing!" he sputtered. "You can't take those!"

"Of course we can," she said levelly. Her eyes had turned menacing. She reached for the cylinder.

"Don't touch that!"

Professor Kupolos threw himself at her but she batted him effortlessly away. She took up the cylinder, did something with her wrist, and wicked looking blades snapped out of each end. She began to twirl the thing. Professor

Kupolos backed away in terror, tripped and fell onto the seat of his pants.

"Do not be afraid, professor," she said. Her tight smile sent icy shivers up his spine. "I do not intend to harm you. I just wanted to demonstrate that we are serious."

Two of her assistants came into the tent, wordlessly collected the artifacts and then climbed into their SUVs, slamming the doors.

"Why are you taking these things?" he asked in a daze.

"Because they are mine!" she snapped, face hardening. Her eyes were like knives, but then she softened. "I suppose I should thank you, actually," she said then. "We had thought these were lost to history. Your photographs on the Net alerted us to their existence."

Professor Kupolos pushed himself up. "Miz Kahn," he said, pleading.

"It is *Miss!*" Her eyes were furious. "Miss *Shah!*"

The color drained from the professor's face. He averted his eyes. "*Mistress,*" he said shakily, "please forgive my impertinence. I didn't know."

Chants were coming up from below the cliff now. The daily protest. Shah Jeanne Kahn flicked a disdainful glance that way.

"But Mistress," the professor ventured after a calming moment had passed, "these are important antiquities. They must be studied."

"I know *exactly* what they are," she said. "They belonged to my ancestors. I do not need to *study* them."

She did something with her wrist again and the blades retracted with a snap. She walked absently to the cliff edge, looked down.

"Men," she said, too low for him to hear. "They always find something to protest about."

She whipped around and strode directly to her SUV, opened the door, paused, and looked back.

"Good day to you, professor Kupolos," she said pleasantly. "And thank you."

With that she slammed the door and the two SUVs pulled away.

Professor Kupolos walked unsteadily to a table, pulled up a chair and sat. He sat there stonily for minutes as the chanting below grew louder and then slowly ebbed. He could make no sense of any of this. His artifacts were gone, his site robbed...

His students began to emerge by ones and twos from the site entrance. They gathered around the tent, loitering in confusion.

"Is everyone here?" the professor asked them. He stood and counted heads, exhaled in relief. "Thank the Mother you are all safe. Is anyone hurt?"

Kate was rubbing her wrist. Her eyes simmered.

"Kate, are you all right?"

"I'm fine," she growled. "Damned Atheannans. They think they can get away with anything."

"They *can*," said Johnson. "They always have."

Kate's eyes went dark. Her teeth were clenched. "Not where *we* come from they can't. I promise you, when I find those b—"

"No, Kate!" The professor cut her off. Americans were so hasty, so ready to fight. He rushed to her, took her by the shoulders. "These are dangerous people." He trembled in recollection, the icy menace of that woman, Shah; that cylinder with those wicked blades.... "I will make inquiries—through proper channels." And then to the group, "All of you, take out your notebooks and document your observations. Do it now while events are still fresh in your minds. Be thorough."

No one argued, not even Kate. His students were disciplined. He took pride in that. They lined up along the tables, pulled out their notebooks and flipped pages. He tugged his own field journal from his pocket, gathered his thoughts, and wrote:

Events of this day as witnessed by Professor Dimitrios Kupolos, Island of Thera. 19 September, 2365 CE.

He scowled at the *CE*, the abbreviation for Current Era. It was a blatantly pandering designation that had recently come into vogue. But he was old, and in his mind justifiably set in his ways. He scratched out the date and began again, jotting down the traditional designation this time, *AD 2365.*

AD, the abbreviation for Alexandros Decessus.

Twenty-three hundred and sixty-five years after the death of Alexander the Great.

∞

LIFE IN CONTINUUM

MacKenzie scowled, spat a string of curses, and toed the mess from his shoe. Jurgens laughed.

"Well, you've sure stepped in it this time, haven't you, Mac?"

Mackenzie answered with a withering glare, which Jurgens met steadily, an amused tilt to his lips.

"I hate this place," MacKenzie grumbled. He turned away from Jurgens before the man could aggravate him further, popped an antacid and ground it between his teeth.

"That's strange," Jurgens commented sarcastically, "since you've spent most of your career here."

"It wasn't *my* choice. Let's move."

The two agents continued along the derelict sidewalk, sidestepping burned out cars and piles of refuse. MacKenzie rubbed his chest against the burning reflux.

"I think we might see some action down here," Jurgens said with insufferable bravado. MacKenzie rolled his eyes and kept moving. His heartburn was killing him. "What do you think, Mac?"

MacKenzie paused and exhaled the heat from his chest. The relief was only momentary. He turned, threw up his hands. Jurgens was right on his heels.

"Believe me," Mac said wearily. There were dark bags under his eyes. "You don't *want* to see action down here."

"And why the hell not?"

MacKenzie surveyed the way ahead. "Look at this place," he said. Jurgens kept his eyes on Mac. "This place is a hole waiting for you to fall in."

MacKenzie opened his arms to their surroundings, a dense urban landscape that had been abandoned for decades. The streets were impassable except on foot, choked with debris, weeds growing through the cracks. Shattered safety glass had gathered over time into drifts, like translucent dunes. High-rise buildings had long ago been stripped of bricks, mortar, and marble up to twenty feet or so off the ground, about as high as someone could reach from a pair of two-by-fours knocked together into a makeshift ladder. The buildings now stood on skeletal piers of rusty steel, as if a flood had risen to a certain level and piranhas had stripped everything below the surface.

"It's not so bad," Jurgens said with more of that aggravating bravado.

"It's your first time in!" MacKenzie shot back. "What the hell do you know?"

MacKenzie turned on the younger agent and glowered. Jurgens was of average height, well built. He wore a regulation black suit, although he'd vainly had it tailored to show off his physique. He kept his hair cropped short, as if he were still in the military. Ray-Ban Aviator sunglasses hid eyes that simmered at Mac's rebuke. Jurgens unconsciously tapped his right hip with the tips of his fingers, some kind of nervous tick. He did it all the time without realizing it. His pistol was holstered there, the new rail gun. The gesture drew Mac's eyes to the bulging outline of the weapon. Mac shook his head in weary recollection. His last partner had been young, too.

"Why'd you carry that damned thing in here?" MacKenzie asked. His voice was resigned. He'd heard it all before.

Jurgens grinned then, flipped open his jacket and pulled the gun. He tipped it from side to side, showing it off. It was an ungainly cudgel of a weapon, nickel plated, with a long oval barrel and a grip that flared out like the head of a blacksmith's hammer, this to accommodate the battery. It had laser sights front and rear, independent beams that could be aligned for a precision shot or separated for a wider shock wave effect. The pistol used depleted uranium pellets that were small enough to be loaded loose into a magazine at the rear of the barrel. It was an ugly weapon, but its magnetically accelerated projectiles didn't just pierce flesh, they liquefied it.

"Because I'm ready for action," Jurgens answered, still grinning. He holstered his weapon. "I've seen the records, Mac. You guys don't seem to live long down here."

"Mostly because of hot heads—" MacKenzie stopped before he could say what he wanted to say, *hot heads like you.* "Listen, Jurgens," MacKenzie resumed after a cooling breath, "you're not liable to see the kind of action that calls for so much firepower. It's mostly kids and indigents, some gangs, fugitives hiding out. Things like that."

"Any action would be better than what I've seen since I got detached from my unit and stuck in the Warrant Service," he countered. "What are you carrying? A nine millimeter, I bet. Glock. Old school."

"Standard issue, Jurgens. You know that."

"Yeah, well—if it comes to it you can plink at 'em while I take out half the block."

"Oh, for Christ's sake!" MacKenzie turned away. He pounded his chest, popped another antacid. Jurgens looked on with a mixture of pity and contempt. MacKenzie was fifty-five years old, right up against mandatory retirement. The man was *ancient.* He wore a buff trench coat over a gray wool suit, patent leather shoes, and a gray felt fedora. He had thin silver hair, which might have once been sandy brown or even blond, and his face looked haggard. He hadn't shaved in a few days. His whiskers were gray.

"Look," Jurgens said impatiently. "We'd better keep moving, yeah?"

"Yeah, sure kid. But listen," Mac poked a finger at Jurgens, "this is police work, not combat. If I shoot someone, I need to be able to identify the body. Get it? So keep that damned thing holstered."

"Sure, *police work*," Jurgens groused. "So when did serving warrants become police work?"

MacKenzie was reaching his limit. "These are convicted criminals, damn it! The worst." He pulled the warrant from his breast pocket, waved it in Jurgens' face. "*We* see to it that justice is served."

"Okay, okay." Jurgens held up his hands. "Whatever you say, Mac."

"Enough of this. Let's move."

MacKenzie walked ahead briskly to distance himself from his arrogant new partner, but Jurgens stayed right with him. They rounded a corner, and then another, as if tracing a route through a maze of decay. Mackenzie stopped abruptly.

"There it is," he said soberly.

Ahead of them was a galvanized chain-link fence, about thirty feet tall. The fence was three layers deep, topped with razor wire. Both the fence and the wire were mottled with gray and white corrosion. Refuse was caught up in it as if it were a gill net.

"That thing is older than I am," Jurgens said, more to himself than to Mac. "I've seen pictures—"

The fence emerged from between two high rises to their left and crossed what was once a small public park but was now an overgrown tangle of vines, weeds and litter. From there the fence canted at a sharp angle and then passed out of view down a block of dilapidated row houses to their right. There had once been a personnel gate straight ahead. The gate was missing now, probably serving as bed springs for some indigent hiding out within, but despite this existing opening someone had still taken the time to snip a hole through the fence off to the left a ways, probably to save the extra hundred feet or so it would take to walk to the gate. MacKenzie found it vaguely unsettling that people were establishing routines here, making themselves at home. He noticed a jumbled pile of debris inside the fence next to the hole, which hadn't been there on his last trip. He knew intuitively that this was to throw up a quick barricade if necessary. The fence was originally designed to keep people in. It now served to keep people out. MacKenzie shivered.

"So what was the deal with this?" Jurgens asked.

"You don't know? I thought you saw pictures."

"I mean, I know it was a prison. I just don't understand why they abandoned it."

"Don't they teach this stuff in school?"

"Only some song and dance about the historic folly of walls, or something like that. It was plague, wasn't it? Or typhus?"

"Both, but that's not the real reason they shut it down. Budget cuts did it. People were moving out even before the city went broke. This downtown area was already in sorry shape by that time, nothing but riffraff, crack houses, meth labs—it was bad. After a lot of hand wringing some genius came up with this idea." MacKenzie pointed sourly at the fence. "But even in there it still cost a lot to keep a prisoner incarcerated. People want law and order, but nobody ever wants to pay. Just get them out of sight, justice on a shoestring." MacKenzie shook his head. "Personally? I think it would have been cheaper to get rid of a bunch of laws instead."

"Humph." Jurgens scanned the area out of habit. Something moved off to their left. He focused. Gone now. "Well," Jurgens said, distracted, "this will be a short hitch for me anyway. I hear they're going to condemn the whole place, turn it into the world's biggest landfill or something." *And then maybe I can get back into a combat unit where I belong.*

"Won't happen," said MacKenzie with stony finality. "The Fat Man likes it here."

"Fat Man? You mean Marcus Constantine?"

"Yeah."

"Who cares about him?"

"You'll find out."

There was something ominous in Mackenzie's tone. Jurgens tapped his pistol absently, asked: "What's to find out? The man's nothing but an old bounty hunter."

"Yeah," MacKenzie said with a distant look, "that's what they say. That's the way he likes it. But in reality—"

There was movement to their left. A bit of mortar fell from a ledge and clinked against some fallen brick. The sound echoed in the stillness around them. Jurgens dropped into a combat crouch, weapon drawn. MacKenzie heard a thin whine as the weapon charged. The twin laser sights probed a far wall, dancing red dots that followed the contours of old shops open to the air, the wreckage of cars, overturned trash bins.

"Damn it! Put that thing away!" MacKenzie growled, stepping in front of the sights. Twin dots bounced on his knees. "You're going to hurt somebody."

Jurgens looked up defiantly. Mac could see his reflection in Jurgens' glasses, a dark distorted figure set against a lackluster gray sky. He didn't need to see Jurgens' eyes to recognize the hard resentment in them. Jurgens seemed to hesitate with indecision, but then he thumbed off the power. The rail gun wound down to silence.

A boy's head peered around a corner, and then the boy stepped out into the open, came toward them cautiously. He was an oriental boy, maybe twelve years old, with a thick mop of black hair and smudged cheeks. He wore a yellowing T-shirt and cut-off shorts. His knees were knobby, his skin deeply tanned.

"He's a CI," MacKenzie said, waving Jurgens away.

"A *confidential informant?*" Jurgens exclaimed skeptically. "He's just a *boy.*"

"Yeah, but he lives here. Stay put while I go talk to him—*and holster that damned gun.*"

MacKenzie turned his back on Jurgens before the man could object. He walked up to the boy and dropped to a knee. The two spoke for a time, back and forth with a lot of gesturing. Jurgens couldn't make out what they were saying. Every once in a while the boy would shoot a hostile glance his way. And then the boy pointed toward the fence. MacKenzie patted the boy on the head, pulled something from his pocket and handed it over. Looked like candy bars. The boy smiled, turned and ran off with his prizes. Within seconds he had blended in to the decrepit surroundings and was gone.

"What was that all about?" Jurgens asked.

"Just clearing the way ahead," MacKenzie said darkly, as if citing long experience. "You never go beyond the fence without permission," he added.

"Whose permission?"

"The Fat Man's."

"What? We're warrant officers. We don't *need* permission."

MacKenzie rubbed his chest, grimaced, and popped another antacid. "Look here," he said after a moment, pointing, "everything inside that fence belongs to the Fat Man. No one—I mean *no* one—goes in or out without his permission. Remember that and you might live. If you don't," a pause and a fatalistic look, "then you won't."

Jurgens adjusted his glasses, tapped at his pistol. "Whatever you say, boss."

"Good." MacKenzie nodded. "This is where the Fat Man plays out his scenarios. You're going to see things," he had that faraway look again, "disturbing things; strange people. Ignore them. We've been granted safe passage. *Don't pull your gun.* You won't need it."

"Scenarios?"

"Just stay close to me, okay. Don't do anything impulsive."

Jurgens didn't argue. There was no point. But *he* decided when to pull his gun, no one else.

"Okay, let's go," said MacKenzie, and he turned heavily toward the gate.

Were it even possible, conditions were worse beyond the fence. So much debris was piled in the streets and along the sidewalks that there was no clear line of sight. Jurgens' eyes were in constant motion, casting sidelong glances around corners, scanning rooflines, open doorways, the tops of debris piles. The fingers of his gun hand flexed nervously. He tapped his pistol. MacKenzie lumbered on as if oblivious, a hulking gray form in a trench coat.

They stepped over a body—maybe alive, maybe dead, they didn't stop to investigate—and rounded the corner of a crumbling brick building. A pack of children ran toward them, maybe eight kids in all, eight, nine, ten years old, all boys. They were racially mixed, barefoot. Their clothes were worn and tattered, little more than baggy T-shirts and rough canvas shorts. They looked like miserable urchins on a Victorian street, but they laughed, they were happy. Wide smiles showed missing teeth.

They're still innocent somehow, MacKenize thought gravely. The children ignored the two agents, just ran on past, giggling and jabbering in their own homemade language. Jurgens recognized the haunted look on his partner's face. He had seen that look before, in wards at the VA. His opinion of MacKenzie softened. So Mac was a veteran, too...

"Where?" Jurgens asked. He didn't need to say more, Mac would understand. The stories were always the same, only the places were different.

"Second Fallujah," MacKenzie answered hollowly. "Before you were born."

"Marine," said Jurgens, nodding.

"Ooh Rah."

"I didn't know. No one told me."

Mackenzie's mind wandered to a vision of an angelic little girl. She had the clearest blue eyes framed with straight black hair, a little mole on her chin. Hers were the most sweetly innocent eyes he had ever seen. Her eyes had found his somehow, so clear and bright. The shouts of warning had sounded dull in his ears, the explosions, the thumps of impacts. It was just the little girl and her eyes, but she was wearing a vest. She could barely walk she was so weighted down with it, and then her hand was moving to a pull cord and Mac was raising his rifle and he felt a jolt and the little girl's head exploded in a spray of red and then she was just a pile of wet rags, little legs sticking out...

Mackenzie came to with a start.

"You all right there, big guy?" Jurgens asked.

MacKenzie spun on his partner, anger in his eyes. "You weren't briefed on anything, were you?" he asked with an edge of disgust.

"I was just told to show up, Mac."

"What kind of man takes an assignment without knowing what it is? Jurgens—what are you *doing* here?"

Jurgens tapped his pistol, whipped off his glasses. It was the first time MacKenzie had ever seen the man's eyes. Jurgens had dark brown eyes.

"Look, *partner*," Jurgens said acidly, "I'm not gonna take—"

They were interrupted by the stumbling footfalls of a man running along the other side of the street. The man was caucasian, his clothes were filthy. He ran with the aged stoop of someone old. He was looking over his shoulder as he ran, as he dodged debris. He was directly across the street now, but he either chose to ignore the agents or else he was too preoccupied. And then another man caught up to him, also caucasian, but much younger, dressed incongruously in a gray pinstriped suit and white wingtip shoes. The second man held a long-bladed knife, a military model with a serrated edge and a deep blood groove. He caught up to the older man, yanked him back with a hand over the man's mouth, and then shoved the knife up to the hilt into the man's kidney. The stabbed man went rigid, his scream constricting in his throat. His assailant pushed him off the knife with the flat of his shoe. The victim bounced when he hit the ground, like a felled tree. The attacker looked around nervously, spotted MacKenzie, nodded briefly and then ran off.

Jurgens was in a crouch, sighting along the barrel of his gun. His glasses were perched on his forehead.

"Get up!" MacKenzie ordered. "I told you to keep that thing holstered."

"What the hell—?"

"I also said you would see strange things. C'mon, let's clear out."

MacKenzie took off so quickly that Jurgens had to holster the pistol while on the run. They went around a corner, crossed a street, and crunched through shattered glass into what had once been some kind of small store. The air smelled like mold. Tufts of pink insulation stained with rust dangled from the ceiling. But they had walls around them, cover, a safe place to talk.

"What was *that?*" Jurgens asked, panting.

"Not the strangest thing you'll see in here," MacKenzie answered woodenly. "Now tell me why you're here."

"I *told* you," Jurgens didn't like Mac's tone, "I was detached from my unit and assigned to the Warrant Service."

"That's bull." MacKenzie kicked at something on the floor. "I've seen your records, too. You're single. You live in an apartment you haven't visited in months. You volunteer for every mission that comes your way. You've got four Purple Hearts and a Bronze Star with clusters. Why, you're a regular hero, not the kind of man who'd get sent to a place like this."

Jurgens looked away guiltily, fidgeted. "I killed a guy," he whispered.

"What?"

Jurgens rounded on his partner, his eyes hard. "I killed a guy, all right?"

"Well, that explains everything," MacKenzie said mockingly. "A soldier killed a guy. Glad we got that out in the open."

"No, look—" Jurgens tapped at his pistol, hesitated before continuing. "We were in Tijuana, drinking, you know how it is."

Mac nodded. "Go on."

"So this Mexican guy comes in, starts talking trash about *soldados*, the usual. Man, the place erupted. I don't know *where* everyone came from. We were all throwing punches, getting kicked and bit. It was a melee, a real Charlie Foxtrot. I popped the Mexican in the throat and, well... Turns out he was some kind of drug lord. Connected. So they put me here, like witness protection. But I hold my rank. And I'll get to go back."

Jurgens had expected either a derisive comment from Mac or else a slap on the back, but instead Mac was staring at the floor, his face a shade or two grayer.

"Who was it, the one you killed?" Mac asked without looking up.

"Some guy named Velasquez. Why?"

Mac's shoulders stiffened. He gazed out on the street, again that vacant look, but combined with something like...foreboding. Jurgens tapped at his pistol, but then his eyes went wide as someone dressed in a full-on clown suit went bumbling past the store front. Then came a clopping sound, and a man in a satyr costume, complete with cloven hooves, followed in pursuit.

Jurgens gaped. "*What is going on?*"

MacKenzie shook it off. "Forget it," he said. "Let's just get this over with." And with that he was back out onto the street, Jurgens trailing in confusion.

The two slipped around another corner. The buildings were close-in on this street, like a canyon. Everything was gray or in dank shadow. A fire popped and sizzled in a barrel, giving off oily black smoke that smelled like... meat. Jurgens looked closer. A blackened human hand hung over the rim of the barrel.

"Mac, you really need to tell me what's going on."

Mac held out a hand for silence. He pressed himself against a wall and peered carefully around a corner. Jurgens came to a halt a few paces back. He tapped his glasses back in place with a finger. "What is it?" he whispered.

"Pssst. Hey you Mackenzie."

The voice came from behind them. Jurgens went into a combat roll, came up on one knee with his weapon drawn. Mac strode past him as if without a care, fully exposed. He disappeared into a dark alley. There was no explaining any of this. Jurgens followed, but he kept his weapon aimed ahead, laser sights searching for a target.

Jurgens could make out two silhouettes in the alley. They were talking. One was obviously Mac, the other was more diminutive. Jurgens came up next to his partner, gun still drawn.

"No need gun," said an oriental boy, a teenager, eighteen or so. The boy had a hostile look in his one good eye. The other eye was occluded, like a white marble. He wore what appeared to be black pajamas, clean, in contradiction to their surroundings. He had a healthy weight and might have been a good looking kid if his face hadn't been scarred by the pox. Laser dots were still tracing the boy's outline. The boy slapped at them as if they were gnats, kept a glowering eye on Jurgens until the agent reluctantly thumbed off the power and holstered the weapon. Only then did the boy return his attention to MacKenzie.

"You go new way," the boy said. He spoke in a native sing-song, as if he were just off the boat, which was unlikely. He pointed down the alley.

"You sure?" MacKenzie asked. He seemed troubled.

"Sure sure," said the boy in one breath. "You go now."

The boy took off for the street while MacKenzie pondered the way ahead, Jurgens loitering at his side.

"Mac, what is it?"

"I don't know," Mac answered slowly, thinking. He slapped at his chest, thumbed an antacid between his teeth and exhaled deeply. Then: "He's changed the route. I don't like it."

"What does it matter?"

"It matters a lot."

"Then let's just go your usual way."

"Can't."

"Why not?"

Mac turned to Jurgens with an expression of... Remorse? Regret? What was it? Jurgens felt an icy chill along his spine. He tapped at his pistol while he waited for Mac to answer.

"Because," Mac said finally, "it might change something."

"Huh?"

"Forget it." Mac squared himself up. "Let's just do what the man says."

They passed through the alley in silence, MacKenzie deep in thought, Jurgens bewildered. They came out onto yet another decaying street, indistinguishable from the rest. All of the turns, the cross streets and bizarre happenings, the shabby gray sameness of it all—Jurgens realized then that he would never be able to find his way out on his own. He stilled his tapping fingers with a reassuring pat of his side pocket. His comm and GPS unit were there. He exhaled in relief.

MacKenzie stopped at the curb, a stoic look on his face. He scanned the way ahead thoroughly, noting every alcove, open doorway, shattered storefront—every place where someone could hide in ambush. They heard shots in the distance, at least a few blocks over, an exchange of gunfire, the deep resonance of a high caliber hand gun, the higher-pitched crack of an answering rifle. Then came two, three, four deep reports, all unanswered. There was a moment of silence. A crow cawed. The breeze ruffled through a tattered awning. And then they heard it, a single, final, fatal shot.

MacKenzie turned to Jurgens. "It's not much further," he said. "This way."

They stayed as close to the walls as the debris and junk along the sidewalks would allow. Something had changed in Mac's demeanor, some sense of—despair? Without thinking, Jurgens was following at a crouch, as if he were on patrol. His hand rested on his holstered pistol. They crossed an intersection that offered a rare, unobstructed view for several blocks on either side of them. MacKenzie scanned left. Jurgens scanned right, saw an indistinct figure sprint across an intersection three or four blocks down. Moments later another figure followed in chase.

"Mac...I'm asking again: What the hell is going on?"

Mac didn't answer, just kept moving. A ragged group of people came toward them, began shuffling across the street when they spotted the agents. There were men and women in the group, all thin and sickly, with pallid, hollow eyes and matted hair. Their faces were spattered with mud or grease. They looked like tsunami refugees. Jurgens scrutinized them as they passed. A few met his eyes as if in recognition. One gestured weakly.

"*Don't look in their eyes*," MacKenzie warned, quickening his step. Too late.

"Some of them act like they know me," Jurgens said. He couldn't tear his eyes away. He was looking back over his shoulder now.

MacKenzie took him by the arm and yanked him ahead. "Don't look at them, I tell you! It'll make you crazy."

"Mac, this whole *thing* is crazy."

"We're almost there. Just hang on."

A shot rang out and a bullet struck a brick wall just over Jurgens' shoulder. Jurgens hit the ground in a rain of dust and mortar, his pistol drawn and searching the far side of the street for a target. MacKenzie ducked left and slipped around a corner. Jurgens kicked to his feet and followed. Mac was just around the corner, his back to a wall.

"*Shhh*." Mac brought a finger to his lips. Jurgens edged in next to him.

"Who's shooting at us?" Jurgens whispered.

"I don't know. Brace me." Mac took off his fedora and threw it aside, grabbed a handful of Jurgens' jacket for support and then leaned over steeply to peer around the corner. "I don't see anyone," he said. "Let's get out of here."

They made a right at the next street and ran for a block. MacKenzie led them around another corner, where they pressed against a wall and waited. Running footsteps echoed behind them.

"He's following," said MacKenzie, breathless.

"I'll flank him, drive him right to you," said Jurgens. He scratched his temple with the barrel of his pistol. A bead of sweat ran down his ear.

"No, we can't. Let's go."

MacKenzie abruptly dashed across the street, leaving Jurgens cursing in frustration. A gunshot spalled the brick above their heads as they rounded another corner, peppering them with sharp chips. Jurgens caught one in the cheek just below his left eye.

"*Son of a—*"

He whipped around, brought his pistol to bear. He spotted a man a half a block or so back. The guy was dressed in rags, like an indigent or a bum. With his eye tearing and his vision blurry, Jurgens couldn't make out details of the man's face. He widened his laser sights, readied to fire for effect. The man kicked backward through an open doorway, out of sight.

MacKenzie was at Jurgens' back, turning him, pushing him across the street. They cut through a burned out building, banged through an alley, and emerged on the next street up. There were people milling aimlessly on this street, not in a group but singly, looking desperate and hopeless. MacKenzie avoided their eyes, but Jurgens met them each. He saw expressions of recognition.

"Why do these people act like they know me?" he asked on the run.

"Because maybe they do," Mac replied, a step ahead.

"What!" Jurgens exclaimed. "Hold up, Mac. Hold up and explain this to me. What is it with this place?"

"No time. Keep moving."

"Make time!"

Jurgens grabbed Mac by the shoulders, spun the taller man around and slammed him against a wall. There was no resistance left in Mac. He had allowed himself to be handled like a rag doll, as if he had given up on life. Mac was gasping for breath, beating his chest with a fist. Jurgens could see bits of chalky antacid between the man's teeth. Jurgens dropped his hands, backed away in shame.

"Look, Mac. I uh—"

"Listen," Mac said between breaths. He was staring listlessly at the sky. His eyes were wet. "It's just up this street, only four more blocks. You'll see it on your right, a big brownstone. Can't miss it. Tell the Fat Man—"

MacKenzie paused. Tell the Fat Man what? That this wasn't necessary and he should have known it? Mac's mind raced. His eyes were as gray as the sky. Had he considered every angle? Had he left himself an out?

"Jurgens?" Mac met his partner's eyes with sudden intensity, *"Don't go in the room."*

"What?"

"And tell him..." A tear spilled and ran down Mac's cheek. "Tell him I'm about to have my first grandchild. For God's sake, tell him not to leave me in there."

Jurgens' brows creased in puzzlement. And then without warning a bullet took off the top of Mac's head.

Jurgens was spinning even as Mac was sagging to the ground. He raised his weapon, sighted on the assassin, who was running for cover, and fired for effect. The upper half of the assassin disintegrated in a spray of gore. The people who had been milling nearby shrieked and ran. Jurgens scanned left and right with his sights, looking for other assailants. There were none that he could see. The street had become eerily silent.

Jurgens turned to his partner.

"*Mac!*"

What remained of Mac's brains were draining into a rusty iron grate. The rest were splattered on the wall above.

"*Officer down! Officer down!*" Jurgens screamed into his comm.

Static.

He banged the comm against his head, tried again.

"*Officer down! Copy?*"

Nothing.

He checked for signal strength. His comm was being jammed...

Jurgens felt nauseous. He had seen death—he had seen worse than this—but something else was going on—something terrifying.

Mac's eyes were closed, thankfully. There was no need to search for a pulse. Jurgens couldn't carry the body, and it would be stripped clean, perhaps worse, before he could return with a team. He agonized for a moment, reached behind Mac's blood spattered lapel and pulled the Glock. He disassembled the weapon, slung the parts down the street and cracked the plastic frame with a brick. He tugged at Mac's wedding ring, fought to get it over the calloused knuckle of a forefinger already going cold. He pocketed the ring, along with Mac's badge, wallet, and comm. Last, he reached into Mac's breast pocket for the warrant.

The warrant was a three-way fold of sturdy white paper, marked on the exposed face with *WARRANT*, along with a docket number. Some of Mac's blood had gotten on it, browning even as Jurgens watched. He unfolded the warrant and read the contents:

Upon his escape from a life internment facility, this warrant is issued for the apprehension of Eddie Stark and the immediate execution of the sentence of LIFE IN CONTINUUM.

LIFE IN CONTINUUM stood off the page in big, bold letters, the seriousness of which gave Jurgens an apprehensive chill. He had never heard of this before.

"What the hell is life in continuum?" he asked himself out loud.

There was some fine print, case numbers and dates of arrest, a judge's scrawled signature, a thumbnail head shot of Eddie Stark, and a facsimile of Stark's thumbprint. Stark was thirty-two years old, already balding. He had an oily complexion, a thin black goatee, and a malicious crease to his eyes. He looked like a sleazy man.

Jurgens slipped the warrant into his breast pocket and then crossed the street to examine the body of Mac's killer. There wasn't much left except for a pair of legs in coarse gray pants attached to a hollow pelvis. No way to identify the guy except with DNA, but this body, too, would surely be gone before he could return.

"Okay," he exhaled. "Four blocks. Big brownstone on the right."

He gave a last, lingering look at Mac's body, and then he turned up the street to complete his mission.

Mac was right, you couldn't miss the place. This had been a trendy neighborhood once, part of the university district. College professors, academic administrators, wealthy graduate students and other highly educated professionals had lived within these quiet blocks of walk-up brownstones. Elegant evergreen topiary would have provided color for the front stoops then, along with window boxes of pansies, daisies and mums. The streets had been lined with stately sycamores, which would have provided cool, overhanging shade during the summers, dusty golden warmth each autumn. The sycamores were gone now, just blackened, splintered stumps. The smaller branches had been used first, then the main branches and finally the trunks, all to fuel fires for cooking and for heat. Once these had been consumed, the stumps themselves had been set ablaze, providing the last desperate pools of moldering heat during the harsh winters. Afterward—and this process only took a few years—winters brought misery and death; and gray ash settled on the city like dystopian snow.

These blocks of formerly stately brownstones were uniformly decrepit now, no different than the rest of the city. The streets and sidewalks here were just as bad as the others, crowded with refuse and debris, and sometimes piles of cracked bones. None of the buildings had windows, or even window frames. These would have gone to the fires during those grim winters after the sycamores had been used up. Some of the buildings were burned-out shells open to the sky. Others had tumbled or had been stripped, except for their shared walls, which often stood naked and alone like somber gravestones, the odd family portrait or child's art still visible in the higher reaches where those walls had once belonged to second or third storey bedrooms.

Jurgens worked his way cautiously through this, alert and wary. He hadn't seen any people since leaving Mac's body. And strangely, he just noticed, he hadn't seen any dogs or cats. A huge mound of brown brick completely blocked the street ahead, like a dam between the gutted brownstones on either side of the street. He was forced to climb over the mound, where it tapered down against the buildings on his right, following a trace that had been scuffed into the mound by other footsteps over the years. But then he got over the mound...and he was astonished at what he saw.

The Fat Man's brownstone *was* big. It was five storeys high, bright and clean, with shiny glass windows and polished mahogany double front doors. Ornate steps led up to the doors. Planter boxes overflowed with color. The street in front of the brownstone was immaculate, all the way to the gutted building across the street. The white center stripe was even painted. And a bicycle lane! The sycamores were mature and green. There were six of them, three on either side of the street. Another mound of brick blocked the street further on. The place was like a secret garden, a vivid island amid the squalor.

It suddenly seemed brighter, like a break in the clouds. Jurgens bounded up the steps two at a time but hesitated at the door. He remained wary, a warning fluttering in his stomach, but at the same time he was relieved by the orderliness of the place. The door knocker was brass, shaped like an hourglass. He lifted it, paused, and then let it fall. The sound it made was low and dense. These doors were not just beautiful, they were thick.

Jurgens was looking over his shoulder when the door silently opened. He was on guard, searching for threats.

Nothing. He turned and was startled. He took a step back, tapped at his pistol. An old—really old—oriental man stood before him in the doorway. The man was dressed in a shimmering purple robe, silk, with intricate gold filigree and a red sash. He wore a matching pill-box hat. His beard was white and thin, hanging to his waist in fragile wisps. His eyebrows were also long and white, arcing up at the ends like wings. One of his eyes was clouded, yellowing, empty. The man had a hunched back.

"Uh, I'm here for the Fat Man, uh, Marcus Constantine," Jurgens announced uncertainly.

The oriental man appraised Jurgens with the one good eye. It was a gray eye, cold. His face was expressionless as he stood to the side, stooping somewhat, one boney hand on the door for support. Jurgens tapped at his pistol as he entered. It was murky inside. Heavy velour drapes covered the windows. The air was thick with the musty smell of old wood and the cloying, syrupy reek of cigar smoke. The only illumination came from scalloped wall sconces, which produced weak orbs of yellow light against maroon papered walls. The silence became absolute once the door was closed, confining, heavy. A clock ticked somewhere.

It was difficult to make out the lay of the place. The furniture was dark, maybe leather or Naugahyde. There were paintings on the walls, set within brooding Victorian frames, but the light was too poor to see details. Also some mounted game trophies, sinister tusks protruding from fierce, shadowy snouts. The oriental man pointed toward a hallway, which looked like a rectangle of gray centered between two heavy wall tapestries.

Jurgens stepped into the hallway nervously. The lighting was dim. There were no doors off the hallway, and no decorations on the walls, only a steep staircase at the end, which yielded a portion of the wan light with each upward step until what was at the top was indistinct and mysterious. Caution surged through Jurgens' mind. He didn't like this. It was too close; too dark. The stench of cigar smoke clung to his clothing and skin like sticky, clinging vines. He drew his pistol and climbed the steps tentatively. A door slowly materialized at the top of the staircase. The door had an iron knob, strangely warm to the touch. He turned the knob and quietly shouldered the door open a crack. A dense cloud of cigar smoke oozed out and swirled around his head like oil in water. It was dark beyond the door, uncomfortably warm. He eased his pistol ahead and followed slowly behind it.

"Ah, the famous rail gun. Or should I say *infamous?*"

Jurgens jumped at the sound of the hoarse, gravelly voice, but still managed to bring his pistol to bear with combat efficiency. Laser sights bisected a gloomy room through wafting eddies of smoke, projecting steady red dots onto the forehead of a large, shadowy figure sitting behind a massive desk. A cigar ember glowed, followed by a puff of smoke. A small lamp clicked on, illuminating a jowly, liver spotted face but little else. Marcus Constantine. The Fat Man.

"Constantine?" Jurgens asked hesitantly. His trigger finger twitched. His armpits were clammy.

Another lamp clicked on, widening their circle of light but leaving the walls in darkness. Constantine deserved his nickname. He was *huge,* spilling over the armrests of his chair. He had dark eyes that were too small for his face, a veined knob of a nose, and drooping ears. His lips were purple and rubbery. His hair was a crown of white with a few anemic strands combed over.

"Raphael Alamos Jurgens," Constantine anounced coyly. "I dare say you have the dark eyes of your mother's people, but the rest of you is all Teutonic."

The man's accent was peculiar. Not British, but still clipped, precise—upper crust.

"What do you know of my family?" Jurgens demanded menacingly. There was no give left to his trigger. One feather squeeze would do it.

Constantine folded his hands on the girth above his waist and grinned. He had all of his teeth, but they were stained, ugly. He chewed his cigar.

"Why, I know everything about you, of course. I am so pleased to finally experience our first meeting. Raphael— we are friends here. There is no need for nervousness. Please put away that ominous weapon."

"*How* do you know about me?" Jurgens asked threateningly. He lowered his gun a degree or two. Laser dots danced on Constantine's lapels.

"It is my business to know. Secrets of the trade, you might say; and besides, my friend, who else in the Service carries a weapon like that?"

Jurgens accepted the explanation, thin as it was, and grudgingly holstered his pistol. He stepped forward to the desk and thrust the warrant into the circle of light surrounding Constantine.

"I have a warrant here for the apprehension of Eddie Stark and execution of the sentence of life in continuum. It's a little messy, I'm afraid Mac—"

"Yes, MacKenzie is dead," Constantine interrupted, "I know. Tragic. We worked together for many years. I will miss him."

Jurgens eyebrows lifted.

"MacKenzie was a good officer," Constantine continued. "He did his job very well. You will fill his shoes now, Raphael."

"Quit that! You don't *know* me. I'm Jurgens."

A sigh. "As you wish, my old friend."

"How did you know that Mac was dead?" Jurgens' voice was edgy. His fingers strummed at his pistol.

"Why, you're here alone, Raph—er—Mr. Jurgens," Constantine answered. If he noticed the suspicion in Jurgens' voice he ignored it. If he noticed the danger in Jurgens' posture he ignored that also. "MacKenzie would never have failed to arrive unless he were dead. Alas, I believe he was due to retire."

"Yes, he was. Damn shame."

Jurgens didn't buy Constantine's story. Then there was that business Mac went on about just before he died…

Constantine flipped a switch, illuminating the entire room. Book cases filled all the walls, from floor to ceiling. Jurgens staggered back, awed. The room was large. There were thousands of books. Thousands. Constantine gloated at Jurgens' reaction, as any bibliophile would.

"Books are my passion," Constantine said with unconcealed pride.

Jurgens walked in a daze to a book case and pulled a volume. It was a very old cloth-bound book, a history of the gangster era of the previous century. He replaced the book carefully and scanned other titles. They were all books of history or natural history, ancient and modern, also memoirs and biographies.

"Are you an historian as well as a bounty hunter?" Jurgens queried while perusing titles, absorbed.

"History is a fascinating subject for me," Constantine explained, dark eyes animated. "I find myself consumed by it. No subject is so often consulted yet so inaccurately portrayed. In my business history must not be misconstrued."

"And exactly what is your business, Constantine?"

Jurgens turned away from the books, serious now. He was ready to be done and gone. Constantine gave him the creeps. But first he needed answers.

"Ah, Mr. Jurgens, there is suspicion in your voice."

Constantine's insouciance was getting to be too much. To the point: "What is life in continuum?"

Constantine chuckled forebodingly, pointed to a chair. "Please sit, Mr. Jurgens. May I get you anything?"

"Answers!"

Jurgens glowered. Constantine sighed.

"Yes, well—Mr. Jurgens, *do sit down.*"

The command was edged with its own menace. Jurgens tensed, lowered himself stiffly into a leather wingback across the desk from Constantine, gun hand ready at his hip.

"Good; very good." Constantine laced his fingers and leaned forward. "Now we can speak pleasantly." A pause; then: "This knowledge is quite dangerous, a Pandora's Box if you will. Are you sure you want to be privy to knowledge shared by such a scarce few?"

"Damn it, Constantine! Enough of this!" Jurgens pounded the desk. "My partner was just killed—*delivering a routine warrant.* My comm is being jammed. I saw strange things out there. I want to know why. Now!"

"You have so many questions, my friend." Constantine spoke in a commiserating tone, but his eyes were like hard beads. "I must warn you, though, that there are many more questions than answers—and some of the answers may not be to your liking."

"You let me be the judge of that."

"Very well, as you wish. But I must begin by asking you a question."

Jurgens impatiently nodded his approval, anxious to get on with it.

"Let's say," Constantine went on, nodding with mysterious amusement, "that in some literary fantasy, like one of my books over there, you possessed a machine that allowed you to travel through time—back to King Arthur's court, for instance; or ahead to H.G. Wells' land of the Morlocks and Eloi. What would you do with that ability?"

"*What?*"

"Mr. Jurgens, this is a thought exercise. Please try to play along."

Jurgens threw up his hands. Constantine continued as if delivering a lecture.

"Would you go back to kill Hitler or Stalin? Maybe you would try to stop the atom bomb." He paused, rubbed his palms. "Or maybe you would go back with that impressive gun of yours to rob Fort Knox. A hundred years ago, say?"

Jurgens glanced at his watch. "Why won't you just get to the point?" he asked bitterly.

Constantine held out his hands in contrition. "My friend, I am trying."

"Cut to the chase, Constantine. What is life in continuum?"

"Exactly what it implies—life in continuum."

Jurgens exhaled in exasperation. Constantine ignored that and continued.

"The trouble with stealing all of that Fort Knox gold, though, is that you would be changing history. When you returned to the present it would be a different present, perhaps even inimical to your well being. And so you would come to realize that even though you possessed the tremendous power of this fantastic machine, there was actually very little you could do with it."

"A nice story." Jurgens rolled his eyes. "What does it have to do with this warrant; this life in continuum?"

Constantine sat back and stubbed his cigar out in a tray. When he raised his eyes again they were malevolent. Jurgens shifted in his seat. Constantine leaned forward again, into the glow of his desk lamp. His face had a ghoulish cast.

"*Everything,*" he said ominously.

Jurgens was tapping a drum beat on his pistol, bouncing on his heels. A shiver ran down his back. Constantine smiled thinly and then resumed.

"But enough of stories for now. You seem unamused. So instead let's discuss this city, this prison. Why is it, do you suppose, that it's not still in use?"

"Uh," Jurgens was flustered by the sudden change of topic, "Mac said budget cuts."

"Precisely! That is it precisely." Constantine stabbed the air with a beefy finger. "They privatized a destitute city, outsourced their corrections responsibilities, and then fenced the place off, all to save money. But it *still* cost them too much," and then in one breath, "not to mention the disease and the cannibalism and everything else."

Constantine took out a fresh cigar and struck a match. He sucked the flame into the cigar, blew out the match with a heavy puff. Jurgens coughed, waved a hand in front of his face.

"You see," Constantine said between puffs, "I think Thomas Malthus would have had a little something to say about their brilliant corrections project. With a prison that suddenly seems boundless, and run by a private corporation—why, you would naturally want to fill it up! It would be cheaper to incarcerate people here for even the most trivial offenses rather than holding them in local jails. It would only be a matter of time, though, before the place would be overwhelmed. Which it was." He spat a bit of tobacco. "And now, after a few years of budgetary bliss, you have not thousands, not tens of thousands, but *hundreds of thousands* of survival-hardened prisoners loose on society and not nearly the budget to deal with it. No one ever wants to pay, you see."

"Yeah, that's what Mac said."

"Mac was a very perceptive man. So if you're the government and you're broke, and you've got to deal with a huge criminal mess—a mess of your own making, mind you—then you start shopping around for the next cheap solution..."

Constantine was being deliberately coy. He studied Jurgens carefully.

"Which brings us to you," said Jurgens.

"Which brings us to me."

Constantine paused to allow Jurgens to draw his own conclusions.

"You assassinate people!" Jurgens blurted. "You're not a bounty hunter, you're a hit man!"

"Oh, Mr. Jurgens, you miss the mark." Constantine sounded disappointed. "It's not as dramatic as all that.

The government couldn't murder thousands of people and hope to keep it concealed." He chuckled at some memory. "The bastards *were* desperate, though. If it weren't for me the poor buggers probably would have *tried* assassination."

"So what did *you* do for them?"

Constantine laughed that off, then caught himself and stiffened up. He proceeded soberly.

"I have a penchant for history, as you have seen, and I have the means to utilize that knowledge." Constantine paused intentionally. His eyes locked with Jurgens. Jurgens clenched his teeth and returned the stare. A vein throbbed in his forehead. "You see," Constantine said calmly, unblinking, "I have a time machine."

Jurgens jerked up at that. The absurdity of the comment showed in his eyes. Constantine recognized that mocking stare. He had performed this exercise before. He pressed on as if Jurgens had accepted the notion.

"But time is a very tricky entity. It can be manipulated but it absolutely cannot be altered. Any interference in history must be carefully researched and detailed. I realized this soon after I acquired the machine, fortunately for all of us. My first thought had been to plunder the past. Could you imagine bringing the wealth of the Pharaohs to the modern day? But that would have changed history, and I doubt we would have survived the repercussions."

Jurgens was stunned.

"You're crazy, Constantine," he sputtered, rising to his feet.

"At least let me finish, Mr. Jurgens."

"No, I'm done with this," Jurgens said with disgust. He was backing toward the door, his hand resting on his weapon.

"If you will sit," Constantine gestured at the empty chair, "I will explain the continuum to you."

Jurgens came to attention at the mention of the word. Constantine smiled, waved the agent back. Jurgens reluctantly returned to the chair. He sat, his eyes fixed on Constantine. "Go ahead," he said then.

"Yes, uh—where was I? Oh, right. The time came when I believed the machine was useless, useless profitably, that is. Scientifically, of course, it had great value. But I am not a scientist. Then I realized the continuum."

There it was again. Jurgens perked up.

"After a time," Constantine rolled the ash off of his cigar, "I learned how to use the continuum—in a way that was both profitable for me and beneficial for the government."

"So what are you saying?" Jurgens asked sarcastically. "You send men back in time?"

"Not exactly..."

"What do you mean, *not exactly*?"

"To send men back in time to randomly toy with the past would be irresponsible. I send them into a continuum instead."

"And just what is a continuum, *exactly*?"

"Imagine a loop, or a circular road, where you walk around and around but never come to a beginning or an end." Constantine's smile was sinister as he explained. "Now imagine if this were a loop of time rather than pavement. You could wander this loop forever, effectively locked in limbo. You would have no perception of this, of course, no idea that anything out of the ordinary was happening to you."

Jurgens snorted and began to rise. Constantine waved a staying hand.

"Now if you are one of our criminals, like Mr. Stark here," he patted the warrant, "and you are sentenced to the continuum—well, rather than being incarcerated behind iron bars you are instead incarcerated behind temporal bars. That's a metaphor, of course, because there are no temporal bars, but it does help one visualize the concept. And here's the real beauty: Escape is impossible and *you require no support whatsoever.* It's cheap."

Jurgens was laughing, shaking his head. "Constantine, you're nuts."

"Is it really so unbelievable?"

"Yeah, it's crazy."

"MacKenzie believed it."

Jurgens laughed even harder. "Well that's convenient. Mac can't deny it since he's dead."

"Yes, sad. To have one's head blown off that way..."

Jurgens kicked out of his chair and drew his weapon. He leveled it at Constantine's chest. Constantine sat unperturbed. He casually lowered his cigar to an ashtray.

"How do you know how Mac died?" Jurgens growled dangerously.

"Why Mr. Jurgens, you told me."

"*I* told you? When?"

"When is irrelevant."

"You bastard! You had him killed. He had a *grandkid* on the way, damn you."

Constantine looked smug. He sucked on his cigar, waved the smoke out of his eyes. "There is always a grand-child on the way," he said. "Or an anniversary or a special trip or a kidney to donate. Mr. Jurgens, there is never a good time to die—and besides, MacKenzie's not dead."

"*What?*" shakily.

"His last words to you were..."

For God's sake, tell him not to leave me in there.

"Oh my God..."

"*Freeze, Rafe. Lower the gun.*"

The voice came from behind him. It was a man's voice, professional. Jurgens went rigid.

"*Gently now. Holster it.*"

Jurgens complied. His hand was shaking. Constantine had a satisfied smirk on his face.

"*Now slowly turn. Don't overreact.*"

Jurgens raised his hands, even though he hadn't been asked. He turned slowly. What he saw yanked the stomach out of him.

"It's okay, Rafe," said the man. "Take a breath."

"Wha? Wha?"

"The blubbering will pass in a minute. I know."

The man winked in amusement. He was holding a rail gun. He was Jurgens' height. He had Jurgens'—*face!*

"I remember the shock, Rafe. They say it's like look-ing in a mirror, but it isn't, is it? It actually feels kind of dirty somehow. Incestuous. But we'll get you straightened out quick and I'll be on my way. Courtesy of you, I get to take a vacation for a few years. And I need it, man. I really do."

"You...you're *me?*"

"In the flesh. And that is absolutely literal."

"*How—?*"

"What did Mac tell you? *Don't go in the room.* Well—you did."

"Ohmygod! This is *real?* He's been telling the *truth?*"

"Every word. Now take a seat. Let the man finish his story."

Constantine seemed to be relishing this. His eyes were gleeful. Jurgens sat numbly, his alter hovering over his shoulders.

"Now to conclude," said Constantine. "What I do is I design a continuum scenario for each man. He is logged with an introduction date and the distance of his temporal exposure. He can be retrieved at any time in case of inquiry. He is not dead, but simply removed from the present."

Realization began to weigh upon Jurgens. He vaguely grasped what he was hearing, couldn't believe that he was coming to accept it.

"Where did this time machine come from?" he asked weakly.

Constantine smiled and leaned back with a greedy glint in his eyes.

"The series of events that led up to my discovery were so preposterously unlikely. The odds—I can't calculate them even now. I won't go into all of the details, but suffice it to say that the couple who formerly occupied this house were professional people. He was a physics professor at the university and she was an engineer..."

"Was?"

"Uh, hmm," Constantine cleared his throat. "Still are, I suppose. I sent them on a little trip—a *circular* trip."

Jurgens edged back nervously. He looked over his shoulder. His alter was smiling down at him, a conspiratorial smile. *Is that really the way I look?*

Back to Constantine: "So you have it here, the machine?"

"Yes, of course."

"Why here?"

"For several reasons. First, the machine is powered by a core sunk deep in the ground below this building. To move it would render it inoperable and, therefore, vulnerable. Second, this, uh, *rustic* neighborhood provides extraordinary protection, as I'm sure you would agree."

"No, I don't agree. A crack assault force could drop in here and take your machine from you before you knew what hit you."

His alter laughed. So did Constantine.

"They've tried," Constantine said, his flabby cheeks twitching sternly for a moment.

Jurgens shivered, tapped nervously at his pistol. The scope of Constantine's power came to him in a dizzying rush.

"No one on Earth can challenge you," he mumbled, eyes downcast. Realization forced the breath from him as if his heart had become too heavy to stay in his chest.

Constantine nodded slowly, a sly smile tightening his nicotine stained lips.

"Don't feel so glum, Mr. Jurgens," he said, attempting to sooth but it came out as a demand. "I'm a simple businessman who has found an extraordinary way to turn a profit. I do not meddle in matters that could adversely affect my current business arrangements. I do not topple governments nor put men in office. I do not need to. These things create intimidation, and intimidation leads to desperation. I do not want to deal with desperate men, including you, Mr. Jurgens. That would be bad for business."

"Why me?" Jurgens asked in a low breath.

"Call it fate, destiny, or pure chance. You will serve a very useful purpose. You have—or will—assist me with extraordinary efficiency, and for that I am grateful. Now, please be on your way. Think nothing more of this, but be available when you're called."

Jurgens passed Constantine a defeated look.

"Who *are* you?"

"I am many people, Mr. Jurgens. Some you know, some you have known, some you will know."

Jurgens was too numbed to say more.

"Okay Rafe, let's go," said the alter. "You have plans for tonight and I don't want you to miss them."

Jurgens' alter took him by the shoulders and steered him out of the room, stayed with him down the stairs, through the hallway, and out the front door. Jurgens sunk onto the front steps, buried his face in his hands. His alter slapped him on the back.

"It all works out, Rafe. Don't worry. It'll be a few years before you go into the room and complete our continuum. Then it will be back to work for me. But until then, as I said, I'm going on vacation. I need—*you* will need—this vacation. So see ya."

Jurgens watched his alter climb the brick pile and then disappear on the other side. He took a deep breath tainted with the vile odor of cigar smoke. He felt gamy. He ripped off his jacket, but the stench stayed with him.

He pulled his pistol, hefted it, examined it in the gray light. He felt impotent; helpless.

"You no escape machine."

Jurgens turned limply. The old oriental man had been watching him through the one good eye. Those were the only words the man spoke. He pushed the door closed. It thumped solidly, like the door to a tomb. It was safe inside the tomb, but outside was dangerous, unpredictable. Bravery was irrelevant. Daring was useless. There were no rules in the Fat Man's playground. Jurgens pulled himself up with effort, consulted his GPS, and staggered despondently into the maze.

Marcus Constantine took a heavy draw on his cigar and reflected upon his latest meeting with Jurgens.

"My poor Raphael," he mused, "you took that hard. You do come around, of course, because you have no choice."

He summoned Lee, the old oriental man, his major-domo, his facilitator, his friend with many faces, as Raphael was further up the line. Lee appeared quietly in the doorway.

"Put a contract on Eddie Stark," Constantine said, chewing his cigar, shuffling papers. "Send word to the street that the Fat Man will give him protection."

Lee gave a short bow and then departed as quietly as he had appeared. Constantine leaned back in his chair and savored his latest scenario. It had been and would be flawless.

It only took three days for Eddie Stark to seek out the Fat Man. Looking from side to side, jittery that his back was to the street, he rapped on the brownstone's polished door and then pounded with his fist. The door glided open silently and Stark was greeted by an old oriental man dressed in traditional silk robes.

"I need to see the Fat Man," Stark said impatiently.

He pushed past the old man in a rush and gagged on the stench of stale cigar smoke. He held a hand to his nose. It was oppressively hot in the house. The old man only had one good eye, and that eye burned with something like insolence. Stark wanted to slap his pistol upside the old man's head but knew better than to try that here. He bit back his indignation, but still glowered at the old man. The old man took this impassively, pointed a skeletal finger toward an adjoining room.

It looked like a drawing room. There was a fireplace going across the way, crackling with heat even though it was actually hot outside. The room was dim except for a line of sunlight streaking through partially opened curtains. He saw leather chairs and a sofa arranged around a coffee table, a liquor cabinet against a side wall. Stark wiped his brow and entered. The cigar stink was thicker yet. He could barely breathe. A dense cloud of smoke rose above a high-backed leather chair.

"I'm Eddie Stark," he announced, breaking a silence that seemed absolute.

The chair eased around, and Marcus Constantine smashed a wet cigar butt into a tray on a side table. Stark gulped. The man was *huge*.

"How can I help you, Mr. Stark?" Constantine asked in a detached tone. His voice sounded like a steel rake on rough cement. He gestured toward a chair. His fingers were like sausages.

Stark sat nervously, both hands in his lap. He had a flighty look on his face, dark bags under his eyes, and three or four days of coarse black stubble.

"Someone's put a contract on me," Stark said, trying to mask his discomfort. "I'm told you can help."

Constantine took some papers from the side table and studied them quietly.

"You seem to be a man who can take care of himself, Mr. Stark," Constantine commented finally. "Armed robbery—served two years of a thirty. Armed robbery and aggravated assault—served three years. First degree homicide, aggravated—sentenced to life—escaped—still at large; and then all this minor stuff. Quite a bit of gun play. You've certainly made a name for yourself. What can I possibly do for you that you can't do for yourself?"

Stark was too intimidated to be concerned about the information the Fat Man had on him. He swallowed hard. His spit was syrupy, tasted like smoke.

"Look," he implored, "they've gotten close three times. I can't shake 'em. I don't know who these guys are or even why they want to hit me. I need your help."

"My service has a price."

"I can pay."

Stark pulled a brick of cash from his coat pocket and tossed it onto the coffee table. Constantine showed no reaction—he knew the amount was substantial. Men like Stark always paid more than their lives were worth.

"Your life is indeed valuable to you, Mr. Stark, but I will require your services as well."

"Tell me. Whatever you need—"

"I need you to kill this man."

Constantine slipped a photograph from the papers in his hands. Stark waved him off.

"I'm not a hit man," he said indignantly. "I'm paying you damned well. Get someone else to do it."

"Then our business is concluded. Good day, Mr. Stark."

Constantine let the papers drop to the floor, turned his chair around and lit a fresh cigar. Smoke curled above the chair as Stark looked on in shock.

"Wait!" Stark blurted. Constantine slowly rotated to face him. His eyes were—disturbingly smug. "Uh, let me see that photo."

Constantine tipped his cigar at the floor. Stark scrambled after the photo and then fell back into his chair. He examined the photo, glanced at Constantine, and then back to the photo.

"Who is this guy?" Stark asked. "Why do you want him killed?"

"Let's just say that he knows more about me than I care to reveal. Ask too many questions and you might find yourself in a similar predicament."

Stark had killed men for lesser threats. He could put a bullet in the Fat Man's head before the guy knew it was coming, but something told him he would never get out of the house alive. He nodded grudgingly.

"Where can I find him?"

"He'll be arriving here shortly. You can lay up for him along the way, the same route you took. You were given a map, yes?"

Stark patted his breast pocket. "Okay, okay," he conceded, fidgeting, "but if I do this, how are you going to help me?"

"I will simply remove you from your assassins. Fear not, Mr. Stark, you are in capable hands."

"Okay then." Stark eyed the Fat Man suspiciously. There was an angle here, he just couldn't see it. "Let's get this over with."

"Good; very good." Constantine laced his fingers. His smile was diabolical. A chill raced up Stark's back. He tried to swallow but his mouth was dry. "My housekeeper will give you some clothes that fit in better with these surroundings. Do you have a weapon?"

Stark pulled an automatic from his waistband and showed it.

"That will suffice," Constantine said dismissively. "Return here when your job is completed."

Constantine took a long draw on his cigar, exhaled it as he turned his back on Stark. Smoke spiraled up to join a dense gray cloud at the ceiling. Stark rubbed his eyes. The old oriental man mysteriously appeared then and gestured Stark out of the room.

Stark was lightheaded from the smoke, wanted nothing more than to get outside into fresher air. He darted for the front door, but somehow the old man managed to get ahead of him, blocking his way. The old man held out a bundle of filthy clothing: gray wool pants, a stained short-sleeved shirt that had once been white, a threadbare jacket. Black sneakers for his feet.

"These clothes stink," Stark complained. "You expect me to *wear* this?"

The old man gave Stark an ominous one-eyed look. Stark's shoulders sagged.

"Okay, okay. I'll put 'em on."

The old man led Stark into a long, narrow room with curving gray walls. Fluorescent-white light glowed from flush round lenses aligned at shoulder height along either side like portholes. There was a metal door at the end of the room. No windows. No furniture.

The old man hovered while Stark grumbled and clumsily changed clothes.

"Oh, man, these are *rank*," Stark complained.

The old man pointed toward the door at the end of the room.

"I get it," Stark said, "the back way out, right?"

The old man said nothing, didn't even acknowledge the question. He took Stark's clean clothes and shuffled out, pulling the door behind him. Stark stared after him, shook that off, and shoved the automatic into his waistband. He moved toward the back door, but the lights went out before he reached it. Man, it was dark! Darker than solitary after lights-out. He stumbled ahead, hands out and searching. A machine-like whirring sound began, growing in pitch. He felt a tingling on his skin, saw flashes of color behind his eyes. Dizziness overwhelmed him and he dropped to his knees. The darkness pressed in on him as if it had weight, as if he were being crushed, and yet he felt strangely light, as if he were floating in warm salt water. Drowning. He screamed. His screams seemed to be snatched away, as if on a wind. Still on his knees, he groped for the door, screaming, crying—terrified.

The whirring noise wound down, like a jet engine throttling back. He felt a knob, twisted it in a panic and yanked. The door opened on a narrow alley between high bricked walls. The sunlight was blinding, even though only a sliver of it made it down this far. He tumbled through the door and rolled to get away. Back onto his knees, he scrambled across the alley, fetched up against the far wall but still pushed for more distance. A runnel of something streamed down the middle of the alley, smelled like— He had the nasty stuff on his palms and on his knees. He grimaced. The door slammed shut. The alley was silent, just some trash rustling in the breeze. He pushed himself up, the wall at his back.

"*What the hell was that?*" he shouted before he remembered where he was. He dropped to the ground out of instinct, nervously scanned the alley up and down. No one there. He exhaled, got to his feet, went to the door and tried it. Locked. Mouthing curses, he trudged up the alley, wiping the filth off of his hands. Once this business was done, he intended to have a little conversation with the Fat Man.

If Eddie Stark took pride in anything, it was that he could shoot. Despite his short stature and nervous nature, he had a sharp eye and a steady hand. Guns evened things. He had learned that early on. He had his gun in one hand and his map in the other as he walked. He had come to the Fat Man along this route, but damned if he remembered any of it. All the streets looked the same: same debris and burned out cars; same empty windows and crumbling walls. *This must be what hell looks like. But is this what hell* feels *like?*

There were plenty of places to lay in wait, anywhere along here would do. But then—he didn't like the idea of holing up. He preferred to stay on the move, to *stalk* his mark. He grinned. Yeah. He cut over to the next street and raced on. There were people in the street ahead, as gray and filthy as he. They looked like starving dogs. He understood then why the Fat Man had wanted him to wear these nasty clothes. He blended right in. He held his gun under his shirt as he ran past. No one paid him any attention. He heard shots in the distance, an exchange of gunfire, too far away to be of any concern.

His mark would be one street over, passing him sooner or later. But where? He followed a cross street to his original route, looked both ways. Nothing. Backtracking, he sprinted for two more blocks, slipped into an alley and crossed again. He peered around a corner. *There he is!* But there were two of them, across the street and a half block up. He tugged the photograph out of his pocket. It was creased down the middle of the guy's face, but there was no mistaking which man his mark was. He licked his lips, leveled his gun and squeezed the trigger.

He missed! *Damn it!* The men sprinted left around a corner. Stark waited a breath, watching the corner in case they came back around, firing. Two breaths, three breaths—he ran in a crouch across the street and into the cover of the alley on the other side. He came out on the next street over, saw the men go right around a corner a full block up. He sprinted ahead, dodging piles of debris. There was plenty of cover on this street, plenty of places to duck if they doubled back.

He slowed at the corner and edged around it cautiously...and there they were again, about to make another left. He ran toward them, raised his gun hastily and fired. Too hastily. The bullet nicked the corner of the building. One of the men ducked and came around, went for his gun. Stark kicked himself backward through an open door, hit the floor and rolled away. The guy didn't fire. Stark crawled back to the door and eased his head out, low. The men were gone.

He took off again in pursuit, turned left and sprinted up the street. He couldn't see them anywhere, but then he passed an alley and came to a sliding stop. He grinned. He knew where they were...

He continued on to the next cross street, made a right and slowed. There were more people on this street, just wandering listlessly like lost children. He stuffed his gun under his shirt and wandered among them. *There!* Up ahead! His mark was standing against a wall, a perfect target. The second man was in the open, also a perfect target. There was a clear line of fire. Just a little closer...

No one was paying attention to him. Why would they? He looked as if he slept in boxes and ate dead cats. He felt that exhilarating tingle of closing in on the kill; the power of the gun. He was well within range now, not even a half a block away. He raised his weapon as he walked, sighted and fired. A perfect head shot! Yeah! Stark imagined a future elsewhere, on a Caribbean beach, Margaritas and a pretty girl; damn, he'd earned it. His mark slumped to the pavement like a puppet with cut strings. He sighted on the second man. People were running and screaming. The second man was spinning around, bringing up his gun, it was...*Ohmygod!*

Eddie Stark had known horror, but never like this. This was a horror that drained every drop of blood; that turned men cold from one heart beat to the next. He didn't wait, he didn't flinch—he ran. He ran for his life even as he knew it was futile...

He didn't hear the shot, that would have been impossible, nor were his synapses quick enough to register any pain. He experienced only an instant of heat before the rail-gun shock atomized his body and cast him in a frothy spray to the wind.

Jurgens examined the body, little more than a pair of legs in coarse gray pants attached to a hollow pelvis. "Okay," he exhaled. "Four blocks. Big brownstone on the right."

∞

CROSSOVER

What's happening to me? I feel like... no, that's not right—I can't *feel* anything. It's more as if I sense things. I sense myself drifting in a silvery light bordered with blackness and stars. I sense that my eyes are straining, searching for something familiar, anything. But this is all in my imagination. I have no eyes. There is a force pulling at me, though, and it is real. It doesn't matter whether I feel it or sense it because the fear churning through my stomach, or rather where my stomach should be, affects me just the same.

It is a primal fear, like an ancient human during a solar eclipse, or an unworthy pagan as the earth shakes. Throughout this entire experience, since I left my body to travel here, nothing physical or otherwise has interfered with me in any way. But I'm only a novice at this. I have lulled myself into a veteran sense of confidence that I haven't earned, and now the force of a hundred tenacious hands is pulling at me in ways I haven't the knowledge or skill to counter.

Another fear, deeper still: *What am I?* Although unbound by physical constraints, I have, at least until this moment, felt resolutely self-contained. But now I sense a fuzzy fringe of diffusion all around me, like a drop of oil in soapy water, slowly but steadily eroding away. I'm losing my memory, losing it in blocks that leave noticeable voids. These voids are like missing spaces, like stutters in my mind. I have to fight—I *must* fight. I must fight with savage animal instinct if I hope to survive.

Oh...oh, no. *I don't know who I am*! I mustn't panic. I must concentrate; I must focus. Remember something; remember anything! Do it! *Do it now.*

I remember a clinking sound, like ice cubes in a glass. Yes...*yes, I can see it*! There's Spencer McQueen, sitting across from me, draining the last sip of bourbon from his glass. Jeffrey's there, too. We call Jeffrey *Doctor Kildare* when we want to tease him, although his real name is Kimbrough. He's swirling his glass around in the wet ring it has left on the table. And I'm...I'm James Whitney. I have a drink in my hand, a stiff Scotch. Laura, my fiancé, is resting against my left shoulder. The alcohol weighs heavily on her eyelids. We're all so young, just out of college by the look of it. I remember! It's graduation night. We four have left the party and gone to a dark, quiet club. We've drunk too much and Jeffrey is finishing us off with a discourse on metaphysical theory.

"So let me get this straight, Jeff," Spence says with incredulity, "*parallel planes of existence?*" Spence still has his hair. His hair was light brown then, and long, tied back in a pony tail with a blue rubber band. He wears a drooping walrus mustache that hides his lips. His eyes are gray in the low light, his brows are creased skeptically. He wipes some stray hair out of his eyes.

"That's right," Jeffrey smiles back with his toothy, pointed grin. His hair is like a curly red bush, with matching sideburns down to his jaw. His eyes are green, dark like spruce, but I remember that they are brighter in natural light.

"So when I die," Spence goes on, "I'm going to crossover and be *me* in another universe?"

"You don't necessarily have to die," Jeffrey slurs, "you may have crossed over already without even realizing it."

"I doubt that," Spence grumbles. He's being baited and he knows it. The bourbon has made him testy. "If I'd had any out of body experiences I would've remembered them."

"Oh?" Jeffrey questions mockingly. "Do you remember all of your dreams?"

"Touché," Laura mumbles with a heavy tongue. She looks so soft when she's drowsy like this, like an image filtered through sheer silk. She has fine blond hair that curls lightly above her shoulders, and the bluest eyes. I love her eyes. She and I are both veterans of Jeffrey's theories, as well as his wit. He's been going on like this since we were kids in high school.

"Now what do *dreams* have to do with it?" Spence protests.

"Maybe nothing," Jeffrey responds, amused, "but have you ever had a dream about something you've never done, like, say, flying a jet; but this dream is so real that you remember the feel of the controls and the smell of the upholstery?"

Spence edges a bit at that. His brow is still creased but I detect doubt in his eyes.

"Or," Jeffrey continues, "have you ever been someplace totally new that you would swear you had visited before? Or even better, have you ever experienced a setting with family or friends that you were sure you had experienced before, to the point that you knew the words the next person would speak?"

"You mean like Déjà vu?" Spence argues. "Sure I have. Who hasn't? But I've read the explanations for this stuff, Jeff. Sometimes your dominant eye records something a fraction of a second before the other eye, so you think you've been there before. And that family scene? It's just a replay of something you saw on television."

Laura is grinning now. Her face is so pretty when she smiles, so alive. Her eyes sparkle, even in the dark, and her lips are so pink and soft I just want to kiss them, which I do. She giggles as our lips touch.

"What you've read is true, Spence," Jeffrey says, unflustered. "Those are valid explanations. But must they be the *only* explanations?"

"Well—why shouldn't they be?" Spence asks, his cheeks reddening. In this poor light he looks as if he has suddenly taken on a tan.

"Because your mind needs to be bigger than that," Jeffrey implores, as if he has been betrayed by something fundamental. He looks my way. "What about you two?"

"Oh, no," Laura waves him off. Now *I'm* grinning.

"Me neither," I say. I lift my glass for cover, take a good jolt of the Scotch and grit my teeth against its potency. "You've been tormenting us with your weird theories for years. Spence needs all the help he can get." To

Spence now, "And Spence, since you'll be stuck with this guy after next week, take my advice: Don't let him drink if you want peace of mind."

Spence and Jeffrey both laugh then, goodheartedly. Laura squeezes my arm, smiles intimately and snuggles closer. In a few weeks we'll be married and starting our new lives in New York City, while Spence and Jeffrey do their post-grad here in Boston. This is a focal point for all of us. And that parallel planes of existence theory of yours, Jeffrey? Close. If you only knew how close.

The pulling is stronger now. It's not a uniform thing, something equally distributed about my, for lack of a better word, *presence*, but a tugging here and a tugging there. A grip slips and I feel an instant of elated freedom before another grip takes hold in a rippling, multitudinous series of yanks and pulls that are dragging me...up or down I can't tell, but I think it must be down. I imagine a painting I saw once, something from Dante maybe, of hideous, writhing bodies pulling a sinner into Hell.

An hysterical fear suddenly courses through me. In my mind I am thrashing in utter panic. The unknown is prying open my mind to reveal fears I do not consciously contemplate. I am running but I am not getting away. Is it possible to die this way, bodiless and cut off from the known? Is that my heart I feel thumping, racing with terror?

No...it's not. I pause to catch an imaginary breath. I sense something, something soothing and steady. Thump...thump...thump... I sense a labyrinthine working of radiated warmth pulsing with each thump. This warmth touches my periphery and effuses through my essence. I can't explain it, but a calm is flowing through me now, like the warmth of a new tundra sun.

I have discovered some other memories, although little more than those related to my current predicament. Blocks of my memory are gone, like pages ripped from a book but, unlike a book, I can't count the missing pages. My memories appear as photographs with pieces torn from them. In one I am a child sitting cross-legged on a manicured lawn. Across my lap lays an aged Golden Lab, gold going white in patches, graying whiskers. The dog looks up at me with that curious dog smile of contentment, tongue lolling lazily to the side. I grasp a stick and throw it side-armed across the yard. The dog lurches eagerly for the stick, and then...nothing—nothing else, just blackness. I have no other memories of the dog. I don't know the dog's name. Strange.

But memories of my current condition appear true in my mind. I feel an urge, no a *need*, to recount them now—to play them like a film. Somewhere among these memories may exist some sliver, some small but vital clue toward an explanation of the events that are overwhelming me...

Spence was a big man. He rested his heavy hand on my shoulder and squeezed, his eyes tight against the tears forming there. The day was dismal, gray and wet with chilling splatters of rain. A priest stood across from me, speaking in reverent tones that rebounded cruelly against my numbed mind. Jeffrey stood away from us, beneath dripping pine needles. His hands were thrust deeply into his overcoat, his face a granite shield of sorrow. He had grown a thin, patchy beard. This caught my attention despite everything.

I heard words in Latin, then the priest made some motion with his hands. I felt prompted to perform my role in this, and released a damp, clodding handful of soil into the grave. It struck the casket with an obscene plunk. I winced at the sound.

"Let's go now, Santiago," I heard as a hushed whisper. That was Spence. He had started calling me Santiago after a trip he had made to Spain a few years back. He had picked up the name from the *El Camino de Santiago* while photographing the pilgrims making the journey. *Santiago* is Spanish for Saint James, but I am no saint. Spence's big hands pulled gently but firmly at my shoulders. I yielded completely as he led me away from Laura's grave.

We gathered at Spence's apartment for a small, solemn wake, just Laura's parents and a few of her friends. Mr. and Mrs. Sheldon were sitting on a couch, holding one another. Their eyes never found mine. People moved silently from the Sheldons to me, pressing hands and whispering condolences. Eyes would catch mine and then dart away quickly. I turned my back on this and tried to distract myself with Spence's work. Enlargements of his best photographs adorned his walls like exhibits in a natural history museum. There were whales blowing in startling blue waters, crystal clear mountains capped with snow, wheat bowing before a fresh wind under an azure sky, the stark reality of a lion's paw poised in mid strike.

A hand squeezed my shoulder. "We all loved her," I heard Jeffrey say. My eyes were fixed, had been fixed throughout, upon the lion's paw. I traced and retraced each extended claw, marveled at the power of the beast and the brilliance of its photographer.

"Jimmy? Jim?"

A gazelle, a split second away from the lion's strike, was literally frozen forever in terror, yet its eyes seemed to show a resignation to fate, a throwing off of the survival instinct for an acceptance of death as a more merciful way. A quick, crushing bite to the neck was more merciful than being consumed alive. A quick leap from Spence's tenth floor balcony would be more merciful than being consumed by grief.

"*Jim!*"

Jeffrey spun me around. I looked blankly at his face but saw only the gently wafting curtains of the open balcony door that overlooked the harbor beyond.

"Jim, are you all right?"

He shook me by the shoulders until the numbness enveloping me shattered like plate glass and fell away. As if descending from altitude, ears popping and sound becoming startlingly clear, I snapped to attention and met his searching eyes.

"We all loved her," he said somberly.

I had never seen Jeffrey so wounded, his face so open and vulnerable. Still, I couldn't suppress a smile. His thick glasses, thin brambling beard, and stand of wiry red hair gave him the comical look of a mad scientist.

"I'll be okay, Jeffrey," I lied. "We all will."

Spence joined us then. His eyes were puffy. I took their hands and squeezed them tightly. "We'll be okay," I breathed. "It helps to know that I'm not alone, that you both loved her, too."

"Look, Santiago," said Spence. He and Jeffrey glanced at one another. Jeffery nodded and lowered his eyes. "You've got some time off—stay here in Boston with me for a while."

"Now that's a good idea, Jim," said Jeffrey, perking up as if this were the first he'd heard of it. "Stay here a while and be with friends. We could *all* use the company."

I nodded my agreement long before my mind said yes. "Yeah, that sounds good," I mumbled.

"Good," Jeffrey said with academic finality. In his mind the problem was solved—the damage contained. "I've got to go now," he said abruptly with quick glances at his watch, "I have a patient at three. Oh, I've moved my office." He handed me his card. "Here's the new address and phone. Drop in on me any time." He squeezed my shoulder and earnestly met my eyes. "Understood?"

"You think I might need a shrink, Jeffrey?" I asked with a pained smile.

"No," he responded dryly, "but you might need a *good* shrink." He winked at me. "We could all use one of those from time to time."

"Oh, yeah? So what do *you* do then?"

"That's easy. I just let Spence get me drunk."

Spence's chin dropped. He rubbed his temples. "Parallel planes of existence," he groaned. "It never ends."

"What?" I asked incredulously. "Are you into that New Age stuff again, Jeffrey?"

"I never stopped," he said with a grin, backing toward the door. We all laughed fondly. Laura's parents and friends looked at us with shocked disapproval. We swallowed our smiles but our eyes were still light. It felt good.

Laura and I celebrated our fifteenth wedding anniversary the June before she died. We went up to Martha's Vineyard for a long weekend. The weather was perfect, cool mornings and warm evenings under a breathless blue sky. Still early in the season, our walks along the shore were intimate. Gulls wheeled and bobbed, the fresh salt smell, the horns of the fishing boats muted by distance—it was magic. I gave Laura a necklace, a delicate crystal rose with ruby-colored petals. Her smile was as brilliant and beautiful as it had ever been, as if she hadn't aged a single year, but there was still that one note of sadness for what I hadn't given her.

Our friends told us, some of them enviously, others with detached wonder, that we'd beaten the odds with our marriage. It didn't feel that way to me. It felt to me that Laura and I loved one another and that time had simply gotten away. I never counted the passing years in my mind, they just seemed to accumulate abstractly until a decade and a half had gone by. They were all years of happiness with no regrets, except for the one—we hadn't had children. Laura wanted children—so did I—but between our careers and everything else that came with living in New York City, time for children, too, seemed to abstractly pass us by. There had always been plenty of time to make a family, plenty of future ahead. It wasn't until close to the end that I really began to notice Laura's quiet remorse, the critical disapproval in her parent's eyes. This became my greatest regret—it torments me even now—that I never got to see the kind of mother Laura would be; that she never got to become the mother she wanted to be.

I was reminded of Laura constantly. A journey through Spence's kitchen recalled Laura's well-stocked pantry. Spence's kitchen was little more than an extra room, a place to collect undeveloped rolls of film and stacks of unread magazines and mail, but Laura's kitchen had been a sensual experience, an epicurean adventure. I believed I could still smell her scent, the freshness of her, mingling with spices and the aromas coming from her stove top. She had created a rustic atmosphere of copper and oak in her kitchen, a warm and reassuring place with tall jars of pasta and stalks of dried herbs within easy reach, flower prints on the walls, fresh flowers on the table. Laura moved through this world with grace and competence, a skill she shared with her mother, combining foods like paints on a palette.

It had been a week and a half since the funeral and I had yet to leave the apartment. Spence had been on assignment for the past three days and the solitude had begun to close in on me. I had approached the door several times for little more than a walk around the block, but at the last moment a tentative weakness would flutter in my stomach and I would back away. It occurred to me to call Jeffrey, but it had become difficult to separate Jeffrey the friend from Jeffrey the psychiatrist. I needed a distraction, not a lecture.

Spence was due back that evening. He would drag in late, tired and hungry, but too energized from his photo shoot to go to sleep without sharing with me completely. If Laura were here she would slip quietly into the kitchen and prepare something special for Spence, a meal that would compliment the stories he would tell, eventually becoming a part of the story itself. I followed her in my mind, took mental notes as she reached into the cupboard for this or that. I heard the flame hiss on the stove, the pans scraping across the burners. I saw the meal take shape, balanced for color and texture, and suddenly felt a need to try this myself, to find my lost Laura that way. I grabbed my coat and stepped outside.

It was a brisk Sunday afternoon. The leaves were still holding on in golds and yellows, and the sky was bluer than one of Spence's perfect photographs. I felt refreshed, energized with a sense of purpose. Laura walked with me. I saw the grocery store through her eyes, and steered toward it. Taking a cart I walked the aisles, picking up this and squeezing that; sniffing this and testing that. I watched Laura's face tighten in concentration as she thumped cantaloupes and delicately squeezed the bread. Affection welled up in my chest. I watched her movements, graceful and precise. I adored her.

At the dairy cabinet I paused in front of the half empty shelves. The fresher bottles of milk had been picked and taken, and those remaining were set to expire soon. Crouching, I reached deeply into the cabinet and pulled forward a few bottles resting against the stainless-steel stocking door in the back. These, too, were soon to expire. I threw them back like disgusting fish.

"Excuse me." I motioned to a stock boy, maybe seventeen years old, who was straightening shelves nearby. "Do you have some fresher milk in the back?"

The stocker looked up at me grudgingly, whipped back a long forelock of black hair with a jerk of his head. He wore a green apron over black pants and a wrinkled white shirt with the sleeves rolled up. He had a ring in his nose. He didn't look happy to be here. "I'll check," he said without enthusiasm.

He disappeared through some hanging strips to my left. I heard a door latch release with a solid thunk, and in a moment the cooler door behind the milk slid open. I crouched low to see through the shelf into the cooler. A foggy mist was forming quickly around the opening. He drug a few crates of milk into view and began pushing bottles toward me. I checked the dates and found them to be the same as the others.

"These dates are all the same," I said to him, wedging my face further between the shelves. I could see a larger swath of the cooler now. It was long and narrow, and the walls looked dank and gray. Rows of dairy crates, stacked six high, were pushed against the far wall. The lighting was dim.

"Isn't there anything fresher?" I asked.

"Sorry, man," he answered with a shrug. "The dairy people are off on Sunday. We don't get any shipments." He looked at me as if this were the most common thing; common knowledge. "Come back tomorrow."

The door slammed shut. I stood back, perplexed. Laura would have known—of course she would have. I mouthed an insincere thanks at no one, left the milk, and pushed my cart to the checkout.

Spence passed through late that night, barely pausing to relax between dropping his equipment and making preparations for his next assignment. He appreciated the food I had bought, although my attempt to prepare a meal had been a failure. We snacked instead, shared small talk. By morning he was gone.

The weather changed suddenly around mid week. The sky turned gray and lifeless, and there was a musty smell of incipient rain in the air. Snow was forecast. The rain came first, cold, falling in heavy drops, followed by showers of gray-tinted slush. My spirits fell with the snow. Loneliness enveloped me in a cold, bitter embrace. I pulled a blanket around my shoulders and stared across the balcony at the gray smeared harbor beyond. I thought of Laura.

The argument had begun on a day very much like this one. First in low tones and then becoming heated, our argument turned bitter. Laura's color had risen and her tone had become sharp, but the hard anger in her eyes had soon given way to a wounded look of betrayal. It is painful to remember her face that way, puffy and swollen from tears. That wounded look in her eyes still haunts me. I remember pausing soberly at the sight of her, my chest tight. I was wrong and I knew it. I was about to slide over to her, to comfort her, reassure her, but I was too late. The chaos took us, and then only blackness.

Children.

Death.

Grief and doubt tore at me mercilessly. I pulled the blanket tighter around my shoulders. The balcony beck-oned me, taunted me with the escape it offered: to traverse that slippery floor, to scale that red iron railing beyond and fall into the relief of eternity. I half pulled myself toward the balcony, half willed myself to stay, shaking as if freezing, torn between the two forces. Some emotional safety mechanism must have come into play—I did not consciously call it. My hand reached out mechanically for the telephone. I ordered a taxi to carry me to Jeffrey.

Jeffrey's office building was a boxy modern design, two stories of dull metal and reflective glass with a flat, utilitarian roof. The building could easily have accommodated four doctors and their staffs, yet Jeffrey officed alone—for reasons I was soon to learn. I pushed through the double front doors into the waiting room and found it empty of both patients and receptionist. I was relieved at first. Had patients been waiting, probing eyes would have turned on me automatically when I entered, scanning for the flaw that had brought me to this place. That flaw was poorly concealed in my face, and I was gratified not to have to share it with strangers.

"Hello," I called out uncertainly. I stamped my feet on the mat and draped my coat over my arm. The office was deafly silent. Somewhere a thump sounded and a compressor kicked on. The lights dimmed momentarily then regained themselves.

"Hello," I called again, peering through the receptionist's window. I looked for a bell or a buzzer but found nothing.

I stepped into a hallway. There were offices off of each side, all empty. The hallway ended at a single, solid wood door that opened quietly into a grand office suite. In this sense, finally, Jeffrey had proved to be conventional. Unlike some academic people I had known, whose offices were cluttered with journals and papers and stained coffee cups, Jeffrey's office was clean and organized, with an aristocratic flair. His desk was mahogany, with a matching high-backed leather chair. His papers were arranged in neat stacks around a leather blotter. The office smelled like leather and wood and books. The carpet was thick, rich brown. All the floor lamps had rubbed bronze stems and green shades, set next to plush leather chairs. An entire wall was shelved with books. There was an adjoining washroom, and a picture window that looked out on a garden and wooded lot. Today, though, the view was smeared with gray snow.

Another remote thump sounded. A compressor disengaged. Otherwise the office was quiet, heavily so. It seemed odd that Jeffrey would leave his office unlocked and unattended. I shrugged and sunk into one of the chairs to wait. I soon nodded off.

My dreams were haunting and chaotic, images of pain and urgency with no apparent flow or symmetry. I had the sense of throwing myself against a wall or barrier, over and over and over again, panic rising and then, finally, failure and despair...and grief.

I heard a dull thunk in my sleep, completely incongruous but vaguely familiar. I tried to catalog it and place it in my dream. Then I heard a swooshing sound, a door opening. I worked to place this sound in my dream as well. It was the sudden wafting of chill air, though, that snapped me awake. My eyes flicked open and found their focus on Jeffrey, who was stumbling toward me stiffly, face pasty and waxy, a toothy grimace frozen on his lips. He was totally naked.

"What the hell?" I cried, jumping to my feet.

"Huh?" Jeffrey questioned numbly, startled and disoriented. He tripped into my arms. I hugged him around the chest, his weight pulling me forward, almost off my feet. His skin had the sickly cold feel of death. His arms were splayed out stiffly, as if rigor had set in. I managed to get him turned around and into the chair. I draped my coat over him, both to keep him warm and also out of modesty.

"Jeffrey, what happened to you?" I shouted into his face. I could see his eyes wandering, trying to focus on me.

"Just hold on," I took him by his shoulders and shook him hard, "I'm calling an ambulance."

His hand shot up then and caught my wrist in a surprisingly strong grip.

"It's okay," he exhaled weakly. "It's okay..."

I studied his face. His eyes wobbled and then found their focus. Forest green eyes leveled on mine in weak triumph. His lips were purple, but they were bent into that toothy, pointed grin that was uniquely his.

"I made it, Jimmy," he croaked. "This time I really made it."

"You made *what*, Jeffrey?" I asked searchingly. Jeffrey's eyes fluttered then and his body began to spasm with chills. "C-c-coffee," he got out through chattering teeth.

I left Jeffrey there and surged through the hall to the receptionist's station, where I found a pot of coffee that had obviously been cooking since that morning. The pot had boiled down about half way, and the coffee was thick and acrid. I grabbed the pot and a chipped mug and raced back, dripping a trail of coffee all the way to Jeffrey's office.

Jeffrey was hugging himself, shivering violently, his teeth clacking like a telegraph key. His skin looked like ice. I knelt at his side and urgently poured a cup, splashing hot coffee on my fingers. I clenched my teeth against the pain, and held the cup to Jeffrey's lips. He slurped the coffee greedily, some of it running down his chin and onto my coat, which was tucked up around his neck. He was so cold the coffee didn't seem to burn him, or if it did he didn't show it. The chattering gradually subsided after a few gulps of the coffee, but he was still shivering, hugging himself stiffly.

"Blankets. Therapy room," he said, holding out a pale arm and pointing the way.

I took off again, found the room and a stack of neatly folded blankets. I scooped these up on the run and practically flung them onto Jeffrey, tucking them around his shoulders, around his legs and feet. After a few minutes his shivering stopped. The life returned to his eyes, and his cheeks began to pink up. I waited, breath abated, for an explanation. Jeffrey was smiling now. It was bizarre.

"I made it, Jimmy. I made it!" he said at last. He was excited, giddy even. His color was coming back quickly.

"You made *what?*" I asked. My concern for my friend had devolved into exasperation. "Quit being enigmatic and tell me—"

He waved me silent and pulled himself up. Bundled in blankets as he was, scraggly beard and all, he looked like a deranged man on a park bench in winter. I sat close to him on the desk. His mind was racing, I could see it in his eyes. They were all over the place, rolling up and down, side to side, but blankly, as if he were searching for the right words. And then his eyes went still and serious, focusing somewhere on the far wall.

"For years," he began, speaking past me, "I've believed that a person's acquired processes, essence—soul if you will—were a self contained entity existing within the body in a symbiotic-like relationship."

He paused to sip his coffee, but also perhaps to gage my reaction. My face must have been blank because I had no idea what he was talking about.

"The original question, though," he went on, apparently deciding that I was paying attention, "was what happens to a person's soul after death? Is it a purely physical thing? Do the synapses just break down and the electrical impulses that trigger memory and thought dissipate into the atmosphere like so many stray electrons? Or are these impulses cohesive and able to exist severally?"

"Huh?" I said, jaw falling.

"But that's just the original question," he went on, ignoring me. He was becoming animated—becoming himself. "This grows into myriad interconnecting questions, from precognition to travel in time and space."

A dull awareness came to me.

"Parallel planes of existence?" I guessed with a groan.

"That's right, Jim. Very good!"

He complimented my comprehension as a university professor would a graduate student, with a patronizing air of superiority. I should have been insulted, but this was Jeffery. I shook my head instead. He wagged a finger at me, still stiff and colorless.

"These aren't like those talks we had when we were young, Jim," he said. "I've been doing research. This is science, not metaphysics."

Jeffrey had brought me to the limit of my patience. I threw up my hands and exclaimed, "For Christ's sake, Jeffrey! What are you *talking* about? I walk in, the place is deserted, and I find you naked and freezing, maybe dying, and you're talking *parallel planes of existence* to me? You know what I think? I think *you* need a psychiatrist."

Jeffrey deflected my words as a parent would a petulant child. He smiled thinly.

"Look at me, Jim," he said after a pause. His eyes were intense. "We've known each other forever. Ask yourself: Am I ranting right now, or do I appear totally lucid?"

I held his gaze, didn't flinch.

"I know this is hard to grasp," he continued levelly, "but bear with me. As I said, I've been doing research. But I couldn't figure a way to set up experiments or controls for an idea that is so—*conceptual.* What I was looking for was more intuitive than observable. I couldn't even propose an hypothesis. I needed deeper insight into the concept first. I tried everything: hallucinogens, sensory depravation, hypnotism, meditation...once I even tried two bottles of bourbon. Nothing worked. But then I remembered Vietnam."

"*Vietnam?*" Jeffrey looked fine, but I swear he was talking crazy.

"Yeah, Vietnam." His eyes wandered for a moment. "Do you remember those Buddhist monks who protested the war by setting themselves on fire?"

I remembered them from the news and in *Life* magazine, orange-robed monks sitting serenely in the lotus position while flames roiled off of them. The smoke was black, oily. I remembered that, too. We were just kids then. The sight terrified me, gave me bad dreams.

"Yeah," I nodded. "It was terrible. I could never understand how they could do it, you know, just sit there."

"Exactly!" Jeffrey stabbed a finger in the air. "Think of the concentration it must have taken to resist the pain, to sit there and burn—to *know* you were burning. It's one thing to idealize an act like setting yourself on fire, but after you actually do it...you can't reason past that. Instinct should make you thrash around and try to put out the fire. So I asked myself: Where was that monk's spirit while his body was burning? Where did he send it?"

"*Where did he send it?*" This was getting to be too much. "Look, Jeffrey—"

"Just read your books," Jeffrey went on as if this were the most natural conversation in the world. "Starvation, torture, hardship—you've seen the photos, the hollow eyes and blank faces. There's something about physical hardship that disassociates the mind from the body. Don't you see? It's so easy."

No, I didn't see, and Jeffrey could tell by the incredulous look on my face. He studied me for a moment, a kind of pain in his eyes.

"I had to move my office here," he said flatly. "My colleagues think I'm a hack. Boy, are they in for a surprise."

His eyes glazed then, going distant, but he shook this off quickly and continued.

"Anyway, I had to create a physical hardship that wouldn't do any permanent damage. I spent a long time on that problem. Then I read about a boy who fell into a frozen lake in Michigan. He was underwater for something like an hour, but they were still able to revive him. And then it came to me. So simple. I moved into this office and had a cooler built into the washroom. The cooler has an automatic thermostat that gradually lowers the temperature. The trick is to sit quietly and meditate while the discomfort increases. I've been at this for months, and then today, for the first time, I had a real out of body experience."

My jaw fell again. It struck me as ironically comical that I had come to *Jeffrey* for help.

"It was a strange sensation at first," he went on, "a kind of weightlessness. But I was still in my body then."

I tried, I really tried, but my eyes rolled at that last. Jeffrey pretended not to notice.

"Then there was this subtle shifting of the walls, like your vision blurring when you've had too much to drink. The next thing I knew, and this is the weird part, I was hanging in the air looking down at my body. No sensation of weight or motion, I was just hanging there looking at myself when the entry chime buzzed. That was you coming in, I guess. Then I was in my body again, freezing to death and feeling as if I had just woken from a dream."

"Jeffrey...I don't know what to say."

And I really didn't. I mean, he looked normal now, that is, for a scraggly looking middle-aged mad scientist.

"You don't believe me, I know." His face became solemn. "Don't worry about it. I need to write this up, take a look at it again when I'm feeling better. I'll call you then and we'll talk about it."

"O-okay. Are you sure you're all right?" I suddenly wanted out of there, away from him, as if whatever was going on could rub off on me.

"I'm fine—really." He tugged at the thin red whiskers on his chin, seemed to ponder something, and then, "By the way, why are *you* here?"

If this bizarre visit had achieved anything, it had taken my mind off Laura—at least for a little while. But there was no way I was going to talk about my problems now.

"I—I just dropped by to say hi, you know, see your new office."

He seemed satisfied with my answer. I was glad.

I spent the remainder of that miserable day—and most of that night—so disturbed about Jeffrey that my thoughts had wandered away from the painful memories of Laura.

It was a troubling diversion, but I was grateful for it. It was not a stretch for me to imagine that Jeffrey's bizarre behavior had actually been part of an agenda designed to distract me from my depression. But in truth, I knew better. Jeffrey had been ostracized by his peers. He was working alone, experimenting on himself recklessly. If something weren't done, I feared I would soon be mourning his death also.

Spence had still not returned, so his apartment was silent and lonely. It was well past midnight before I finally nodded off. I must have begun dreaming of Laura the instant my eyes closed, at least that's the way it felt. My dreams were pleasant at first, probably having me smiling in my sleep. I dreamed of happy times, recalled vacations and holidays and a particularly poignant evening in front of our fireplace during a dark, winter power outage. How had I celebrated what was most dear to me when life still seemed endless? How had I appreciated it?

Doubts, indecision, frustration—oh, how she had wanted children.

My dream turned about with cyclonic fury.

Laura died in a car accident. I was with her when it happened. I can recall events now so clearly, events that occurred much too quickly to absorb at the time. The entire tragedy runs like a full-length movie in my mind, although the events were over in less than a minute. I can play this movie, I can pause it; I can rewind it, examine it frame by frame in exacting detail. I can gage reactions, counter-reactions and available options—they are now so easy to see. A little slower, a little faster; look up a little sooner—if any of these had occurred Laura would still be with me today.

Laura was driving that night. We were heading home from a ski weekend at Windham Mountain. It was cold out, sleeting. The wipers grated painfully over the crusting of ice sheeting the windshield. Visibility was poor. The drunk driver crossed into our lane suddenly, but must have realized his mistake at the last minute. He swerved back into his lane but lost traction, sending his car spinning toward us in disorienting, oblong arcs. The rear of his car struck us on the upswing, sending us into a counter spin. Our engine raced, our tires growled and shuddered, but all I heard was my own heart beating wildly and Laura's short panicked breaths.

We were in our old station wagon, a classic 70s Town and Country with faux wood grain trim, which Mr. Sheldon—Carl—had given to us as a wedding gift, and which we had kept all of these years because, well, why buy a new car in New York City? Laura was an excellent driver. I hated to drive, so she always did it. She kept us on the road through the duration of the spin, handling the wheel nimbly and lightly, resisting the urge to slam on the brakes. But Laura couldn't control where we would come out of the spin, nothing could have. We hit the lamp post left fender on.

The impact was violent. I can't adequately describe the sound of it, just hollow, crushing, horrible. Things inside the car came loose and flew around as if weightless. Glass rained down, a lot of glass—more glass than our car seemed to possess. Metal screeched and compressed, yielding, yielding, yielding until the steering column plunged backward like a ram. The wheel snapped away and spiny pieces of column and linkage impaled Laura to her seat.

She was conscious, but she didn't cry out. Blood spurted from her chest in crimson pulses. She grasped the column like an embedded spear and tried to pull it out. This was futile. She gave up quickly and collapsed against the seat, blood spattered arms lying at her sides, palms open. She had a stunned, disbelieving look on her face, as if her imminent death just couldn't be. I would like to think that in her final moments she thought of me, but I'm sure she didn't. Her mind was rightfully focused on her own plight, and whatever memories or thoughts she had time to review.

My own composure was not nearly as stoic as hers. I was wrenched from my own numbed shock by dapples of cold that touched my face like icy fingertips. Sleet coming in through the empty windshield was hitting the dashboard and flinging into my face. Everything was so quiet and surreal. The street lamp was bent over, casting its orb of silvery light at an unnatural angle. This light was all around Laura, like a halo, like an ethereal glow. Her eyes were fixed ahead but blinking rapidly. I struggled with my seat belt, couldn't get the damned thing to release, so I pulled myself up and out of it, hunched over against the ceiling. I slid across to Laura, slipped my arm behind her to pull her toward me, heard as well as felt a sharp inhalation of breath.

Laura's body was fixed and unyielding. I looked down in confusion and saw the steering column pinioning her. I had to shake my head, rub my eyes and look again. This couldn't be right. Where had that shaft come from? Why was it in Laura's chest? Her living warmth was soaking into my clothes. That's when my head cleared enough for me to understand what was happening. I cried out and pulled away too roughly. Laura inhaled sharply again, the only expression she could offer against shocking pain. I wanted to comfort her, to soothe her, but any touch, any movement brought her instant agony. My mind was lost; my grief primordial. When her chest heaved for the last time I cried beyond anguish—beyond humanity.

What occurred after that I do not remember. I am probably fortunate for this. Two people died that night. The drunk's name was Murray Brest. He was fifty-six years old, divorced, the manager of an equipment rental store. He had two grown children, no grandchildren. His daughter attended his funeral. His son did not. Murray's car had skidded harmlessly into a ditch along side the road. His car was mostly undamaged, but his turn signal lever was found embedded in his skull. The highway patrol had no idea how this could have happened. As for me—I walked away without so much as a scratch.

The dream wouldn't let me be. It replayed as always, with Laura sitting mortally wounded, the distance between us greater than a stellar jump. I fought to cross those inches, those light-years, to her assistance, impotence tearing at the fabric of my soul. I awoke in a soaking sweat, tangled in gamy sheets. The air was hot, heavy and suffocating. Breaths were painful efforts. I flung off my dripping top and crossed to the balcony door. The weather outside had settled into a quiet, crushing cold. I slid the door open roughly, practically dislodging it from its tracks. The frigid air was bracing, pure and clean. I gulped it in as if I had been underwater for too long.

So there I stood, on a balcony ten stories up, well past a cold, impersonal midnight, bare from the waist up, my skin becoming thick and leathery from gooseflesh. My mind acquired a sharpness I hadn't experienced in a long time. The stifling veil of solitude and grief I had suffered under these past weeks gave way to a clarity of mind and thought that I welcomed like a life saving drug.

I swished the slushy ice off of a vinyl patio chair and sat, hesitantly at first, but then fully back against the freezing cold cushion. I ignored the discomfort and willed myself to revel in the cold and the pure air it had brought. Reassuring sounds came to me, like anchors of reality in an otherwise surreal attitude: the hissing drone of far away traffic, the regular burst of a fog horn, the occasional caw of a night bird. I felt the cold as a detached entity, separated from me by a comforting blanket of mental peace and relief. It seemed, at last, that I could sleep without being tormented by grief and anguish.

I dreamed, deeply, with the pleasure and contentment of remembered love, my soul filling and mending. I arose in my mind, ascending from that tenth-floor balcony and in full sight of my condition. It was dreadfully cold, and only reasonable for me to fear for my unprotected skin, but the look of peace on my face erased all worry. I hovered this way for some time, or such that time can be measured in a dream, uncogent of anything but blessed relief from the toll of continuous despair. My thoughts fell inward, as if into a well, until I sensed a barrier to my expression, a semi-solid membrane like the wall of a living cell.

Now this was unexpected, something I had never before experienced in a dream. I snapped to attention, if this can be done in a dream, and reviewed my surroundings with dream enhanced vision. The world was the world, as the world is supposed to be. The sky was moonless and dark, sheathed in low cloud. Spence's red brick building loomed obtrusively before me, his balcony jutting out like a cliff ledge. There I sat, upright and with my chin on my chest, still sleeping peacefully. Rotating then I saw the harbor and a much broader view of the world. All seemed as it should, except...except that perspective seemed to be distorted about the periphery of my vision, turning inward like a tunnel wall. A silvery white light began to fringe my vision, like a halo encompassing all I could see. All I could see...condensing, becoming measurably smaller in increments of dream time until the silver white glow overwhelmed my material vision.

I rotated again to refocus on my body, that fixed point of dream reference. I saw myself there, but through narrowed vision, the contours and outline becoming vague and undefined. Then...motion, as if I were being pulled through a membrane by osmosis, but motion on a galactic scale. My earthly awareness perceived incredible velocity, although I felt no change in inertia, no gravitational forces whatsoever. Silvery white light involved all of my senses.

And then this sense of motion abruptly stopped.

A silvery white light flickered and shone before me like the leader to a spool of film on a movie screen. The light appeared to have infinite length, narrowing into delicate filaments in the directions I perceived as up and down. In width it had uniform edges bordered by the densest black. It was a ribbon of light, a parade of photons.

Rotating, I observed uncountable numbers of these glowing ribbons spread out through space, from flickering filaments close-in to twinkling pinpoints further off, like distant stars. I sensed auto-motion, and this distanced me from the ribbon ahead. As I moved away I sensed the ribbon pulling at me, tugging at my core, but not like a restraint, more like a homing beacon. I continued to move away, gradually and without direction, until the light of another ribbon began to involve my peripheral senses.

This new ribbon of light seemed no different than the first. I wafted around it for an immeasurable time, which could have been an eye blink or an eternity, and then I moved on to others, as if flitting from tree to tree in a forest. I had no sense of the distance between the ribbons. My earthly intuition told me that the distances were vast, but whether on a galactic scale or a quantum scale I could not tell.

After a time, having explored many identical ribbons and having found them to be completely indistinguishable, I drifted back toward my point of origin, pulled by a gentle force along an intangible tether. Had I understood the importance of that force I would have clung to it in abject fear, as if roped to the sheer face of a high mountain. But there was no need for fear. This was just a dream, a visually stimulating but otherwise completely dull dream that had provided me no insights or revelations. This dream wasn't even the stuff of conscious memory, doomed instead to be forgotten once I awoke.

But then Laura appeared in my mind, uncalled. I experienced a moment of guilty resentment. My lips frowned in my sleep. The tranquility I had sensed throughout my dream was suddenly gone, displaced by torment of the usual intensity. I slipped into recollection of the accident, the course of my memory coming to rest upon every minute detail, an unbearable rain of anguish that wouldn't stop.

In a dream that had become a nightmare, with ribbons of light flickering all around me, I detected a change in the pitch of mine, the flickering becoming erratic—slower perhaps—with the occasional moment as if time had stopped, like a freeze frame, a picture of the past. The dog I played with as a boy—flicker, flicker, flicker—a football game in high school—flicker, flicker, flicker—Jeffrey before the beard. These were bizarre juxtapositions. They made no sense. And then she was there. Laura—the accident.

Like film skipping in a projector, sequential snapshots flashed before me, coming to rest on a photo of two cars converging in a dark, icy night...

Flicker.

The cars draw closer...

Flicker.

Closer yet...

Flicker.

They collide...

Flicker.

They spin out of control...

I was overwrought. How many ways is it possible to experience the same tragedy, the same hopelessness and despair?

"*Santiago!*" I heard this in a booming pitch.

Flicker, flicker, flicker...

"*Jim!*"

I am shaking now. No, I am being *shaken*.

"*Damn it! Jim!*"

Flicker, flicker...flicker...flick...

The ribbon flashed silvery white, fading into a low, yellow-orange sun mirrored against the early morning still of the harbor—then motion and a head-on collision with a red brick building...

I grasped the chair's arms with a death-like grip and inhaled the breath of a drowning man. Spence took me by the shoulders and yanked me to my feet.

"My God, Jim, you're freezing!" he exclaimed, panic in his voice.

I was too numb to move or speak, but acknowledged his assistance with a grateful look in my eyes. He drug me inside. I could feel the pressure of his great big hands, a reassuring comfort. He covered me with an electric blanket, fumbled for agonizing moments with the cord, then finally got it plugged in. I felt the warmth ease through me like an old, welcome friend. I felt my jaw come loose suddenly, as if ice had just melted there. I heard Spence speaking emphatically into the telephone. I smelled coffee. Soon the chills came. I gathered the blanket under my chin, clenched my teeth and squeezed my eyes.

"Are you okay, Jim?" Spence asked. His tone was urgent. He offered me a mug of coffee, which I took with both hands and raised to trembling lips. The warm, soothing effect was immediate. "What were you *doing* out there?"

"I fell asleep," I answered him stiffly. "Stupid thing to do."

"Stupid? You could have *frozen* to death!"

"Look," I barked at him defensively, "I went out for some fresh air and I fell asleep. Could've happened to anyone."

"I doubt that," he said, eyeing me suspiciously. Or was it just my imagination? "Anyway," he went on, "your color's back. I think you'll be okay. Jeff's on his way over."

That tore it.

"Why'd you call *him*?" I practically yelled. I'm not sure why I was so upset.

"Hey—!" he began then checked himself. I could see the color rise in his face. He shrugged his shoulders, turned his back and walked away.

To convince Jeffrey that I wasn't suicidal was difficult. To solicit an interpretation of my dream without arousing his suspicion was even more so.

"Jim, you know..." Jeffrey began. He was pacing with his hands clasped behind his back. "...I loved her too. We all did. But—and I don't mean to sound insensitive—you've got to let her go. This thing isn't healthy."

I was bundled up on Spence's couch, watching Jeffrey pace, annoyed. Spence sat in a recliner across the room, his feet up.

"I know, I know, I know," I repeated, hoping my assent would get him to drop it yet knowing that it wouldn't. Jeffrey came up next to me and rested his hand on my shoulder.

"I suggested that you take some time off," he said, meeting my eyes clinically, "but now I think you should get back to work—find something to take your mind off of this."

There was really no reason to argue; nothing to be gained.

"You're right," I said after a prudent pause. "I'll stay through the weekend, go back to the city on Monday."

Jeffrey nodded his approval. So did Spence.

"Good, good," Jeffrey said, problem solved. He took a seat and worked clumsily to change the subject. "So, Spencer, how was Mexico?" he asked.

"Uh, good, really good," Spence answered awkwardly. "I got some great shots. And you? How's the research going?"

"I've had an episode," Jeffrey replied proudly. He smiled enthusiastically. His eyes sparkled. So *episode* is what he called it. "I started writing it up just last night, but I'll need to repeat the process at least once before I try to publish. As a matter of fact, Jimmy walked in on me right in the middle of it. It's funny; he found me the same way you found him this morning. Odd coincidence, isn't it?"

An odd coincidence, indeed.

Spence was in town for the rest of the week. I would never see Jeffrey again. Spence did his best to keep my mind off Laura. I appreciated his efforts, but new thoughts had begun to come to me. This research of Jeffrey's—it was obvious that he was serious about it. Spence, Laura, and I had always laughed it off, as if Jeffrey were tilting at metaphysical windmills. It made for interesting bar conversation but did not resemble real science at all. Still...

The underlying theme of Jeffrey's lectures had always been the physical reality of the soul. He argued that the soul must be energy, able to be transmitted, received, or amplified, much like radio waves, and conforming to physical laws. His main complaint was the lack of a word to describe the soul in scientific terms, a way that would not cause academic eyes to roll. Jeffrey had always been certain of his ultimate success, but less so of his ability to prove it to his contemporaries. Now I questioned my own skepticism.

Just what had happened to me in my dream? I had been subjected to extreme physical and mental distress.

I had observed myself and my surroundings from a vantage point I had never before seen, and I had recalled those observations clearly. I had experienced a variety of sensations while apparently having no physical form. I had witnessed the accident, not as a participant, but as an *observer*, with the ability to recall it to a point by force of will alone. And if Jeffrey was right, what would these out of body experiences of his be like?

They would be like my dream.

And then a revelation came to me with biblical impact. It took my breath. Literally. If I had seen the accident then I must have traveled back to it; and if reliving this event was a physical thing, as Jeffrey believed, then I should be able to change its outcome!

I had never felt so elated, so fundamentally relieved. A wellspring of hope rushed through me like a torrent. The experiment would be easy to duplicate. I considered consulting with Jeffrey, but...no. I was afraid this would be too much even for him. Telling Spence was out of the question, he already thought I was crazy. I made my plans in solitude, therefore, and awaited the proper time.

Spence hopped a plane Saturday afternoon. He was bound for Tierra del Fuego to photograph penguins for *National Geographic*, with a side trip to the Falkland Islands on the itinerary. We said our formal good-byes then since I would presumably be in New York when he returned.

The weather had cleared remarkably at week's end, and my spirits matched the pure blue sky and brisk gusting winds. I spent the balance of Saturday waiting in anxious anticipation, each passing minute registering like a countdown. I didn't sleep. I sat before the clock and willed it forward, pushing and pushing and pushing until its face seemed to blur and its hands spun like window cranks. Sunday morning came at last, a bright, eager morning. The clock's hands slowed their advance and came to rest at 10:00 a.m. It was time.

The grocery store appeared much as it had the previous Sunday, quiet and with few shoppers. The lone cashier, caught in a long, stretching yawn, did not notice me, nor the two stockers who were hustling boxes up and down the aisles. I slipped through the hanging strips, still unnoticed, found the steel dairy cooler door and pulled hard against its weight. The catch released with a loud thunk. I froze at the sound, but no one came. I pulled the door open just enough to squeeze through, as if opening it further would give me away.

Once inside, I quickly pulled the door toward me. It closed with another solid thunk, cutting off all outside sound, making me feel more confident as I surveyed the interior. The cooler was roughly fifteen feet by thirty feet, and dimly lit by a row of bulbs recessed into the low ceiling. The wall to my right was composed of sliding doors that gave access to the dairy shelves outside. The wall to my left was gray with an icy sheen. Stacks of dairy crates were lined against it. I proceeded toward the farthest corner, my breath condensing around my head like a helmet of fog.

Reality began to intrude then, an uncertain trepidation about the trespass I was committing; a foreboding of embarrassment should I be discovered. I forced myself away from these thoughts, to concentrate on the one goal and nothing else.

I worked my way into the far corner, dragging crates away from the wall, arranging them into a barrier around me. At last I knelt in the corner and considered my work. If anyone happened into the cooler I would be completely hidden. It felt safe. I was able to proceed uninterrupted, but I still glanced about furtively as I pulled off my clothes.

The crushing cold air assaulted me before I even got my shirt off, raising thick gooseflesh. I clenched my teeth so hard that my jaw muscles throbbed from the tension. I hopped from foot to foot as the icy cement floor drove frigid needles into my soles. I spread out my coat on the floor and hopped onto it, realized then that I should have brought a blanket or a pillow to sit on. I lowered myself onto my coat instead and sat with my legs crossed. This was it. I pulled my feet onto my ankles in the lotus position, what I remembered of the posture of those burning monks. I wasn't on fire as they had been, but my skin still felt as if it were burning in the cold.

The shivering came not gradually, but in convulsions, which I fought against with tensed muscles and clenched teeth. I was mostly numb by then, hugging myself about the knees, rocking back and forth in jerking movements. Any thought of meditation or sleep was ridiculous. This was a bad idea, a stupid idea.

I began to despair.

I was embarrassing myself; I felt like a fool. I had melded Jeffrey's dubious research with a dream of troubling origin in order to produce this result: a man sitting naked and shivering in a supermarket dairy cooler. And of Laura, I thought with profound sorrow, who is truly gone, what would you make of this? Her face filled my mind, bringing tears that misted away into the fog of condensed breath around me. My Laura, whose love had given me purpose and whose beauty had given me pride and all of those things that had made me whom I had become, the loss of which had left me devoid of light and being and the multitudes of little things unnoticed until they are gone.

What a waste. What a sad, sad waste...

...The membrane pressed firmly against my senses, the osmotic force pulling me through the silvery white light; and like a cork popping from a bottle, I shot through this into a vast forest of glowing ribbons.

I would have thought it impossible to be disoriented in such a condition, nevertheless I hovered there for some immeasurable time, the flickering projector image playing before me. At last I gathered my senses, reacquired my purpose, and focused my thoughts intently. This time, as the flickering became slower and the occasional still image flashed my way, I noticed myself moving downward along the ribbon, as if traveling homeward along a vertical highway. All the while the faint tugging of the invisible tether connected me to my point of origin.

Flicker...flicker...flick...

The scene, now too hauntingly familiar, appeared before me: two pairs of headlights converging in the darkness. I regarded the scene—quizzed it. What was my plan? To enter and stop the accident, that was my plan. I needed more time. I concentrated deeply and descended several more frames.

Our car was alone, a minute or so from the accident. I willed myself firmly against the image, the mechanics of this form of travel coming to me only through instinct. I sensed the bitter cold wind of that night. Soon I was upon the car, through the car, and among its occupants.

"We can't wait, James," I heard Laura say, pain in her voice, lips trembling faintly.

"There's time," I pleaded with her, "another year; two at the most. Then we can afford to move out of the city."

The conversation brought a pang of guilt that had me dripping virtual tears. I pushed my consciousness close to Laura and thought: *we can start a family right now if you'll stop the car. Just stop the car. Stop the car!*

"I'm *thirty-eight years old*, James," Laura said. "Another year or two might be too late."

She sounded so wounded. Oh, God...

I now pressed against my other self. *Take the keys, Jim! Take the keys!*

"Listen, honey," I was saying in a patronizing voice that made me want to cry, "I want kids too, it's just that— Is that car swerving?"

The headlights were approaching. Panic shook the core of me. I reached out to grab the keys, the wheel, anything, but I had nothing to grab with.

"I don't know," Laura replied, suddenly attentive. She ducked to see between splotches of ice. "He looks okay to me."

Something crossed my eyes, *his* eyes. He was edging toward her. "Okay, honey," he sighed, resigned. "I promise—"

I was in a frenzy. *Stop the car! Stop the car!*

Impact—spinning—the growl of tires on ice. Laura's stoic control. The light post. The collision. The steering column ramming into Laura's chest. The shock on her face. The disbelief. Blood pulsing...

Anguish ripped at my soul viciously. I cried a mournful wail and pushed away from the horror before me. I was ripped from the scene as if from a decompressing airplane cabin, and emerged in the void with the ribbon flickering its pattern. My grief was excruciating, like progressive weights stacked upon my skull. I drifted there for uncountable time, not caring whether I lived or died, or if those conditions even existed for me anymore.

The next sensation I felt was the lack of one. My lifeline, the tether I had sensed tugging at my consciousness, was gone! I started in a panic, willed myself up the ribbon with furious speed, then down again, stopping and starting like a hummingbird to a climbing flower. My reference was gone! I couldn't find my way back! Through force of will I concentrated deeply, but the flickering pattern of silvery white remained unchanged. I was lost—marooned—in a dark ocean below foreign stars. Loneliness compressed me like dense crushing cold. My vision narrowed to a pinpoint of perception until, like a spent candle, it quivered and blinked out and my mind was plunged into absolute blackness.

I can see it now quite clearly, something to do with relative time—the time I spent here versus the time my body spent in that dairy cooler. I can imagine my skin freezing to icy hardness; my blood chilling and running viscous until my heart could no longer pump it. Jeffrey had said this state could be maintained for quite some time, but how much time had passed in the physical world? In my oxygen-deprived brain, synapses had broken down like breakers being thrown until my body had finally died. My lifeline had been broken; my reentry into the physical world was no longer possible.

How much time has passed I cannot know. The unknown groping force is drawing me along the ribbon. It is taking me up, not down as I had feared. It is taking me higher than I have traveled before. Along the way I sense the essence of myself dissolving, even these recounted memories disappearing in blocks of random patchwork.

Thump...thump...thump...

I can remember fear but I am not afraid. Warmth and contentment have enveloped me in a comforting embrace. My mind is at work, doing work of which I am vaguely familiar.

Thump...thump...thump...

Circulating primal thoughts; imprinting instinct where I find none.

Thump...thump...thump...

A silvery white light I somehow recognize; the eternal warmth of innocence. A newborn baby is being laid upon its mother's stomach, the ropey umbilical still attached. I am drawn into this new life; I sense its purity. I issue commands without knowing why. A heart beats faster—thump, thump, thump—a stomach growls and I raise a tiny fist to my mouth. I am...can't remember...my thoughts fading...fading...

Drawing breath; blood coursing through labyrinthine workings; hunger gurgling upward into a pitiful cry; bits of me flinging away, fragments catching here and there.

I am...

...fading.

∞

Kirk Ward Robinson was born and raised in south Texas, and has since lived in every continental American time zone. He is an inveterate hiker and cyclist who prefers to travel and explore the world that way. His wide-ranging career has included roles as a chief operating officer, bookstore manager, stagehand, bicycle mechanic, and executive director of an educational non-profit organization in cooperation with the National Park Service. Robinson has been twice named to Kirkus Reviews' *Best Books:* in 2012 for *Life in Continuum,* and in 2015 for *The Appalachian.* These days he maintains a small ancestral farm in the hills of Tennessee.

www.kirkwardrobinson.com

www.ingramcontent.com/pod-product-compliance
Lightning Source LLC
Chambersburg PA
CBHW070428120726
47910CB00003B/689